Other Tor books by
Hilbert Schenck

Steam Bird

CHRONO-SEQUENCE

HILBERT SCHENCK

TOR

CHRONOSEQUENCE

Copyright © 1988 by Hilbert Schenck

First printing: June 1988

A TOR Book

Published by Tom Doherty Associates
49 West 24 Street
New York, N.Y. 10010

Library of Congress Catalog Card Number: 87-51400

ISBN: 0-312-93079-8

Printed in the United States of America

0 9 8 7 6 5 4 3 2 1

For Anne, with love

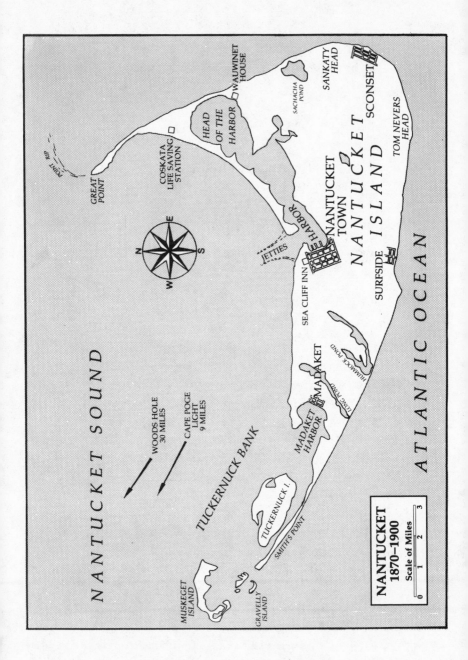

NANTUCKET SOUND

WOODS HOLE
30 MILES

CAPE POGE
LIGHT
9 MILES

TUCKERNUCK BANK

MUSKEGET
ISLAND

GRAVELLY ISLAND

TUCKERNUCK I.

SMITH'S POINT

MADAKET HARBOR

MADAKET

LONG POND

HUMMOCK POND

SURFSIDE

SEA CLIFF INN

JETTIES

NANTUCKET TOWN

NANTUCKET HARBOR

COSKATA
LIFE SAVING
STATION

GREAT
POINT

POINT RIP

HEAD
OF THE
HARBOR

WAUWINET
HOUSE

SACHACHA POND

SANKATY
HEAD

SCONSET

NANTUCKET ISLAND

TOM NEVERS HEAD

ATLANTIC OCEAN

NANTUCKET
1870–1900

Scale of Miles

0   1   2   3

It is inevitable that a great deal of ecology must be descriptive, yet it is surprising that when interest changed from the description of the structural aspects of vegetation to the examination of the changes which occur, the essential parameter of any changing system, time, has so seldom been mentioned. Succession has formed the subject of innumerable papers in the last forty years, yet in only a handful has the rate of the process been discussed. Even where the evidence was clearly available in the form of historical data or in the annual rings of the woody plants, the idea of time as an essential part of the process did not seem to occur to, or perhaps seemed unimportant to, the authors. . . .

"Yet these papers were written in a world in which speed was almost defied. So divorced has succession become from its legitimate spouse, time, that some ecologists have felt the necessity to invent a new term which leaves no opportunity for the time element to be overlooked; we no longer have a succession but a chronosequence!"

The above is from Alan Burges' Presidential Address to the British Ecological Society in 1959, *Journal of Animal Ecology*, 29:1–14.

"On Tuckernuck Island a gargoyle, locally known as 'The Yoho,' peers across the shoals toward our island in communion with some cryptic shrine of the Muskeget lares. We have not been alone in wanting to discover that lararium."

"Muskeget is wild, beautiful, productive, enlightening and unique. It is vulnerable to man, ephemeral even without man. Ephemeral for the sea will eventually claim it all. It is saltating in response to natural forces—its time is running out; so may be ours."

All quotes from *Time Lapse Ecology, Muskeget Island, Nantucket, Massachusetts* by David Wetherbee, Raymond Coppinger, and Richard Walsh, New York: MSS Educational Publishing Co., 1972.

·1·

AN
AUCTION
AT
PHILLIPS

Eve Pennington walked briskly down the stairs to the basement showrooms of Phillips, Blenheim Street, and pulled a well-marked catalogue from her handbag. She then turned into the small book-display room, its every wall covered with mostly full wooden shelves, and began prowling along the lines of books. Her long, manicured fingers carefully leafed through this or that dusty, leather-bound treasure, her sharply defined lips pursing, her well-outlined eyebrows often drawn into a thoughtful frown as she consulted the estimated price list stuffed inside the catalogue. Eve was a tall, slim, attractive woman in her early forties, pretty in a severe and cool way, and like many single, academic women around her age, she had grown about her over the years an invisible protective shield of friendly impersonality. Most of her exchanges were now either chatty or professional.

Eve moved deeper into the small book room, her eyes brushing aimlessly over the somewhat disheveled section of scrapbooks, manuscripts and postcards, when a thin, cloth-bound ledger with no title on its torn, rough cover caught her wandering eyes. She yawned and peered at her watch. Eleven-forty. She was meeting her good friend, Dr. Julia Stetson, an astrophysicist in London on a two-year appointment to Imperial College, for lunch at noon, but the restaurant was only as far as Dean Street.

She reached and pulled out the ledger, gently dislodging a box of postcards that partly blocked it, and opened the loose, broken cover. It was some sort of manuscript, written in a round, legible hand in brown, faded ink. On the title page she read: "Being a true account of the verbal stories given to me, Thomas Cope, by Captain Henry Macy, of Nantucket, in the State of Massachusetts (America), and by his wife, Mrs. Captain Henry (Joanna) Macy, and regarding certain amazing and possibly occult events connected with the island of Muskeget, a small place lying five miles west of Nantucket Island."

Eve bit her lip and frowned at the yellowed page. Nantucket? Muskeget? She riffled through the pages of the journal, stopping to read a few words here and there. Near the end were the witnessed signatures of Captain and Mrs. Macy followed by what appeared to be a brief appreciation of the stories in the same hand as the rest, signed with the initials, T.C. Eve checked the lot number, thirty-four, then found the entry in her auction catalogue.

"34. Cope (Thomas). Handwritten MSS in bound account book relating supposedly supernatural events witnessed by Nantucket (American) fishing captain and wife, mostly on small island (Muskeget) near Nantucket, dated 1892 in Cope's hand, about 42 pp. Covers somewhat distressed."

Eve crossed the room, idly glancing at some handsome old maps scattered on the central table, depicting the Scilly Isles. "Ian, what's this thing about?" she said to a young man sitting at his small desk in the darkest corner of the book room.

Ian McPherson, a cheerful, nearsighted Scotsman and book freak from Edinburgh, was the present cataloguer and organizer of the monthly Phillips book auctions. He smiled up at Eve, his wide, magnified eyes large and warm behind thick glasses. "Good morning, Professor Pennington," he said, taking the ledger into his hands with the same loving care he gave to all his charges. "Ah yes, this thing." He looked up and smiled at Eve. "Well, it's part of that collection of occult and psychic stuff, starting at around lot one-seventy. Did you happen to notice it?"

Eve frowned and shook her head. "I wouldn't give ten seconds to that Victorian hocus-pocus, Ian."

Ian shrugged. "Yet in a way the people involved were only trying to do what your friends, the astronomers, were already doing, Professor. I mean by that, explaining away the universe."

Eve gave him a bright, friendly look. "I'm sorry, Ian. I'm being terribly narrow-minded," she said at once. "So what is the account about? Ghosts? Poltergeists?" She looked at her watch. "I don't have time to sit down and read it."

He slowly turned the pages. "It's been some months since I looked at this . . . Ah yes, I remember. There are these *fish* that come. Well, it's really a kind of tall story, at least, I think you Americans would call it that. Evidently this fellow Cope made trips to America to collect psychic accounts. He was part of that bunch around Dr. Soal in the 1880s."

"Fish?" said Eve, taking the book back and staring at the title page again.

"And there's a birth in there. I think I remember that," said Ian, "and a fishing captain's wife has her say too."

Eve fumbled with her catalogue. "What's the estimate . . . ?"

Ian peered down at his lists. "Twenty pounds." He pursed his lips almost guiltily. "Well, if it were a ship's log or an account kept in a lighthouse or life station, it could be worth good money, but it's really just an interview account, all written at the same time apparently. Whatever value it has is its being in the handwriting of Thomas Cope, who now and then interests some people."

"Who was Cope again?"

"A wealthy psychic investigator, which translates to a credulous believe-anything individual, I suppose," said Ian. "Sort of an early Charles Fort. You know, he collected strange and wonderful tales and tried to prove spirit visitations, the supernatural, the fourth dimension, whatever, from it all." He looked at her, smiling quizzically. "I should think you'd be eyeing that Bion, Dr. Pennington?"

It was almost noon and Eve turned to put the battered ledger back on its proper shelf. She gave him a large grin. "Ian, I don't need you to tell me that Bion is a lovely thing. But, lordy, a three-hundred-pound esti-mate! I wouldn't be able to pay my way back to the U.S."

Ian shrugged cheerfully from his gloomy corner. "It may not make that price, you know. It *is* in French."

Eve laughed merrily and four old men poking around the shelves smiled to themselves at the cheerful sound. "Ian, you know that's why it's valuable. The later English editions are a dime a dozen."

"Not quite. Try twelve-hundred quid a dozen," cor-rected Ian, and then in his best Colonel Blimp voice, "Bloody frogs! Can't read a blinkin' word they write, wot?"

Eve waved good-bye. "See you at two, Ian," she said, then added as though explaining something to herself, "Actually, I spent a summer on Nantucket," and went off to her lunch where her friend, Julia, decided that attending the book auction would be fun.

So the two tall American women, smart and slick in their trim pants suits and gotten-up faces, made an attractive pair in the shabby, green Phillips salesroom. They sat in the midst of the old Jewish book dealers in thick sweaters under worn suit coats, and here and there, an occasional younger dealer in jeans and a turtleneck sweater.

As Lot Thirty-Four approached, Eve glanced down at Ian's estimate of twenty pounds. All right, she thought in sudden resolve, if I can get it for that, I'll do it.

The lots were not brought upstairs to the sale, but simply announced in sequence. When Thirty-Four was called—the auctioneer first reading from the catalogue description—Eve held back. At ten pounds she came in at twelve. The auctioneer immediately got fifteen and

Eve went to eighteen. There was an agonizing pause, then from the back of the room a finger-flick response to the auctioneer's last try for twenty pounds. "I have twenty pounds, can I now get twenty-two," he said. "Twenty-two pounds on Lot Thirty-Four, anywhere? Going at twenty, then . . . ?"

"Yes!" screeched Eve, suddenly overwhelmed by the stretched moment and madly waving her catalogue.

"Thank you, madam," said the courtly auctioneer, nodding down at Eve. "I have twenty-two pounds. Now, twenty-five? Is there twenty-five? Twenty-five anywhere?" It was now evident that the interest had gone out of Lot Thirty-Four and the auctioneer rapped his small hammer, gripped around its head, on the top of his high auction box. "Sold to you, madam, for twenty-two pounds," and he waited for Eve to give her name.

"Eve Pennington," she said promptly in a strong voice, and Ian waved cheerily from behind his account books next to the auctioneer's box. Eve's eyes were bright and she turned to smile at Julia, who grinned back and whispered, "Oh, Eve, it *is* exciting! No wonder you come to these things."

"And more to come!" Eve hissed back. She had that sudden, sixth sense, one that now and then strikes experienced auction-goers, that she was going to have a good day.

When the first edition of Bion's important early treatise on astronomical and mathematical instruments lagged at one-hundred pounds, Eve held her hopes in check, knowing that price was simply ridiculous. At one-thirty it lagged again and now Eve sat up straight, intently waiting.

"One-forty, only one-forty on this important work in its original binding, ladies and gentlemen? Ah, thank you sir. Now, one-sixty? One-hundred-and-sixty-pounds?" He paused to look at Eve, who was the other bidder. She gulped and nodded.

"Thank you, madam. Now, one-eighty? Only one-hundred-and-eighty for a first—the French—edition of Nicholas Bion's *Mathematical Instruments*? One-eighty anywhere . . . ?"

It seemed to Eve that he went on like that forever and she clenched her teeth wondering if she dared come in one more time at two hundred. She squinted her eyes as the repetitive intonations went on and ground her teeth so hard that it was not the rap of the gavel that brought her back to the auction room, but the sudden clap of hands by Julia and her cry of, "Oh, Eve, you got it! How lovely!"

"Pennington," intoned the auctioneer quietly to the account people at their desks, and as Eve looked up grinning, Ian clasped his hands over his head, shaking them like an American prizefighter and beaming out at her.

Then, only four lots later, Eve bid in and then bought another large, handsome volume, William Leybourn's famous treatise on dialing and surveying, dated 1678, for a mere pittance, fifty-five pounds. Eve knew she had to quit, not just because she was way ahead but because she was out of money.

When the occult books at the end of the auction began to come up, the two women edged out of the salesroom and Eve paid her bill at the office for her three books. Her face was flushed and her smile was wide and brilliant. "I've always dreamed of owning the first Bion, but I never thought I could afford it. If the truth be told, I guess I still can't," she said to her friend.

Julia shook her head. "Eve, you couldn't even get a week's worth of shrinks for that money. And instead, you've got *years* of archaic, technical French to plow through."

When the auction ended, Eve was the first in line at the door of the book room where Ian exchanged sales receipts for purchased books. He proudly plopped the huge, ridge-backed Bion in front of her, and she gently opened it to a plate of navigational instruments, the huge page unfolding again and again. "A book fit for a king," breathed Eve, touching the thick, ivory-hued paper.

Ian put the Leybourn down next to the Bion and grinned. "That's exactly what it says on the title page. One of the Louises, fourteen or fifteen, I think."

Eve folded up the plate and closed the Bion, then opened the slightly smaller copy of Leybourn's *Surveying*. "Look, Ian," she said, pointing at a plate on the use of the theodolite, "see what he uses as an object, a target. Not some new, technical marvel of the day, but a picturesque, Germanic ruin, all wrecked stones and trees growing through roofs."

Ian McPherson looked down at the etching, then up at Eve Pennington's now-passionate face, as she stared delightedly down at her old book and its charming, copperplate etching of ruin and progress intertwined. Ian was a young man of poetic sensibilities, and he was both moved and amused that this older, attractive woman, filled with a kind of intense, yet he thought a bit empty, enthusiasm for old books and early science, should have seen the most poetic aspects of the Leybourn plates at a glance.

"Yes, we have quite managed to educate the poetry out of them by now," said Ian. "Modern surveying texts are decidedly cheap and narsty by comparison, and probably a whole lot less clear."

Eve fitted the two books into a large plastic shopping bag she always brought to auctions for this purpose and turned to go. She paused, blinked uncertainly and shook her head, then turned back. "Hey, what about my other book?" she said in a low, confused voice.

Ian looked down at the slip and grinned. "Sorry." He walked over and took the battered ledger off its shelf, then came back and put it in her hand. "Forgot that you bought that other thing. Hope it's interesting."

"Bye-bye, Ian," said Eve, waving, "and thanks for all your help."

Before Eve and Julia managed to flag down a cab in front of Phillips, Eve had convinced her friend to come up for drinks and a simple supper to celebrate the great bargains. As they opened the car door, a tall man, perhaps thirty-five, dressed in a dark business suit, burst out of the front door of Phillips, then paused to look around. Seeing Eve and Julia, he ran down the steps and stopped in front of them.

He nodded politely, but his face was a mask. "By any chance did you ladies happen to buy Lot Thirty-Four today? It was a handwritten journal."

Eve nodded. "Yes, I did."

The man turned to her and again spoke with stiff politeness. "Would you mind telling me what you paid for it?"

Eve shrugged. "No, I guess not. Phillips lists all the prices anyway. It was twenty-two pounds."

The man nodded impassively. "I arrived at the auction late. Car trouble. Would you accept fifty pounds for that lot now? I realize . . ."

This had happened to Eve at the end of auctions before and she had a ready answer. "If you'll give me your card, write the date and lot number on the back, I'll promise to call you first if I should decide to sell it." She said this with a cool, distant voice. As she spoke, she saw his face harden.

"You won't quote me a price now, then?" He stared at her with narrow eyes and leaned forward with an insistent gesture. "I travel and I'm not in London very often. I'm prepared to pay a fair . . ."

"I'm *awfully* sorry," said Eve icily, now opening the cab door wide and sweeping Julia in ahead of her. "If you'd just give me your card . . ." She smiled thinly, now through the cab window. The man made no answer but stepped back and turned.

"Thank you," he said absently, then went quickly up the steps into Phillips again.

As the cab scooted away, Julia turned and grinned over at her friend. "Sounds like you made good buys all the way around today. He certainly was ready to pay plenty for that battered book. What is it, anyway?"

The hostility within the stranger had very much disturbed Eve for some reason and she slumped back in the cab seat and stared down at the bag of books on the floor. "Oh, I don't really know," she said in a tired, small voice. She sighed. "It was just some sort of impulse, I guess. I looked at the title page and I saw it was about Nantucket and an island near it."

She peered out the window, then at Julia, and her face was pinched. "When I was fourteen, my family went to Nantucket for one summer, the four of us. We rented a little house way out at the west end, at Madaket. There was lovely swimming, you could choose calm and sandy, or big surf, and we went sailing often in a little catboat. My sister was a year younger than I was, a very beautiful, gentle girl. That summer was the happiest our family ever had. Next winter my sister died in a car crash. On her first damned date! And the sixteen-year-old punk who wrapped his family love-boat around a utility pole walked away from it!" Eve shook her head. "My mother was destroyed by that, became a drunk. My father found another woman and went off, just *left* us. Nothing has ever seemed farther away to me than that sunny, happy summer."

Julia, hearing the desolate tone, suddenly hugged her friend. "Hey, you know what your problem is? Post-auction adrenaline-high downer, that's what! Gin and tonic is the indicated restorative."

By the time she reached her cozy, fourth-floor Hampstead flat and mixed the drinks, Eve did feel much better. There was certainly no denying that thick, brown bulk of the Bion that sat heavily on her desk, and next to it the somehow more businesslike Leybourn.

Eve caressed the Bion and opened it to a plate of engraved and decorated drawing tools. "Leybourn is an engineer's book, very much a male production," she said sipping her drink, "but the Bion is more feminine, more delicate. See how his dividers arch so gracefully . . ."

Julia dropped into a comfortable chair and gratefully took a long pull on her drink. Her wide, handsome mouth curled in amusement at her friend. "You really think analysis is inherently beautiful, Eve? I mean beautiful in a visual, an aesthetic sense?"

Eve stared down at the books. She shook her head and gave a thoughtful frown. "I don't know. It seems to me that astronomy, the kind we do today, just *is*. I mean, it isn't beautiful or not beautiful. It works. You can predict. Where the beauty is, has to be, is what we make of it," and she went and poured herself another drink.

She smiled at Julia. "Bion shows how to create a sundial at any angle of inclination or bearing entirely by constructions using only a straightedge and compass, no protractor marks, no millimeter lines. First you make a special rule and lay off scales, all with the compass, then you construct and erect the dial itself with its correct angle of style, and you can do it for any place on earth. That's what I think is beautiful. Taking the motion of the earth and the sun and putting them down on a flat sheet of paper with pencil, compass and edge. It's the *doing* it, having the *understanding,* that's what's beautiful. I mean anybody can figure orbits on a digital computer with somebody else's program."

Julia shrugged. She was from California, well beyond two husbands and into a career in astrophysics with NASA. "I don't know anybody with a beautiful job, nowadays," she said thoughtfully. "I suppose poets and painters, some of them, used to live with beautiful ideas and things, but look at the ugly, sick, incomprehensible garbage they're all cranking out now." She stared directly at Eve and lifted her glass. "Being an employed, active woman physicist or astronomer today may not be exactly beautiful, Eve, but it has to be better than pumping babies out between your legs and dropping dead like those wives and sweeties way back then. You won't find a single woman's name in either of those monster books."

Eve gave her friend a cheery smile. The gin made her feel happy and relaxed. "Lordy, Julia, let's not get going on all of *that* stuff. C'mon, I've got some lovely huge pork chops in the fridge. Let's have a glut!"

After supper, Eve walked her friend up the hill to the Hampstead tube station and they stopped in a pub on the edge of the Heath for a nightcap. Julia leaned forward, her elbows spread on the bar like a man, and carefully sucked the brown foam off her stout. "Not too long before you go back, Eve. Happy about that?" she said from a mouth outlined in froth.

Eve took in a thoughtful breath. "I guess I am. I haven't been very busy here. Everything is just so leisurely at these English schools."

Julia wrinkled her nose. "Slack is a better word. Well, as they keep telling me at Imperial, we're going down the tube. Why fight?"

"If they are, it's because of those rich kids' prep schools, and of course Oxbridge and the nasty way they talk." Eve shrugged. "You've just got to go deeper for people than the snobs are willing to go."

Julia shook her head. "There are some real ones over at my zoo. Boy, and I thought some of them at Berkeley were precious!" She whistled out a sigh.

"Poor Julia," said Eve with a big grin, putting her hand down warmly over her friend's, "you have had bad luck. But good old Dr. Right is out there someplace, fiddling with a duplicating machine, changing plates at the prime focus, hands smelling of hypo."

"Fuck Dr. Right!" said Julia in a low, hard voice, her

face close to Eve's. "I don't need men most of the time and they're mostly bastards nowadays, anyhow. Scared to death. Can't be Dr. Big Shot quite the way they used to do it. You're doing it the right way, Eve, believe me! I tried the other and I know. You've got your career and your science history hobby and all your friends."

Eve nodded and drank down her ale. "And I do have Jack, well, now and then," she said thoughtfully.

"Jack Goldman is a wimp," said Julia positively. "He's the best there is in spectrographic analysis. I'll give him that, and only that."

Eve smiled and tossed her head. "Jack sleeps with some very attractive women, well, sometimes he does, and I include myself in that group. I mean he's not completely wimpy. Not like Noel."

"Don't rub it in about Noel," said Julia with a rueful smile, dropping a one-pound note on the bar top and getting down off the stool. "Noel is one of the main reasons why the British lion is wearing chartreuse snuggies and drinking its tea with a droopy paw."

The two women kissed warmly at the tube station entrance, and Eve walked the short distance to her flat, staring up at the starry sky and a sliver of moon, thinking about going back to Boston, seeing Jack again, picking up her life there and going ahead. But that thought made her unsure and as she let herself into the flat and looked at the glasses with their melted ice on the living room table, she wondered how Julia really dealt with her loneliness, with that yearning to be cherished. Julia is tough, tougher than I am, she thought sadly.

The Bion lay open to a plate of handsome sectors, their two delicate parts spread wide like so many pairs of legs, like women's legs ready for sex. Eve poured herself one more drink and stood looking down at the books. How much there was to find then, and how beautifully elegant the finding became. She would never be a really important astronomer. Her specialty, extrasolar dark-body analysis, was highly probabilistic, highly specula-tive, based on the tiniest of incremental signals from the largest and most expensive instruments, gathered tenta-tively across vast distances. Quite the sort of thing a woman might get into, in fact, sort of the needlepoint of astronomy.

Eve shook her head in disgust. That was just unfair and stupid, she thought, and self-pitying too. Most of astronomy today involved that kind of nit-picking. They were all making thousands of tiny stitches in a tapestry that the Bions and the Leybourns had gleefully unfurled three hundred years ago like a huge flag.

She idly picked up the battered ledger with its "34" tag still taped to its front and began to read the first page, but the ale and the final gin and tonic made the words slip away and she turned off the lights and began to undress, knowing that she would certainly fall asleep quickly. Lying on her back she grinned up into the darkness, thinking once more about the huge, ancient books.

The next morning was a warm, sunny June day and Eve walked to the tube station, then rode to her ten o'clock lecture at Queen Elizabeth College where she taught. The term, never very demanding, was now running down to its end and soon the students would be immersed in their year-end exams, although her class did not seem very exam-focused in the warm, drowsy morn-ing.

After a lunch with some of her department colleagues,

Eve sat at her desk for a while, doodling with this or that minor job, but by two in the afternoon she had decided, with a kind of increasing determination, that she would go home and read that damned journal she had bought at the auction. She rode north in the tube but the day was so hot she decided not to stay in her now-oppressive top-floor apartment but to hike up to Hampstead Heath and read her odd treasure in the sun and open air.

The Heath was dotted with strollers and sitters, enjoying the rolling, open fields. Eve found a comfortable seat on a grass tussock and started to read the handwritten account, but was attracted by the sudden sounds of merry-go-round music and other clashing, noisy indications that a fun fair was taking place down in a long valley just to her south. She rose, gripped the book in her hand, and wandered down the hill, through a grove of trees. She came out on a scruffy, trampled midway with a few small and rackety rides and the usual opened-out caravans with pitch-and-toss games, wheels of chance and disheveled slot and coin-flip machines standing forlornly on splintered wooden stands.

Eve stood watching the children riding on the small, nongalloping merry-go-round when in an instant she felt a sudden jerk as the ledger was snapped out of her hand from behind. She whirled instantly, making a snatch after it, but the young man who had seized it was now running back down the narrow midway.

"Stop thief!" screamed Eve. "Help! He's stolen my book!" The small, dark figure of the man turned and he sprinted into a space between two of the caravans, but at that instant a large and heavy gypsy stepped down out of his caravan into the same space and the man ran right into him.

Eve sprinted down the midway crying out at her loudest, "Thief! Thief! Thief! Hold him!" and the large gypsy did just that, seizing the much smaller man around both his arms in a bear hug and lifting him off the ground.

"'Ere, 'ere! Wot's this then?" he rumbled in a dark and menacing tone. "Pinched the lady's purse, eh? Dirty little bugga!"

Eve ran up to the two men and immediately seized the book, which the small man still had gripped in his right hand, and strongly and quickly jerked it back. "Why did you *do* that?" she said in a loud, frightened voice. "What is this about?"

The squinting, pasty thief was completely unable to answer and indeed, his pimply white face was becoming quite red as the large gypsy continued to squeeze him against his vast chest. "Bloody snatch thief! I'll teach yer to be muckin' about my show!" and he squeezed all the harder.

"Oh, dear, please don't hurt him," said Eve at once. "I've got my book back." She took a deep breath and tried to stop shaking. "I'm sure he won't do it again, sir."

The young man had now started to groan quite piteously, and the gypsy suddenly let him drop so that he fell down on his hands and knees with a loud thud.

"Narsty barsted!" said the gypsy, his large, dark face now quite flushed with anger and indignation. The thief made no move but remained on his hands and knees gasping, and his very helplessness seemed to enrage the gypsy even more until he suddenly put his large boot against one of the small man's shoulders and gave him a great push so that he rolled completely over several times in a swirl of dust and ended up flat on his back. He made no move whatever, but stared up at the gypsy, his eyes darting, trying to judge what would happen next. A crowd of perhaps twenty people were now gathered around the three of them and Eve put her hand on the gypsy's arm.

"Sir, *please!* You've been most kind. Don't hurt him any more."

The gypsy looked down at the flattened figure. "I might just kick 'is rotten 'ead in," he said in a voice dangerous and thick. His large hands were working together.

At that moment a series of loud "'Ere, 'ere's!" came from behind them and two tall police constables pushed through the growing crowd and stared at the gypsy, then at the man on the ground. "An wot's this then?" said the tallest of the constables to the hulking gypsy. "Can't pick on someone your own bloody size, mate?"

Eve stepped up to the policeman and shook her head vigorously. "It's not a fight. That man on the ground snatched my book from under my arm and ran off with it. This kind gentleman," and she indicated the gypsy, "happened to catch him and hold him before he could get away."

The other policeman reached down and seized the small man by the arm and silently half-helped, half-lifted him to his feet. "Snatching things, eh?" said the first constable. He turned to Eve and asked, "Wot did he take, missus?" but before Eve could answer, the gypsy, who had been closely watching the silent thief, suddenly made a grab for his wrist.

"'E's lookin' for a way to run . . . !" said the gypsy in a rush and at that instant the little man lifted his right wrist and took a hard bite of the gypsy's gripping hand.

"Bloody 'ell!" shouted the gypsy, letting go of the thief who turned in a flash and dashed back along the midway at extraordinary speed, darting behind a caravan. But to Eve's astonishment, the two policemen did not jerk off their helmets and rush after the criminal, as Eve had seen them do once or twice down in Picadilly, chasing a pickpocket, but simply shouted, "Stop you! Stop in the name of the law!"

The gypsy took two or three long steps in the direction of the vanished thief and then turned in an open rage on the policemen. "Wot's the matter? Not payin' you buggas enough to chase snatch thiefs? Bloody 'ell . . ."

The taller policeman, who had shouted after the thief, now frowned quite coldly at the gypsy. "Kicking a man lying on the ground is an offense too," and his voice was hard and impersonal. "You tell me my job one more time and you'll go down to the station." Then he turned slightly to stare at Eve and it seemed to her that his eyes were somehow more intent, more purposeful than this dreadful little episode demanded. "Now, missus, just what did he take from you?"

"This book that was under my arm," said Eve, but she did not offer the object to the policeman, even though he had his hand out. She had suddenly decided that nobody was going to touch that book again. Eve smiled in what she hoped was an honest manner and opened the ledger with her left hand while skillfully palming a five-pound note she had rapidly folded up inside her skirt pocket in between two of the empty pages. It was a bit of smooth, professional sleight of hand. "Oh, I don't think he wanted the book," said Eve calmly. "He must have seen me put this five-pound note between the pages. I was just going to change it."

The policeman now stared at stern, level-eyed Eve, the book again shut and tucked tightly under her right arm and the five-pound note idly fluttering between the fingers of her left hand.

"Bloody faggot 'alf-arse law enforcement," mumbled the gypsy, his face a mask of disgust as he stared in contempt at the policemen.

"You keep your big mouth shut!" said the policeman in a tone of complete menace, then turned with less certainty to Eve. "We don't need to chase him, missus," he said in a level voice. "We know who he is." His eyes looked Eve up and down and a silence fell on the group.

Eve took a deep breath. "Officer," she said, "if you need my name and address, I'll be glad to give them to you. I do think that man should be punished."

The second, silent policeman pulled out his notebook and wrote down the material Eve told him; and the moment he was done, Eve nodded to the gypsy, saying, "Thank you sir," and then to the policemen, "Now, if you don't mind, I think I'll go. Please call me if you need anything more." She walked rapidly through the thinning crowd while the policemen stood peering after her, then she strode up the hillside, cutting across through long grasses and hilly meadows. As she did so, she began to tremble again and her teeth to chatter. "Oh, boy," she whispered to the open heath, then looking down at her book, "this is no place to read *you!* What have I got here?" Eve had a definite sense that the two policemen were not quite right, not what they seemed. But as she thought that, an even more disturbing thought was born. What if they were policemen, maybe not exactly police constables, but still part of some official force?

"That," said Eve to her hot, silent apartment as she breathlessly let herself in, "is the sort of idea that crazy people have!"

She mixed herself a light and icy gin and tonic and collapsed into her most comfortable chair, then unbuttoned and took off her sticky, sweaty blouse. The scruffy ledger lay open on her lap at the title page, and Eve began, carefully, slowly, and thoughtfully, to read the "amazing" stories transcribed by one Thomas Cope, Englishman, mystic, and tall-story hunter.

·2·

THE MACY STORIES

I possess some modest facility in the art of rapid notation now coming into application in the more progressive commercial establishments of London and have thus chosen to transcribe the more or less verbatim accounts of Captain Macy and his wife into a kind of field notebook with additional comments and observations as may amplify the stories. As I have suggested elsewhere, scientific enterprises succeed to the extent that their observed phenomena can be simplified, then reproduced easily and at will. Psychic studies, on the other hand, depend wholly on a seemingly random succession of unique events. The description of these events thus lies at the central core of the entire discipline and any assessment by the student of the source of the descriptions may well prove as important as the purported events themselves.

I had learned of the Macy experiences on a tiny island off Nantucket near the New England coast from a sea captain who had written me concerning certain personal observations involving the fakirs and holy men of India. These proved to be the usual collection of indirections and sleight-of-hand manipulations typical of such bizarre entertainers and I found the captain's offhand mention of a "damnably odd business some years back off the American coast" far more compelling. This account, unique at least in my experience, interested me greatly.

The island of Nantucket, having become something of a watering place, is easily visited during the summer months and Captain Macy was kind enough to meet me at the ferry dock and sail me to his domicile on the island of Tuckernuck, a few miles to the northwest of the town of Nantucket. The Macys lead a plain yet comfortable life on this modest strand and accepted me with that ready hospitality that is characteristic of many rustic Americans.

The captain himself is a small, wiry man with a full grey beard and a lively, peering pair of eyes. Any serious student of the supernatural often finds himself facing rather obtuse and sometimes bewildered individuals whose need to believe in the marvelous grows, root and branch, from the very ordinariness of their lives. I was immediately heartened to find the captain, though relatively uneducated in a formal sense, a shrewd and keen observer of his daily world. Best of all, he neither believed nor disbelieved in the existence of paranormal and psychic events. To put the matter simply, he was interested in, and concerned by, what he observed yet retained an open mind to any explanations.

After a hearty and well-cooked supper of various sorts of seafoods, the captain walked with me to the west end of his island and, offering me a comfortable rock on which to perch near the summit of a modest hill, pointed to a tiny, low, rather barren island to the west, little more than a sandbar, in fact, then gave me the following account. I have tried to duplicate something of his accent and figures of speech, but only when these do not obscure the factual essence of the episode. T.C.]

"At that time there were no lifesaving stations, or even much in the way of humane houses [The Massachusetts Humane Society, a group of Boston shipowners and Christian-motivated women of substance, began around the middle of the century to provide houses of refuge, lifesaving apparatus, and lifeboats for the rescue of distressed mariners along the New England coast. T.C.] along these shores. I guess there were maybe three shacks along the south side of Nantucket for mariners washed ashore after a wreck, but none on Tuckernuck nor on Muskeget. Muskeget is a little, low island, surrounded by bars and shoals, and a thoroughly bad spot for a vessel of any size. Just before our wars with England there was a kind of hospital or contagious ward on the Gravelly Islands, which were part of Muskeget then, where they kept poor folks with the smallpox. I guess it was an awful place and the Nantucket selectmen finally got rid of it. It's my belief that whatever it is that haunts these waters maybe got started up then.

"The Gravelly Islands are completely gone away now, washed right out to sea, but they were never much to mention, just a few acres of rocky piles sticking up a few feet at high water. Everybody has heard some stories about what went on at that so-called hospital. It was just a place to put people who were infected so that they could die a long way from anyone seeing it. The officials in Boston paid some doctor to look after the place, but it might have been kinder if they had just tossed them poor folks over the side of a whaler in the middle of the ocean.

"I don't know much about haunting or spiritualism, but it does appear that those shoals around Muskeget might be haunted. Tuckernuck folks call the ghost the Yoho, although I'm not so sure it's just one particular thing. In my opinion it's a kind of influence that had grown out of all that suffering that was brought to that little place in the smallpox hospital.

"Anyhow, my first real connection with the Yoho, or whatever it is, came in the late sixties. Like I say, there was no humane house, nor any house at all, on Muskeget. It's just a sandbar mostly, with some scrabbly stuff growing here and there. And the damn island moves. Kind of shifts along eastward, year by year. By that I mean the west shore gets washed off and the eastern bar keeps getting bigger.

"It was an awful night in December, blowing from the nor'east like billy-be-damned and snowing too. Couldn't see a quarter of a mile, if that. Somehow, I had a sense that there was something wrong out there, and I could see that my wife was kind of worried and upset too. I went out and walked toward the west end of Tuckernuck, up onto this bluff, and it seemed to me that there might be a lost vessel out in that snowy wind. Still, I kept telling myself that I couldn't possibly see fifty yards past the end of the island.

"The next morning was cold and everything was covered by plenty of snow. I couldn't lose that awful, dark feeling, so I decided to take the dory with the spritsail and make a run down by Muskeget to see if everything was all right. Now, in fact, there had been a wreck the night before. A big sloop, a packet from Chatham, the *Daisy*, Captain Manter, had struck on Tuckernuck Bank north of us and broken apart. The two crew members were just gone. They were never found, but Manter and his young son, Billy, had come ashore on Muskeget hanging on to some wreckage.

"I could see there were pieces of a vessel blown onto the Muskeget beach so I landed and right away found Billy and his father. There had been no place for them to take cover on that low, flat island, no place to get warm. They were lying in the grass. The father had taken his boy in his arms and was trying to breathe into his mouth, to keep him alive, so their two mouths were frozen hard together. Captain Manter had his coat open and he had tried to get his boy inside it, tight to his body. The captain's elbows stuck out on each side and his arms were right around his son. They lay there, the pair of them, just completely frozen together, and it was the awfullest sight, and the saddest, I ever did see. There was a slight cover of snow on the two of them, so it was hard to see at first just what they was, and when I brushed this off, well, I just fell down on my knees and started to weep. Them tears just flowed, I can tell you! I've never felt worse than I did at that moment. But it was right then that a very odd thing happened. It was then, I guess, that I sort of met the Yoho.

"What happened was this. I had my hand on Manter's icy face, kneeling in the snow crying like a baby, when there was suddenly a house, there, right next to us. It was a humane house, like they have now along the dunes on the backside of the Cape and other places where vessels may come ashore in the winter. There was nothing fuzzy or dim about it. It just sat there, solid, with a door and a window, and believe it or not, the chimney was smoking! Think of that, there was actual smoke and I could smell the wood burning!

"I got up. The house wasn't ten feet from me and I headed for that door. I wasn't scared or anything like that. I was, maybe, only half-thinking, what with them poor bodies on the ground and all the rest of it. So I put my hand on the latch, and I swear to this day that I felt the thing lift and heard it click when I opened the door. Inside were bunks set against the wall and a big, glowing stove in the middle. So for a second I just forgot that there wasn't any humane house on Muskeget and I turned to bring Captain Manter and his son into that warm room. You know, for a second I really thought I might just thaw them out and they'd be all right. It's crazy, but the house being there was crazy too. Of course, when I turned back, the house was completely gone. The snowy beach grass was there instead, with no sign of anything else.

[In my paper to the society two years ago regarding the sensory aspects of hallucinatory episodes, I noted that of the five senses, the sense of smell and of taste tended to be the least stimulated, probably because they play a relatively small part during many intense emotional situations. Captain Macy's house-of-refuge vision is unusual in that it was fully formed; he *smelled* the smoke, *heard* and *felt* the latch, *saw* both the inside and outside of the structure. T.C.]

"You suppose that was just my imagination, fired up by that dreadful, sad accident, and sometimes I think so too. But the one thing I knew then was this. That Yoho was saying something to me and that something was: build a humane house on Muskeget. Yessir! I hadn't the slightest doubt about that, none whatever, and as it turned out, it was surely the right thing to do.

"I wrote letters to the Massachusetts Humane Society and the Boston Marine Society telling about the need for a house. My wife writes the Kings English pretty good and she helped describe the accident, but of course they never have moved very quick up in Boston, and probably never will. [While in Boston I visited the archives of the Humane Society and found Capt. Macy's letters. Two phrases, possibly due to Joanna Macy and referring to Muskeget, are oddly suggestive: "It is a strange and dangerous place, yet *we do not fear it*. What we know is that *people there need protection.*" The question becomes: What must people be protected from if not from fear? T.C.] So I built the house myself when I had the time, and some people from Chatham came over to help and gave some money, so we had the thing up by the next summer. The humane people voted a hundred dollars for the stove and other things, so we got the place into pretty good shape. It was tight and friendly, right enough, and living so close, I kept an eye on it and made sure some fisherman didn't steal the firewood stacked inside.

"Now the business with the house mirage, or vision, or whatever it was when I found Captain Manter and Billy, was something I saw alone. But what happened next was seen by plenty of people. There's plenty still living on Nantucket who were there and will confirm the story.

"That next year we had a bunch of easterly gales in November that were plumb awful! Two whaleships were lost afore they even got out to sea, and I don't know how many coasters were stranded or wrecked. About the third day of the storm, people at 'Sconset and Surfside on Nantucket saw this big three-master driven and banging along the offshore bars and rips and heading for God-knows-where. They followed her west on horseback until they got to Madaket and Smith's Point, which in those days kind of stretched south of Tuckernuck and was the most westerly part of Nantucket.

"The vessel finally come to rest west of Smith's Point and just about abaft of Muskeget in the midst of a terrible smother of rips and shoals. Her masts had mostly gone over the sides, but we still hoped to get a line-throwing gun to Muskeget to shoot a line across her before she came apart completely. The gun and outfit was brought on a buckboard from the humane station at Surfside and then ferried out to Muskeget in a catboat.

"Well, we got a line square across her the second try, but there just didn't seem to be much activity aboard. There was maybe twenty of us on the Muskeget beach by then and we had a big driftwood bonfire going so's they could see us and what we were doing, but the people on the schooner just didn't take the line or nothing. Now it may be that they were waiting below. The waves were breaking across her decks. She lay quartering to the easterly surge and it was something, I can tell you. Still, we yelled and shot off a couple more blank charges in the gun and tried to get them to come up and pull out the breeches buoy line.

"It was almost dark and we're all of us standing in that cold wind staring out at the wreck when I saw, plain as day through the glass, that a woman come over to the side of the vessel and then just fell over into the water. Well, there was a big moan went up from us on the beach and some of them dropped down on their knees and started to pray.

"We could still see the woman. She didn't seem to be sinking, and through the glass I could see why. She was lying on the backs of a great school of fish, churning and thrashing around next to that vessel. They were porpoises, hundreds of them, and they was just like a floor that was alive. They were so tight together that I don't believe that woman ever really got into the water at all. Instead, she started to move in toward us, to shore. It was really the fish brought her in, a great large mob of them all tight together and moving through the rest.

"Well, I never saw anything like that, ever. We went down to the water's edge and there were the fish. They just covered the whole ocean. There were so many of the things, and they were so close together that they had stopped the waves from breaking. Why that sea between us and the stranded vessel was so choked up with fish that there just wasn't room for anything else to happen. In the middle of it, moving toward us, was maybe a dozen of them fish with that woman supported on their backs. There was no mistaking it. We had a big fire going and it made plenty of light. We waded into the water to get that woman and the fish were all around us. They rubbed up agin us, paying us no heed at all as far as I could tell. And they were warm! The water was warm! You put your hand on one of those fish and he was hot, like a hot brick wrapped in flannel.

"They brought the woman right into us, into maybe two feet of water and then some of us carried her ashore. And when I looked back, them grinning fish were still there in the firelight. They all had their snouts pointing our way and they were watching us. Then they just sank and were gone away. It was several minutes afore the waves began to break on that beach again.

"My wife, Joanna, had got the humane house ready, with the stove going and all, so we carried the lady right inside. She certainly looked poorly to me, but Joanna and old Mrs. Pease from Madaket started taking her clothes off and it was pretty evident right then that the lady was laboring to bring out a child.

"We men went back to the beach. We hoped that more of them would try and come in, but none ever did. What happened after that you'll have to hear from my wife. But I just want to say right here that in my opinion that night was a true miracle. It wasn't anything normal or usual, of that I'm absolutely certain!"

[It should be clear from this transcript that Captain Macy believes he was experiencing, during his discovery of the Chatham wreck, a precognitive episode, a foretelling of the future. Philosophically, the psychic investigator is, or certainly should be, most suspicious of any such prediction of future events. Whatever "force" induced Captain Macy to build the humane house "knew" the house would be needed some years hence when the laboring woman came ashore. Yet one hardly requires a crystal ball and a gypsy medium to define the need for some sort of shelter on Muskeget Island. The place lies in the midst of swirling waters, vast sand shoals and deadly, powerful currents. Wrecks occur frequently there and loss of life is a commonplace. I asked the captain how many vessels had been wrecked on, or in the vicinity of, Muskeget during the years following his vision, and he shrugged and responded, "Plenty, at least a dozen, I would guess." Why then, I asked, did he associate this particular wreck with the woman with the episode of Captain Manter. Captain Macy peered at me in the quiet dusk and he did not shrug. "Wrecks is

wrecks, Mr. Cope, and one's pretty much like another,
but when there are two separate, odd matters at the
same exact place, it makes sense to me to connect them."
I explained to the captain that precognition, a trifling
with the flow of time and the sequence of events, raised
the most difficult and intractable questions in all of
natural philosophy. He thought a while and then shook
his head. "I don't think I'm claiming the house was built
for that special wreck or that laboring woman, Mr. Cope.
It was built because it was needed and when that vessel
came by, the next year or ten or twenty years on, it was
put right to use." By whom, I asked him, but he sighed
and looked soberly out at the darkling sands of
Muskeget. "If I knew that, Mr. Cope, I'd be someone
different, maybe someone bigger and richer, from what
I am." Indeed. And we would be richer in ways far
different from the bulge in one's purse. T.C.]

Eve put the open journal on her coffee table and got
up to get another drink. What the hell was that all about,
she wondered. Not the usual ghost story, at least. Eve
took a pull on her almost-neat gin drink, then began to
stride around her flat. Some things about the Macy story
intrigued her, especially the question of why anyone
would want to steal it. And then that odd sense of
planning in the Yoho's activity. First build the house,
then bring in . . . what? . . . the woman with the baby?
Or would any shipwrecked mariner have done as well?
No, that wasn't it, because there were others who came
ashore there over the years. The captain said so. And
why did Cope pick up on Macy's letter to the Humane
Society, where he said they did not fear Muskeget, yet
needed protection? Eve rubbed her eyes and shook her

head. Macy and Cope were talking about power, about something strong but not menacing.

Eve stood thoughtfully staring out the window, hardly noticing that a small white car had stopped in front of her building. She glanced down and saw, in a moment of confusion, that there were policemen getting out of the car, but before she could step back from the window, one of the men looked up and caught her glance. Damn, they had seen her, knew she was home!

Eve darted back from the window, seized the journal and the two other large books from the auction and dashed into her small john. She dumped her dirty clothes out of the hamper, dropped the three books in, and threw her clothes back on top. As she shut the hamper, her buzzer began to sound.

She dashed back and pressed the talk button. "Yes?"

"Police, Dr. Pennington. Might we speak with you a moment?"

"Yes, of course," she said absently, pushing the door-lock button. She rubbed her eyes and tried to remember where her passport was at that moment. She walked into her living room for a swallow of her drink and pulled a sweater over her head. She felt pushed, pressed by them. They hadn't even given her time to read it all.

When Eve opened the door to a single, heavy knock, she saw the same two policemen from earlier in the day, but now the small, ferret-faced thief that had snatched her book was handcuffed to the silent one. "Dr. Pennington," said the taller constable at once, "is this the man who snatched your book?"

"Absolutely. There's no doubt. I'm sure the man at the carnival would identify him, too."

The policeman hardly seemed to have noticed what

she said. "We'll need what he took, miss," said the man, "for evidence. We'll bring it back in the morning. And we'll need you to sign a statement."

Eve took a deep breath and tried to smile cheerily. "Oh, dear. Well, I mailed those books I got at the auction off to America. I'm going home in a couple of weeks and I don't want to be loaded down with stuff, so I mail anything I get now right off."

The man looked at her with a stony face. "It's not here then, the book he stole?"

"It's in the mail," said Eve firmly, "but I don't see what difference that makes. I paid twenty-two pounds for it yesterday at Phillips, at an auction. I'll be glad to sign whatever you want about the theft."

"You mailed it?" said the constable slowly. "From around here, I suppose?"

Eve nodded. "Yes, from the office near the Swiss Cottage tube station. I really don't . . ."

The man nodded at her. "I'll be back in the morning," he said in a slow voice, "with a statement for you to sign. Twenty-two pounds it cost?" and he made a note.

Eve nodded again, wishing they would go but not wanting to suggest by glance or gesture that she didn't want them poking around in her flat. The moment seemed to drag endlessly as the tall policeman made some more careful notes, then looked at her from under dropped lids. "I guess there isn't anything more right now," he said. "We'll be in touch with you." He turned to his silent partner and the short prisoner. "Let's go," he said to Eve's immense relief, and she eased the door shut with a reassuring click behind them, then dashed to the window to watch them come out of the front doorway, but they seemed to act the same when seen from three flights above as they had at her door. They said nothing to each other, but the silent officer and the small man got in the back seat and the other policeman climbed in the front and started the little sedan, which Eve saw had a Metropolitan Police shield on the front doors. Eve watched them roll down the avenue out of sight and let her breath out in a whoosh. She went and fished the books out of her laundry hamper, threw over her cross-bolt burglars lock and mixed one more drink.

"Okay, Mrs. Joanna Macy," she said in a tight, excited voice while sitting down with the book again, "now what?"

[Mrs. Macy is a handsome woman, slightly taller than her husband, and possessing a round, cheerful face. Her speech and manner show somewhat more education than the captain. Like her husband, there is a sturdy honesty about her that I found both refreshing and encouraging, although one suspects that Joanna Macy is probably a bit more ready to believe in the paranormal event than the captain. The sunset was ended and Muskeget was lost in dusky shadows when we returned to the Macy homestead where Joanna plied us with a cool drink of some sort of tart fruit punch ably assisted by what the captain described in his colorful manner as, "the best dang Medford rum money can buy." I should note here that although there seems to be considerable drunkenness along these lonely, offshore islands on the New England coast, the Macys have not allowed rum, nor the dreadful American whiskey, to cloud their lives and judgments. As we sipped the excellent product of Medford, in Massachusetts, the captain turned to me and smiled. "Mr. Cope, these yarns we're spinning for you

don't come out of any bottle. When the weather and the
sea gets worked up, the last thing anybody needs is a tum-
bler of this," and he gestured at the rum bottle. T.C.]

"I was born Joanna Cambell into a strict Scotch
Presbyterian family, but I've never been an especially
religious woman. I guess religion never actually did
anyone much harm, just so it doesn't get in the way of
common sense. It seems downright unlikely to me that
on a world as big and busy as this one, the Creator would
fool around with this or that little trick or miracle while
letting most of it go straight to hell in a hand basket most
of the time. So I don't see what happened on Muskeget
that night, what with the wreck and woman and all, as a
religious matter. In my opinion, to put it simply, that
island was alive and maybe is still alive. Something called
those fish to bring that woman to shore. Something was
working there that can get inside of things that live and
make them do what it wanted. I was born in Glasgow, in
Scotland, but my father had come down from the north,
from those wild places, and he told me that if you live
close enough to the edge of the land and the edge of the
sea, if you listen hard and watch close, you can get a sense
of places that are different from what most people see
and hear.

"That woman off the wreck was about dead when we
got her inside the humane house. I know something
about having children, what with birthing four myself
and helping with plenty more. There weren't all that
many doctors at the west end of Nantucket, so we all had
to learn the ways of getting a baby out of a woman. That
woman was a hard case, all right. You could see that. She
was pretty well scarred and bruised and unhealthy
generally. Mrs. Pease looked at me and her old eyes were

sad. 'She's dying, Joanna,' she said, and her face was white and thin. 'We aren't going to get that child nohow!'

"It looked like that, but I wasn't going to give up. 'Push on it!' I said in the woman's ear. 'Try! Try!'

" 'She's dead,' said Mrs. Pease in a voice sadder than the winter winds. 'She isn't breathing.'

"Well, it seemed so for a minute, but I just couldn't believe that those fish would have brought her to shore like that just so's we could bury her and the baby too.

"Then she started to breathe again, all by herself. It was a funny breathing for a laboring woman, regular, long breaths, and as she did that she really began to labor, to push hard. I put my hand in and I could feel that baby's head. It was moving down, but things were awful tight there. The woman just wasn't in good shape for doing this. I didn't know what to do then. The woman was pushing and her face was red as a beet. I guess I began to lose heart. I could see the woman wasn't going to last much longer, no matter what we did. I've seen some hard moments and bad things along this coast, especially in the winter, but right then my courage just flew out of me and my hands shook, my legs were water and I looked up at Mrs. Pease. 'Pray,' she said to me, 'there's nothing else to do.'

"But that wasn't exactly all we could do. There was something else, though I didn't have the courage, or maybe the determination, to see it.

"The woman hadn't said a word since the men carried her out of the water. But right then, she spoke, only it wasn't exactly her speaking. It was the baby talking from inside her. 'Help me!' it said. 'Cut! Cut! Help me!' You could hear it plain, right out of her belly.

"Mrs. Pease kind of pretended she didn't hear it. She

figured it was Old Nick himself, come to diddle us. But I knew what was said and what was meant. Those words steadied me like nothing before or since. 'All right,' I said, and I took Captain Macy's clasp knife I'd borrowed to cut the cord and I cut into her both ways.

"The woman gave a great last shove and a groan and the baby came out in a big, awful tide of blood and water that went all over everything, Mrs. Pease, me, the floor of the house. I lifted up the baby and put a sheet around it, trying to wipe away the mess. It was a girl, and I guess the prettiest baby I ever saw brought out. She didn't cry a bit. Just looked at me out of big round eyes. 'Thank you,' she said. Think of it! Just born, covered with slime and blood, but her mouth moved and she said thank you to me so natural that I guess I smiled and the baby smiled back.

"'She's gone, Joanna. She's dead,' said Mrs. Pease, and, sure enough, the moment that baby had come down into my hands, the woman had stopped breathing. Just like that. No gasps or rattle or choking. Most people, even the old ones, don't give up so easy. Right at the end they seem to know it and they make one more try, to sit up, gasp, cry out, whatever. But I'm not sure that woman was alive those last few minutes. And once the baby was out, whatever was keeping her going just sort of let go of her and she stopped living without a sound.

"Well, there was one more odd thing to happen. I was holding the little girl trying to think about it all and Mrs. Pease was sitting on a bunk looking at the floor. Her face was kind of puzzled, though she talked about it all later, and plenty at that. I should say that at that time my youngest, Tommy, was six, so I was hardly what you'd call a nursing mother. But that little girl started to cry then, just like any baby would, and I started to flow right into my dress from both sides. I never saw anything like that. I had more milk than I'd ever had with any of my four and I just unbuttoned and put that little girl on me and she took to that milk as happy and quiet as any baby could.

"Whatever was there on Muskeget could do what it wanted with us. Make us live and die and talk and give milk. It was a wonder, all right, and I can't say I understand it, but that was no ordinary haunt. Everything I ever read about spooks and ghosts claim they come back to fix old wrongs or complain about old evil doings or show us how awful past things were. But there was none of that in this business. Whatever was there knew what it wanted to do, how it wanted things to happen. I believe that, even if I don't know exactly what the final end of it was, or is.

"Nothing about that schooner, her captain, or any of her crew has ever been discovered. No bodies ever washed ashore and the boat was smashed to small pieces before the night was ended. We found a broach on the woman's dress later with an inscription on the back, 'Love to Miranda,' so we decided to name the little girl Miranda Macy. I love her now just like my others, maybe a little more what with everything that's happened. She's a beautiful woman, Miranda, and a smart one too. Grew up with us, worked hard, saved her money, and now she owns one of those tourist hotels over in 'Sconset. Runs it better'n any man ever could.

"We buried her mother on Tuckernuck, in the little east-end cemetery and Henry cut the stone for her grave. Plenty of people still remember the business with the fish, but I guess I'm the only one around now who really knows about the birth and how that happened. When Miranda comes to see us, I ask her if she has any special feeling about Muskeget or the humane house there, but she says, no, nothing more than what we've told her about how she got started in the world. She's a fine young woman, Miranda is. If that Yoho or haunt, or whatever it is, wanted to save somebody, maybe to make up for all the poor, sad folks who died in the smallpox hospital, well, it couldn't have picked a better person to save.

"I guess that's about all I can tell you about our experiences with the occult, as you call it, Mr. Cope. Here and there you still hear some talk about the Yoho, how it lives in the fogs, how it comes at you as a beak or on the rush of big wings, and how you can find cloven hoof marks on the sands of Muskeget or the west end of Tuckernuck. But people naturally call something evil when they don't understand it or what it does. I don't see the Yoho as either good or bad, especially, but just as itself with its own purposes. And how many people can you look in the face and see their purposes anyway? Very few, I think."

[Other men on Nantucket verified Captain Macy's story about the porpoises and, in fact, some of them gave me explanations. Now and then porpoises have been known to group together in the water to support a drowning man, sometimes close to shore but more frequently in the open ocean near a whaleship. The animals have been known to attach themselves to a particular vessel and follow it across wide ocean expanses. The presumption is that a school became attached to the wrecked schooner and behaved in the manner described, although all the men I talked to agreed that most such episodes involve many fewer animals than in this case.

I visited the quaint village of Siasconset (called universally here, 'Sconset) and interviewed Miss Miranda Macy, a very attractive and lively young lady who runs an excellent boarding house (called universally here, a hotel). She could not throw any further light on any of her parents' stories. I asked her if she had, perhaps, started talking at an earlier age than most children, but she only laughed at that and said she was really quite an ordinary person. She then commented, most winningly, I felt, on her adopted mother's story, more or less as follows. "Mr. Cope, as an Englishman you probably believe that most of your neighbors in Scotland are dour, unromantic, and without imagination, but my mother is not at all like that. Deep down, she really does believe in Yohos and the little people and headless ghosts in castles, so much so that she is always ready to give any of them the benefit of the doubt. Do you see what I mean, sir? When she came to that moment with my other mother in the house, when she had to cut, what else would happen but that I would ask her to do it? Certain Irish fairies can supposedly make the newborn speak, you know. My mother is a very courageous and admirable woman and that story just makes me love her all the more."

Miss Macy then realized that she was, to some extent, calling into question my own interests, and she immediately stopped and apologized.

"I don't mean to imply, Mr. Cope, that psychic occurrences have never happened. It's just that until you or I live through something as intense as that moment in the humane house, I don't see how we can really judge her story honestly."

"What about Mrs. Pease?" I asked her then and I was interested, perhaps encouraged, to see that this question immediately threw some doubt on what she had just suggested.

"Mrs. Pease was an old woman when that happened. She died when I was four." Miranda spoke slowly and looked at me directly. "My mother is a very strong-willed person. I think she might have been able to make Mrs. Pease see or hear whatever she wanted."

I asked her then, myself, if she had any sense or feeling about the area around Muskeget Island and she answered that she had none that she could notice, other than a natural affinity to the whole area where she spent a happy and busy girlhood. Miss Macy is a levelheaded and capable young woman. In her situation, I think I might try to have as little as possible to do with a past event that could otherwise label her as a strange and exotic specimen on a very conservative island that values such things not one little bit.

Before I left Nantucket I hired a catboat for the day to sail me to Muskeget so I might walk around the place myself. There are other small buildings there now, a gunning club and some fishing shanties on the south shore, but the humane house still stands almost in the center of the island. I entered this and sat down on an old rocking chair, hoping for some sense of whatever magic had infused this place, but there was nothing. It is decidedly in the nature of these phenomena to come upon us when we are least ready to receive them, and to deny us *absolutely,* when we face and dare them to appear. T.C.]

Eve closed the journal and tossed it on the coffee table. She stretched and, feeling hungry, went out to poke around in the icebox, staring with deep dissatisfaction at some chunks of thick, tough British bacon. She mixed a drink and made her thoughts come together on the Macy stories. They were certainly a likable bunch, thought Eve, shaking her head in real admiration. God, imagine, the baby says "Cut" and she does it. Talk about tough!

"Not a psychiatrist in a carload with that crowd," she said suddenly to her empty flat. Eve knew that her academic friends, with their turtlenecks, their dope, their shrinks, and their clever talk were not likely to do anything spunky like that. And neither could I, she thought sadly.

She dropped into her comfortable chair and opened the journal at the end. Even old Tom Cope, she had to admit, was no fool or phony. He really seemed to be an honest man, not afraid to write down ideas that tended to go against the supernatural stuff he was seeking.

Idly she began to leaf through the empty back pages of the ledger and two pages beyond Cope's comments found the following, in a completely different hand: "Miranda Macy did have other important moments on Muskeget. See story in Yankee yarn-spinners book. Also, I have her own account of some later experiences."

There was no signature or initials after this brief note and nothing else on any of the other pages. Eve sighed and hunted up the Phillips catalogue from the recent book auction, then carefully went through it line-by-line, seeking any other lots that might pertain to this matter. She especially peered at the occult listings at the back, but they seemed to be entirely European or English in origin. She could find nothing else that seemed related to Muskeget in any way.

The question was, Eve asked herself, did she really care about this crazy bunch of very tall stories because of the tales themselves or because someone else seemed to want the book so badly?

She couldn't answer that. Something about the whole business continued to both attract and elude her. She was fuzzy from the gin. I've got to go easy on the booze, she thought to herself, and thinking this, went to mix another. The baby said, "Cut!" she thought again. If any of that *really* happened, *any* of it, then Thomas Cope had, for a second, caught a tiny piece, a thin corner of something bigger and grander than all the astronomy ever imagined! What the hell was it? What?

·3·

TWO
ENCOUNTERS

That next Saturday night, Eve Pennington had a date. Ancient, distinguished Professor Forbish Wingate, dean of British science historians, had asked her to see a new play in the West End and then go to dinner at a Japanese restaurant that she had suggested. The play, one of several running at that time dealing with the deep malaise of the British upper-middle class, bored Eve almost to angry tears. Fortunately, she came to it with a few shots of gin under her belt and so managed to doze through most of the second act and the onstage whimpers about how perfectly *awful* it was to have a meaningless, exploitive job that paid you thirty thousand quid a year.

Afterward, in a noisy pub, Dr. Wingate pursed his grey, wrinkled lips and gave Eve an apologetic smile. "Sorry about that play, Eve," he said cheerfully. "There aren't all that many things around, really. I didn't think you'd care too much about *Richard III* done in the language of the Ukraine or that one at the Alburrey where they scream at each other for a solid hour."

Eve grinned lopsidedly at the old man and patted his arm. "I'm not much of a playgoer, Forbish," she said at once. "And I *know* the food is going to be good. Thank God that author isn't cooking it up." Eve shrugged and tried to collect her fuzzy thoughts. "I just can't abide the idea that the more money you have and the more varied and interesting your job, the more miserable you should become. I mean, what if those people in that play had to do *real* work?" She suddenly remembered the stories of Nantucket in the ledger. "We smart people all seem so weak nowadays, Forbish. What's going to happen to us, anyway?"

They went off to the restaurant and were soon settled in a quiet corner, having one more drink and eating some delicious raw fish. "We'll be sorry to see you go, Eve," said the professor. "I can't tell you how much your help meant at that conference. And everyone says your paper on the construction of lunar dials was the best thing on the program." He looked at her out of pouchy, red-rimmed eyes. "Have you ever thought about doing the science history thing full-time, Eve?"

She nodded and took a gulp of her dry martini. "Oh, I've thought of it lots of times, but there just aren't any departments in America that could fit me in. Hell, there aren't any departments in America at all, really. Oh, maybe a teeny one at Harvard, but not much else. I have to eat. I don't have a rich daddy like those people in that play."

The old man gave a thin smile. "Perhaps something could be worked out over here," he said in a quiet voice.

"It wouldn't pay what you get now, but then, you wouldn't have to work so hard either."

"Well, you're sweet to say that," said Eve at once, smiling warmly at him. "It would be fun to be here, doing my hobby full-time and getting a crack at all that lovely stuff that keeps going on sale."

Professor Wingate nodded. "Yes, well, Noel tells me you had an impressive day at Phillips last week. Got yourself a French Bion. I'd love to see it sometime."

Eve, ravenously hungry from all the drinks, attacked her crispy tempura with much concentration, trying to chew rapidly so she could keep up the conversation. "You know, Forbish, I got something weird at that sale that might just interest you. You've done a couple of things on those Victorian occult crazies . . ." and she went on to rapidly describe the ledger and its stories, then to tell how at least two apparent attempts had been made to get the book away from her.

And as the gin and the tasty food and the warm dark coziness of the restaurant helped her to spin out these stories, Eve failed to notice that Professor Wingate had stopped eating and was holding a white cup of warm sake shadowing the lower part of his face and lips, peering at her from eyes that, though usually rheumy and red, now had points of black alertness at their centers.

Eve babbled on about the auction, the stories and the policemen, eating and drinking in between her comments, not noticing that the professor was not saying anything much beyond an occasional grunt or an "Oh?" to keep her talking.

"Well, what do you make of all that?" she said finally, putting down her fork and looking at him suddenly and directly.

Forbish Wingate's face in the dim light of the single candle on the table was seemingly expressionless. "The policemen came back the next day?" he asked in a low voice.

Eve nodded. "The tall one did. He had me sign a statement telling what happened, only a few words really. I haven't heard anything since."

"And what do you think about it, Eve?" he said in a cool, serious tone. The food had helped reduce that gin-buzz in her head and Eve had a sudden thought that maybe she had said too much. She had, after all, lied to the policemen, and maybe old Forbish Wingate was one of those law-and-order types who really believed in totally cooperating with authority. She didn't actually know him all that well, she suddenly realized.

Eve lifted her eyebrows and tried to grin. "I've thought about it a little. The only thing I can come up with is some sort of buried treasure, perhaps something left there when the smallpox hospital was on that little island. Otherwise, why would people want that journal?" She shrugged. "Of course, maybe nobody really does want it all that much. Like they say, even paranoids have enemies," and she tried to give a tinkling laugh that somehow came out as more of a croak.

The old man rubbed his chin and then his hollow, wrinkled cheek. His eyes watched her steadily, with no shift or blink. "I wonder if I might borrow that ledger, Eve?" he said slowly and intently. "I have a certain interest in Thomas Cope, and what you're describing sounds like a rather important addition to his material."

He paused, since she seemed to make no response, then tried to take a more casual tone. "Cope, you know, had a thing about animals as, perhaps you might call them, psychic instruments, indicators of the supernatural. The business with the fish is exactly the sort of thing he would have studied with avidity."

"Sure," said Eve, "you can borrow it. But under the circumstances, I don't think I'll mail it to you. Stop in my office on Wednesday, when you're up at my place for your lecture, and you can pick it up then."

Professor Wingate let his eyes drift thoughtfully around the restaurant, then fixed them on Eve again. "All right," he said finally, "eleven in the morning convenient for you? Or whenever you say."

"Eleven Wednesday is fine," said Eve, sipping on a sweet and tasty liqueur and wishing she could stop babbling so much when she had a few drinks in her. "Unless, of course, somebody manages to snaffle it away before then."

"I do hope you will keep it safe," said the professor seriously. "It might turn out to be quite valuable, you know? By that I mean intellectually valuable."

They parted outside the restaurant and Eve thanked him warmly for the evening and the "perfectly yummy food."

The professor nodded formally. "See you Wednesday," was his parting statement.

Eve resisted a last drink when she got back to Hampstead and climbed into bed instead, where she had a slight case of the whirlies. She wondered how secret agents and detectives, in the thrillers she occasionally read on planes, were able to drink so heavily and still manage to do their jobs. Yet Forbish Wingate was no nuclear bomb designer or remote-sensing satellite engineer. He was the goddamned president of the British Society for the History of Science, the dullest, driest bunch of fuddy-duddies, rich hobbyists, and useless dilettantes in all of Merry England! But she didn't want to give him that ledger, she damn well knew that, and as the bed steadied under her and her eyelids drooped toward welcome sleep, she decided what to do.

Next Monday, Eve arrived at her office at eight-thirty in the morning and had the astronomy beadle let her into the copier room. "Up early, Professor?" said old, toothless Harry, giving her a rather flattened, but quite genuine, grin.

Eve put her finger to her lips. "Don't you say anything, Harry. The others get so defensive about not being here early and then start explaining about their trains and all. And anyway, we're lucky if the students show up by eleven. I just have a bunch of duplicating to do and that awful copier takes so long."

By nine-thirty Eve had two copies of the Cope journal complete, but she decided to omit the final note about the other material on Miranda Macy from the copy for Professor Wingate. She bit her lip and tried to remember if she had mentioned that note to him Saturday night. How she had babbled on! Well, if she did, maybe he missed it in the midst of all the other stuff. Eve rubbed her cheeks and stared down at the ledger and the copies. Why is it that I always want to confess things, she thought in annoyance. Christ, I've got more guilt than those damn fools in that stupid play!

Eve got back to the empty office she shared with two younger men in the astronomy department and thought hard about where to hide the ledger itself. Along the back wall of the big room was a tall set of flat drawers for star maps, atlases, and photo blowups of hundreds of deep sky features. Next to these were several file cabinets containing similar things, folded or fitted to an 8-by-11-inch size so they could be stored inside standard envelopes. Eve took a new envelope from the stock cabinet and sat down to type on its upper corner, "Alpherotz, Infrared & U.V." and stuffed the ledger inside, then filed the envelope in its proper alphabetical sequence. To find that, she knew, they would have to pull hundreds of envelopes out.

She shoved one complete copy of the account into her desk and by then it was just about time to meet her class.

When she came back to her office at noon, she saw that Professor Wingate was sitting near her desk in a straight chair, perusing some science history journals. Somehow Eve had expected that, but she let her eyebrows pop up in surprise. "Hello, Forbish," she said. "I thought I wouldn't be seeing you until Wednesday."

The old man gave her a friendly grimace and jumped gallantly to his feet to shake her hand. "It turned out that I had a couple of errands up here, so I thought I'd drop by . . ." but before he could continue, Eve stepped over to her desk and lifted up the remaining duplicate of the journal.

"Well, here it is, the whole thing from start to finish. And you can keep that. I made one for myself." She handed him the stack of papers.

He stared at her without expression. "Well, Eve, I'd prefer the original. In these handwritten documents, just the stress of a pen can speak volumes."

But Eve was sober now and she was suddenly fed up with being so nicey-nice with these laid-back Englishmen in their cold masks. She pushed the papers at him and her mouth was a set red line. "I'm *awfully* sorry, Forbish. Quite frankly, I happen to think that somebody is trying to get that book, for whatever reason I don't know. I don't expect you to believe that, but it would be utterly stupid for me to give you the document when I know perfectly well that you won't guard it the way I would. You have a copy just as I do, so the thing won't be completely lost if it should turn up missing." Eve stopped talking and her set face showed that the topic of the original ledger was exhausted.

The old man shrugged and then smiled from narrow eyes. "Of course. I'm sure this will get me started in an entirely adequate way. And if it should turn out to be important . . ." He shrugged again. "Well, perhaps I can see the treasure itself someday. You know that it's possible to make estimates from a document of this sort as to how many sittings were involved, sometimes even the time span between the recording of the stories."

"Forbish," said Eve from her own fixed smile, "I promise that you'll be the first one allowed in the bank vault," and she gave a quick laugh.

Professor Wingate inclined his head at Eve. "Thank you for doing this," he indicated the sheets, "and I'll see you at your much-awaited party next week."

Eve smiled more brightly now and wiggled her fingers in a friendly farewell gesture at him. "See you then, Forbish," but when he had gone she replayed his words and their tone again. Everybody knows something that I don't, she thought angrily. What the hell is it?

During a solitary and inedible lunch in the college cafeteria, Eve decided what to do next. The only thing she might know that Wingate might not was that there were other, presumably later, accounts linking Miranda Macy and the island of Muskeget. So Eve dashed off that afternoon to the West End and Phillips again and found the place quiet and the reception area occupied by a lovely young lady in very tight slacks and a bulging, frilly blouse.

"May I help you, madam?" the girl said formally yet quite warmly to Eve, for she saw in Eve's smartly-styled suit and carefully-fixed face a kind of kindred, if older, soul.

Eve's wide red lips spread apart in a real smile at the young woman. "Is Ian McPherson around, do you know?" she asked in a bright voice.

The receptionist returned Eve's smile in a flash of perfectly white, perfectly straight teeth. Now she spoke as herself. "Oh, 'e's downstairs pottering about in 'is little cave, I expect. You just go knock 'im up, luv," and her tone and expression said that Ian was both funny and very nice and that either of them might properly find him a very warm chap.

Eve waved her thanks and clattered down the stairs to the closed door of the book room. She knocked tentatively, then heard from inside, "Who?"

"Eve Pennington, Ian," she said at once. "Can I see you for a sec?"

The door opened and a grinning Ian welcomed her into his book-filled sanctum. There were books piled everywhere, on the floor, on tables, on chairs and chair arms, on shelves, and moved into the very middle of the room was Ian's small desk and his long sheets of handwritten copy for the next auction catalogue. "Just in time for tea, Dr. Pennington," he said expansively, "which is actually any time since the water's on the boil all day."

Eve sat down, after carefully unloading a chair of its

books, and smiled. "That's quite a dishy sweetie at the front desk, Ian. Did she get Miss Britain at Earls Court last year?"

Ian shrugged. "They're always trying to put up a big front at the front office, you know. *Phiiiliiips heaaaahh*," he intoned in a nasal, stuffy British voice.

"She has quite a back too, Ian," said Eve. "Oh, lovely. Thanks," as he handed her a steaming cup of tea. "I know you're busy, but I just had to come by and ask you a question."

Ian nodded at her, then expertly threw their tea bags into a dark and bookless corner. "Whatever I can do," he said.

"Do you remember that last auction, the occult things?" Ian nodded and she went on. "Well, first, did the owner of that stuff have any more? Was that a whole estate or what?"

Ian thought a moment. "It was an old lady, not an estate. She had a few more things, if I remember rightly. Some of them weren't worth bringing here. They would have realized nothing and I hate to see people totally clean off their bookshelves and leave only dust. There may have been a few things she kept out of sentiment. You know, books that were inscribed or written by somebody she knew."

Eve now looked intently at Ian and she spoke in a low, conspiratorial voice. "Ian, I know you're not supposed to do this, but could you tell me who that owner was and where she may live?"

Ian laughed heartily at Eve's seriousness. "I think that lonely old lady would love to see you, Dr. Pennington." He got up and went to a file cabinet and rummaged around, finally producing a printed card. "Mrs. Rose

Stringfellow," he said, handing Eve the card. "Henley-on-Thames."

Eve copied the address. "Does she have a phone?"

Ian McPherson took back the card and peered at it. "I'm afraid not. Old Mrs. Stringfellow is not especially well-off. That's why she sold the books, I expect." He sat down and put his hands behind his head. "She wrote us and I drove out to look at her books. Brought it all back, all the stuff that was in the sale last week." He sipped his hot tea, staring at her with bright eyes. "Don't tell me you're getting hooked onto the psychic stuff?" he said suddenly.

Eve had felt very much alone these past few days. She said to herself, I have to trust somebody, and Ian did actually have the journal here for a while and let it go to the sale. She looked around the little, crowded room and took a deep breath. "Ian, please call me Eve. And please listen for a few minutes . . ." and she quickly told him about the Macy stories and the seemingly deep interest shown in them by various people.

Ian listened with a clouded, thoughtful face, sipping at his tea mug. When Eve finished, he spoke at once. "There's something else you ought to know, Eve," he said. "About a week after the catalogue for that sale went out, two plainclothes policemen came here and went through our catalogue mailing lists for the book sales."

Eve frowned her puzzlement at him. "Wasn't the ledger here then? Couldn't they have taken it or borrowed it?"

Ian nodded. "Definitely. Reputable auctioneers, our descriptive name for ourselves, are most careful to cooperate with the coppers on *any* request. They could have taken the whole damned sale with them if they wanted. The one thing we can't be connected with is stolen or doubtful goods. Mr. Fitzhugh, the general manager, personally brought those men down to see our lists."

Eve shook her head. "Well, that's just crazy, Ian. Why would they come here, fiddle around, then go, and after the sale try to get the book back from me by theft or whatever? It doesn't make any sense."

But Ian had jumped to his feet and his alert, handsome face was lit by a sudden flash of interest and excitement. "But you're talking like John B. Watson, Eve! Holmes would just look *harder*. Sense is exactly what it does make!"

Eve pressed her lips together in a rueful grin. "You just discovered the story of my life. That's exactly who I am and always will be, Dr. Watson."

"Watson had his qualities, Eve. And as a dues-paying member of the Baker Street Irregulars, I should be a little better at this than you are. Let me give you my Holmesian understanding of the affair." He leaned against a bookshelf and took a final pull on his tea mug, then set the thing precariously on a tottering pile of leather-backed classics. "Let's assume that every event you've described to me is, in fact, connected to that journal you bought at the sale."

He waggled his fingers at her. "Now the coppers that came here to look at my lists were the real thing. They've been here before and, anyway, Fitzhugh wouldn't be caught by two phonys that he'd never seen before just because they had some sort of badge or identification. You're absolutely correct in thinking they could have either taken or borrowed the mystery journal then. They could have pulled fifty books out of the sale, to mask their real interest, and we would have just stood there hoping to get them back sometime. They didn't go near the books. What they did was to check my file of subscribers to the catalogues against a short list of their own. From the time they took, I would assume they had perhaps a dozen names, no more. They didn't spend ten minutes with that file box."

Ian rubbed his head and then waved a finger at her again. "So what does that imply? Simply that they knew about the journal, knew what was in it, and were interested in just who might buy it. They had some ideas of their own, their own list, and so wanted to see if any of those people would be getting catalogues. The description of the journal in the catalogue must have alerted them."

Ian took a step forward, but had to stop short before a wobbly book mountain overturned. "So what happens? You buy the book, either by chance or . . . ?" He shrugged at her and raised questioning eyebrows. "And somehow there is another group, another, let's say, less official group which knows something about this business, but not as much. They are at the sale, watching group one, and when you get the book, the official, plainclothes people somehow identified you to this second group, which they may not have even known about. Now the new people don't know what's in the thing you've bought, and they try to get it away. First the fellow at the door here, then the snatch on the Heath and the hanky-panky with the doubtful coppers at your flat."

Eve's eyes widened in disbelief but Ian plunged on.

"Now, think about it, Eve. You said that neither the shorter constable, nor the thief they supposedly caught, ever said a word in front of you, right?"

Eve nodded. "The little man groaned when that huge gypsy squeezed him, but that was all."

"Right!" said Ian excitedly. "Well, I'm claiming that the ones that came here to Phillips were the real ones, so those others must be fakes and perhaps only one of them could speak properly. I mean, our way. Think about what your reaction would have been if the other copper had said something to you like, 'Izz zees ze teeff, madam?'"

Eve broke out in a huge smile. "What a *wonderful* imagination, Ian! Now it's Russian agents, dressed as constables, prowling Hampstead Heath. And looking for what?"

Ian shrugged and answered cheerfully. "Russian, Israeli, Arab, French, maybe even your own famous spooks, that is what you call them, isn't it? My point is, there have to be *two* groups, don't you see? One knows, or thinks it knows, what it's doing. The other is following the first to find out too."

But Eve firmly shook her head. "The only trouble with all that web spinning is this. How does Professor Forbish Wingate fit into it? I know a little about indirection and tricking people to do what you want and I swear he didn't set me going on that journal and the stories. The liquor and the food did that. Old Wingate just sat there taking it in. I blabbed my guts to him. Maybe I was a little tight, but I'm certain that he had no real interest in my triumphs at the auction until I got to my descriptions of the Macy stories and the fact that other people seemed to want them. From that point on, he couldn't think of anything else."

"Okay," said Ian at once. "Holmes would just see that as *new* evidence, something that tells us an important fact. Professor Wingate isn't in either of the police groups, but he still knows something about what they know. Why? It must be because he's a specialist in a little, backwater field, the History of Science, right? So whatever secret it is you've found, actually, purchased from us, it's somehow connected with some discovery made by science historians."

Eve laughed sharply. "That's like suggesting that two mating guppies can produce a great white shark. One of the reasons I keep thinking about getting into science history full-time is so I won't have to do anything that will end up hurting people someday, and I can stop taking money from NASA and Defense. I don't know any secrets, Ian. I don't want to know any."

Ian spoke in a serious voice. "Suppose for a second that those stories in that journal are true. Suppose they are part of a whole group of such stories from which somebody can learn how to do those things, cause hallucinations, order fish around, make a baby talk and start a mother's milk flowing. You don't think those kinds of skills wouldn't attract the attention of exactly the sort of people you say you don't want to work for? I think most governments would trade all kinds of lives and treasure for a shot at that secret, that sort of ability."

"Well," said Eve, wrinkling her nose in thought, "I have heard the Russians are big in psychic research, parapsychology, all that stuff, although they don't seem to have gotten very far with it. But Holmes, old chap, with all this activity and interest, how is it that nobody wanted the journal enough so that I simply stumbled on it? Why, that man could have had it for much less than the fifty pounds he offered me afterward."

"He evidently didn't know it was important until *after* you bought it," said Ian. "And Holmes would never accept any theory that you got it by pure accident. He would always look for a connection, some way in which you specifically relate to all the rest of it."

"You mean, my being interested in science history?" said Eve.

"Perhaps. That is certainly a connection. Why did you buy the thing, anyway?"

Eve tried to think back a week to her inspection of the books. "I really don't remember noticing it in the catalogue, Ian. I was glancing along the shelves where you had the postcards, scrapbooks, and manuscripts, just in case I missed something, I suppose, and I picked it up." She paused, trying to remember. "Then when I saw that it was about Nantucket Island, and especially about Muskeget, I guess my interest was just caught."

"You've been to those islands?" asked Ian.

"Lots of people have been to Nantucket, Ian. It's a very tony summer resort now, very expensive. But I've been to Muskeget too. When my family spent a summer on Nantucket back in the sixties, we used to sail over there for picnics. It was deserted, sandy and buggy, but kind of an interesting, lonely place. And there were a couple of little, abandoned houses to play in."

"So that's a connection too," said Ian at once.

Eve lifted her sharp, black eyebrows. "I guess it is. Certainly if I'd never heard of it or been there, I wouldn't have paid much attention to that journal." She stopped talking to shake her head. "This is just so *strange*. I can't seem to let go of it. I don't believe all your Sherlock Holmes stuff for a second, but *what* is it about?"

But a new idea had seized Ian McPherson and he was now squeezed in behind a tower of books, digging into a file drawer. "Hang on, I had a thought, or maybe a memory . . . ahh . . ." He pulled out a file folder and opened it to some inventory lists, then read intently. "Right! Listen to this, Eve. That Bion and the surveying book you bought, plus a few other good early science items, those came in from Mrs. Stringfellow too, but later, maybe a month later." He rubbed his forehead. "Now what was it . . . ? Yes, she had gotten them as a bequest, from some relative who had died the previous year . . . or was it two years? Something like that. Some solicitor wrote her and asked where to send the books, so she just contacted me and asked if they could go in the sale with the others. Well, there weren't more than a dozen, I think, but they were all good items, so of course I said yes." He stared at Eve as he put the folder back in the file. "Well, Eve . . . ?"

She stared back. "Now you're saying that they baited the hook. Who are they, Ian? This is all so loose. It really doesn't quite hang together."

Ian came back to sit down at the desk. "Well, it couldn't until we know more about it. If I were you, I'd go for a talk with Mrs. Stringfellow. See if those added books were really okay, you know, above suspicion. See what else she has to offer."

Eve Pennington got to her feet and reached to take Ian's hand. "Dear friend Ian," she said and her voice was warm, "I told you all that crazy stuff just so you could tell me I'm a book nut with a persecution mania, and instead you've stuck me in the middle of an occult spy thriller. You can meet old Forbish and play detective with them all. Please come to my going-away party next week . . ." and she bent over to scribble her address and the time of the party on a scrap of paper.

Ian nodded and smiled warmly back, thinking how really smart and solid a person she was, and how attractive. "I'd love to come and say good-bye," he said.

Eve grinned at him. "If you brought that bird of paradise from upstairs, Ian, you'd be the star of the show. I guarantee it."

Ian stretched and leaned back in his swivel chair to peer over a leaning tower of books, then winked at her. "Do you really see me as such a man-about-town, Eve? I'm actually a genuine antiquarian book person, truly loving the musty, dusty tomes and the creaky philosophies of days long gone."

"Phooey," said Eve. "We're both romantics, you and I. That's why we like this old stuff . . ." and she indicated the disheveled city of book towers surrounding them. "I mean passion *meant* something then, Ian." She waved a hand and turned to go. "Bring anyone you want or come by yourself, Holmes, but keep your wits about you above all else. Because," she squinted from the doorway at him, "because the deadly Professor . . . uh . . . ah, what's his name?"

"Moriarty," said Ian, winking again.

"Right, Professor Moriarty may be lurking among the other, much tamer professors sucking up my gin and Julia's dope." She shut the door and left Ian staring at the book room ceiling. There was a core of sweetness behind Eve's up-front manner, Ian knew, and he carefully, and happily, folded up her address and put it in a special place in his wallet.

·4·

A VISIT TO HENLEY-ON-THAMES

Although Eve had no Tuesday classes, she briefly dropped by the school to retrieve the hidden journal and to look through her mail before heading for Paddington Station. A high-speed, intercity express took her swiftly to High Wycombe, but then there was a forty-minute wait for a slumbering diesel railcar to begin its fitful trip along the mostly tree-girded single-track line to the Henley terminus. The day was warm and bright and Eve looked obliquely at her two fellow passengers, an older man and woman, wondering if they were there because she was there. But they both got off at a roadside halt and the vibrating railcar arrived in Henley bearing Eve as its only passenger. She knew what "Ian Holmes" would say to that. The coppers knew about Henley and probably why she was coming there as well, and so did not need to follow her.

The main street of the town was lined on both sides by narrow one- and two-family homes, mostly set directly on the edge of the sidewalks, and she had no trouble locating the tiny Stringfellow house, its two window boxes filled with spring flowers coming into bloom. As she rang the mechanical bell set in the door, she turned to look along the deserted street, thinking again about people watching her from dark, second-floor rooms out of blank, blind windows.

"Yes, can I help you?" A short, squatty woman with thin white hair and a kindly, wrinkled face peered out at her.

"Mrs. Rose Stringfellow?" asked Eve at once, and the small, old woman nodded cautiously at her with an almost birdlike gesture. Eve took a deep breath. "My name is Eve Pennington, Mrs. Stringfellow, and I teach at a college in London. I'm a friend of Ian McPherson, the young man who sold your books at Phillips. I wondered if I might . . ."

But Mrs. Stringfellow's watchful expression had given over to one of openness and trust. "Would you like to come in, dear? Eve, is it? Did you buy some of my books? Oh, do call me Rose, luv." She said this in such a rush that Eve did not even bother to offer a hope that she was not disturbing the old woman. It was obvious that Rose Stringfellow was both lonely and delighted to have company.

"That would be very nice, uh, Rose," said Eve quickly and stepped into the dark, musty little room.

Mrs. Stringfellow pulled up some shades to make her small parlor a bit brighter and cocked her head at Eve while pointing at the most comfortable chair. "Do you have time for tea, dear?" said Mrs. Stringfellow and when Eve nodded an, "Oh, yes, thank you," delightedly dashed out to her small kitchen and began the clinks and tinkles of cups and silverware being organized on a small tray.

Eve looked around the small, cluttered room with its worn, overstuffed furniture, its dusty plants on the window ledges and the dark, murky photographs and landscapes on the walls. The big floor-to-ceiling bookcase along the back wall was the only unusual furnishing in a front room that otherwise looked like thousands of others, in Henley and everywhere else in England, bordering narrow streets like this one. With a slightly sinking heart she saw that the bookshelves were mostly empty, except for some sewing materials, piles of letters and other scattered bits of Rose Stringfellow's quiet and solitary life.

The kettle soon began to whistle and in a minute Mrs. Stringfellow was back with the tray of tea things. After finding what Eve wanted, in the way of milk, lemon, sugar and hot water, she carefully put Eve's cup and saucer on a small table next to her arm. The old woman gave a satisfied sigh of completion and sat down herself to sip from her own cup, to make sure the tea strength was right, then smiled openly at Eve. "Now," she said brightly, "are you interested in old books? I'm afraid I sold most of mine at that auction. You're American, aren't you?"

Eve took an obligatory sip of hot tea and nodded to praise its welcome warmth and acknowledge her Americanness. "Well, I'm interested in some old books. I wonder if you can remember this one?" and she held out the battered journal to the old woman.

Mrs. Stringfellow took the book in her hands and opened it, then smiled at Eve. "Oh, yes. That was one of my husband's favorite stories, you know. He got that book from Thomas Cope, when Mr. Cope was an old man, after the first war."

Eve blinked at the woman in surprise. "Your husband *knew* Thomas Cope?" she asked in a low, alert voice. "And did you know him too, Rose?"

"I met him once," she said. "My husband's hobby was what used to be called the occult. Things that go bump in the night, you know?" and she smiled half in affection and half in embarrassment when she said it. Mrs. Stringfellow caressed the old ledger and stared down at the title page. "We went there, you know, Ben and I. To that tiny island they talk about in here. Just before the last war started, it was."

Eve caught her breath and tensely leaned forward, suddenly forgetting her tea and her cool reserve. "You've *been* to Muskeget? But *why* did you go there? What . . . ?" Eve stopped and realized it would be better to start at the beginning. She took a long sip of tea and sat back, trying to relax. "I don't mean to be snooping, Rose, but would you mind sort of giving me a little history of all this, some background about you and your husband. I have lots of time . . ."

Mrs. Stringfellow positively beamed at that and also settled back comfortably. "Dear, I do love to talk. I'll be glad to tell you whatever I can. Ben and I had a nice, companionable life, but really a very quiet one. Still, *anything* I can tell you . . ." Eve was smiling supportively and Mrs. Stringfellow briefly shaded her eyes to consider some distant memories.

"Well," she said, "Ben was in the trenches, in the first war it was, and he was hurt, almost died, I guess. I didn't know him then but the experience gave him, you might

say, an interest in the afterlife. He used to tell a story
about being in a hospital, in France, and getting up one
hot night. He couldn't sleep, so he walked to an open
window to get some fresh air and I guess the light behind
him sort of cast a shadow against the thick fog outside so
that as he walked toward the window, it seemed like
another man was walking toward him out of the night.
Ben thought he recognized the figure. It was his best
friend, who was still up at the fighting. My husband
spoke to the figure, asked him how he was and what he
was doing there, until finally he realized it was just his
own shadow on the fog outside."

Mrs. Stringfellow shook her head and her voice was
thoughtful. "Later, Ben learned that his best friend had
been killed in action, at just about the same time in the
early morning that Ben thought he saw him walking up
to that hospital window." She shook her head. "With
some people, coincidences like that can have a big
meaning. To Ben it was a kind of proof that there was
more to the world than could be explained, that supernatural things could happen. I guess you could say that
night really changed his life."

Mrs. Stringfellow looked fondly down at the journal.
"I met Ben when the war was about over. They sent him
home because of his wound to a training camp and I was
a secretary there for one of the officers, a typist. Everybody wanted to go to work then to help with the war,
and of course the money was good too.

"Anyway, we got married and it turned out that Ben
had a nice little income and a house in Sussex left him by
his parents. Nothing too big but enough so that he didn't
really need to work very hard. I never took much stock
in all that supernatural stuff, but Ben wanted to believe it

very much, and it did give him something to do and think about.

"Back then there were some important people who believed in the ghoulies and the gruesome. Professor Lodge, a famous scientist, was one, and of course Sir Conan Doyle who had written the Sherlock Holmes stories. Ben and I went to seances and did the Ouija board, and Ben collected and read all those books that were sold last week. He wrote now and then for a journal and sometimes he went to interview people who had heard or seen spooks or odd things."

Mrs. Stringfellow gave Eve an almost guilty smile. "It was interesting all right, and sometimes it was even a little bit frightening, but"—she shook her head—"I thought most of it was like those tunnel-of-love mechanical spirits that moan, and clank chains, and flash green eyes at you. I can't say I was ever much convinced by any of it.

"You wanted to know about Mr. Cope. My husband corresponded with him for years. I guess several of those psychic investigators did. Mr. Cope was very old then and he had known most of the famous psychics and mediums at the end of the eighteen hundreds, so people went to see him like a kind of pilgrimage to what they might call a guru now. My husband went two or three times. You had to go there because Mr. Cope never went anywhere else. It was a big house up in the west of Scotland, a long, hilly trip, and I never had the heart to try it until Ben got me interested by telling me about Mr. Cope's house. So the next summer I went north with Ben on the train. It took most of the day, but I'm glad I went because Mr. Cope was a very interesting and gentlemanly old man. Ben said he made his money in cotton mills or railways or something like that. He lived up in the open on the high fells in this big, dark house with several servants, a car and driver, and some barns and cattle.

"We were only there one night, but Mr. Cope gave us a wonderful dinner with wines and all different courses and desserts, and all through it my husband and Thomas Cope talked right along like old friends about the supernatural and what various strange happenings really meant. You could see it was something that really interested them both."

Mrs. Stringfellow jumped up to pour some more tea for Eve and herself and then sat down again, thoughtfully, on the edge of her chair, clutching the ledger. "I don't remember all that was discussed, although it seemed to me that Mr. Cope had some original and interesting ideas for a man in his nineties. But what I do remember is at the end of the meal, when we were having our coffee out in front of a big, open fire, my Ben suddenly turned to Mr. Cope and asked him what, of all the strange things he had studied in his life, he would most like to know more about or continue to investigate. Well, Mr. Cope stood right up and limped across that flickering room with his two canes to a big wall of books. He reached right up to it, I remember that especially, he didn't have to look for it or wonder where it was. He just pulled it out, stumped back and handed to my husband this very book," and she indicated the journal on her lap, looking over at Eve.

Eve nodded. "And did he say why this was the one case he would like to keep studying?"

Mrs. Stringfellow nodded. "He had several reasons, I think. He said he knew the people who gave the accounts and they were completely reliable; I remember him making that point strongly." Mrs. Stringfellow leafed through the journal, glancing here and there. "He said that most things like this have no apparent purpose, no human sense about them, but that this one clearly did." Mrs. Stringfellow caught a name from a page and nodded more strongly. "He said to my husband, I remember that, 'What about Miranda Macy? What happened to her? Read those accounts, Ben, and then ask yourself that question.' He thought it was important to see where the woman born on that island had gone and what her life had been like. 'How many human beings are marked by destiny like that woman?' he said to my husband."

"This was all he had?" asked Eve. "That journal was all that Cope gave your husband?"

The old woman nodded. "That and his advice. But my husband thought often about it after we got home from that trip. Oh, yes, Mr. Cope died that fall, so we never went again. Ben wrote to book dealers and librarians on Nantucket and Cape Cod for books about Muskeget and about Miranda Macy."

"And he found some!" said Eve at once, jumping up to lean over and turn the journal pages to the final note in a different handwriting.

Rose Stringfellow glanced down, then up at Eve. "Yes, that's Ben's writing." She looked puzzled. "But you must have Miranda's account in the other book that was sold with this one?"

Eve shook her head. "There was only one item in this lot. And there were no other handwritten journals of this sort listed at all. Are you certain . . . ?"

Mrs. Stringfellow nodded vigorously. "I'm sure it was put in the sale. I remember keeping those two together with a rubber band, since they were on the same subject. Oh, dear, well, I suppose things do get separated."

Eve stared at Mrs. Stringfellow. "Do you remember anything that was in that other account, Rose?"

"It was my husband's interviews with Miranda Macy. She was Miranda Street then."

Eve stood up straight, her eyes wide in amazement. "You *met* Miranda?"

"Yes, but she couldn't talk then. She was in Nantucket Hospital with throat cancer. Anyway, that's what they would call it now . . ."

But Eve was looking in agitation at her watch. It was after one. "Rose, can I get us some lunch? I'm really keeping you at this much too long."

The old woman rubbed her hands in embarrassment, looking down at the floor. "I don't know as there's all that much out in the kitchen . . ."

"*Please* let me go buy some lunch. Please, Rose. I can't tell you how interested I am in all that you're saying." Eve turned to the door. "I'd love to get us lunch if you'll just tell me what you'd like."

Mrs. Stringfellow gave Eve a grateful smile. "Well, if you're going to that place at the end of the street by the station, a bottle of that dark bitter would be nice. As to the rest of it, well, you just get what you would like and that will be fine with me. Oh, and while you're gone, I'll take a prowl around and make sure that other book isn't still here."

Eve almost jogged down the sidewalk so as to waste as little time as possible. So perhaps they had filched a book, she thought. The Macy accounts they knew about, or didn't care about, but this other . . . ?

She staggered out of the small store under the load of

a dozen bottles of black, local bitter and a large bag of cold cuts, cheese, bread, cakes and whatever else she thought Mrs. Stringfellow would like. She would get Ian aside at her party and ask about the second book, she decided on the way back. He might at least remember if it ever got to Phillips. The thing had to have been snitched long before the visit of the police. Otherwise it would have been listed in the catalogue.

When Eve pushed open the unlatched door, Mrs. Stringfellow put her hands on her hips and sternly shook her head. "Now you just shouldn't have done all of that, Eve. I wish . . ."

But Eve carried her purchases through to the tiny kitchen and turned fiercely to the old woman. "Rose, you can see that what you're telling me is of intense interest to me. A few pounds"—she gestured at the groceries and beer on the small table—"is nothing in comparison. Please believe that."

Mrs. Stringfellow patted her arm. "Let's open a bottle of that bitter and the stories may get even better. This is the *nicest* day, Eve!"

Soon a buffet of cold cuts, cheese, and new tomatoes, helped by more beer, was spread on the tiny kitchen table and the two women were eating and drinking like old friends. Rose sighed, but quite cheerfully, and continued her reminiscences. "Miranda Macy married a young man, Horace Street, on Nantucket. The story of all that is in this book Ben got from America when he wrote to those booksellers." Mrs. Stringfellow handed Eve a thick plain book in scuffed yellow boards. The black title was simply, *More Yankee Yarns*, and the author, in smaller black letters at the bottom, was William D. Lincoln. Eve opened the book to where a paper mark stuck out and found a chapter entitled, "An Evening with 'Skipper' Chase."

"Is this the other book your husband mentions in his note in that journal?" said Eve.

Rose Stringfellow nodded. "Mr. Ian said it wouldn't sell and I should keep it. But when Ben read that story he was determined to find Miranda Macy." She looked at Eve from serious eyes. "Well, I have to say that Mr. Cope did make a true prediction, that night we had dinner with him. Miranda Macy certainly did have some kind of lifelong connection with that little island."

"Can I buy or borrow this book?" said Eve, staring down at the nondescript yellow cover.

"It's my present, luv," said the smiling old woman at once. "I only wish I had the other to give you. That was even more interesting. Much more personal, as I remember it." Mrs. Stringfellow paused and looked again at the Macy journal, lying open to her husband's brief note at the end. "Funny that I sent those two books in, come to think of it. That nice Mr. Ian said they wouldn't fetch much," she said, half to herself. She looked at Eve in puzzlement. "When I got back from America last summer, I needed money and it just seemed to me that I should . . ."

"You went to America last year, Rose?" interrupted Eve, watching her closely. "Did you go to Nantucket?"

Rose Stringfellow nodded happily. "I certainly did. My brother, the one we went over to see just before the war, had these nice children, and the oldest went and bought me a plane ticket, and then he met me . . ."

Eve blinked and rubbed her forehead. "Before we get to that, could we talk some more about Miranda Macy, or Street? Did your husband go to America specifically to see her, or what?"

"Not exactly," said Mrs. Stringfellow. "My husband wrote here and there, trying to find out what happened to Miranda and one day he got a letter from her directly. I guess it was the fall or winter of thirty-eight. At that time I was hoping we could take a trip to America to see my brother. We didn't travel very much. Ben was quite a homebody and the war was coming and I knew we would never go anywhere then. So I guess you could say that the letter from Miranda was the final thing to convince him. That summer of thirty-nine we went across on a big liner."

Mrs. Stringfellow stared at Eve and now her smile was soft and distant as she remembered. "That was a fine trip, Eve, a time I still like to think about. By the end of July, when we got to Nantucket, Miranda Street was in the hospital for the last time. She was a handsome woman, even then, tall, thin as a rail, her face like a hawk with the skin all pulled tight over her bones. And of course she couldn't talk.

"We visited with her every day, and Ben brought his journal. He would write a question in it and then she would write the answer underneath. That way, he kept track of what he'd asked and how he'd asked it. I think Miranda truly liked us, and she still remembered Mr. Cope, so that helped."

Mrs. Stringfellow stared at Eve from level eyes. "You might think that being with a dying woman every day is an awful way to spend a summer holiday, but it wasn't depressing at all. The time that my husband spent in the hospital was good for him and good for Miranda, I'm certain of that. I think she wanted to sort out her life, and writing things down, answering questions, was a good way to do that. As to my husband, he was really excited about what she was telling him. All his life, ever since his wound in the war, he had been . . ."—Mrs. Stringfellow frowned and thought about the correct words—"well, an unimportant man, rather a small person. Not to me, you understand, not for a second, but I guess he seemed that to himself. The whole occult business turned out sad and humiliating for some of the noted men who were in it, but my husband was never big enough, even in that little, forgotten thing, for anyone to know about him. With Miranda Street he finally felt he was doing something important on his own, and it filled him with enthusiasm. He so wanted to do it right."

Rose looked at Eve and her eyes were dark with puzzlement. "I don't know *why* I sent that book to the sale now, I really don't. Oh, well, soon it won't matter a bit, will it, Eve? I guess it never mattered very much at all," and her voice was so low and suddenly discouraged that Eve reached across the small table and strongly seized the old woman's hand.

"Rose, I don't think we, I mean we educated people, know what matters and what doesn't anymore," she said in a firm voice. "Maybe what Miranda was telling your husband was the most important story in the world. You think what's on television or in the papers is important? I think it's mostly stupid and ugly. God isn't giving us miraculous births anymore. What your husband sought was no small thing."

That seemed to cheer up Mrs. Stringfellow and she took a long drink of the bitter and her smile returned.

"We would have stayed all that summer if we could have, but the news from Europe was just terrible and we were scared we'd get stuck over in America with no money and no way to get home, so we had to end it. I guess what I remember most from Miranda's stories was the fact that she went to that little island, that Muskeget, to die the year before. She admitted that to Ben. But then they had a big storm, a famous hurricane, and Miranda was on the island but she didn't die. Some men came and saved her, took her off, and after that she was mostly in a hospital. I can sort of understand how she felt. She'd been born on that place, born under very strange circumstances, and with her so sick and all, it probably seemed reasonable to go back there and end it."

"Did she have any ideas or explanations for all this?" said Eve. "I mean for her connection with the place?"

"I don't know as she did, really. But Miranda wrote down, and I remember it plainly, that she went back to the island to die with her lover."

Eve sipped from her glass of bitter, her eyes fixed on Mrs. Stringfellow's face. "Her *lover?* Did she mean Street, the man she married? Did she think he would come back at the end in some way?"

"Perhaps. He died in the first war, you know. And maybe she meant the island itself, or some part of it." Mrs. Stringfellow shook her head. "We finally had to leave Nantucket and go to our ship in New York. The war started while we were at sea and it was quite exciting, what with the zigzagging and the blackout. It took us almost a week longer than the schedule, but we got back safely and from then on, the war simply became everything. My husband was in the Home Guard and did some fire watching, so the war was a good thing for him. It gave him plenty to do, but the supernatural business quite faded out of our lives."

"And Miranda?" said Eve.

"On the trip home, Ben wrote down some more questions for Miranda Street and sent them off when we got to England. A month or so later we got the letter back with a note from a doctor on Nantucket saying that Miranda had died in August. That really ended my husband's studies of the occult, you might say. It was just as well, I suppose. There didn't seem to be any place to go with it all.

"When the war was over, my husband's money was about over too. Everything was hard then and we had to sell the house in Sussex. It's certainly good that we got this little place then. Otherwise"—Mrs. Stringfellow squinted at Eve and shook her head—"I'd be in council housing someplace, or maybe an old persons' home. I get lonely, Eve, but I think it's good and right to look after yourself. Do you know how I feel?"

Eve nodded. "That's one thing freedom really means, I think. Having both the right and the guts to be lonely. So you two didn't go back to America or Nantucket again?"

"I never went with Ben. He had to get a job after the war, in a store. He was a clerk. We lived very simply and Ben died suddenly in fifty-eight." Mrs. Stringfellow dabbed her eyes. "I miss him still. We were never what you might call passionate, but he had a good sense of humor and even when I joked about all the occult things, he just joked right back. 'You're going to keep me going straight, Rose,' he used to say. 'Without you, I'd end up

riding a broomstick on the back of the North Wind.' He
had a little poetic turn, you know."

"But you finally went back?" said Eve.

"Last summer. My brother's oldest son, Jim, wrote me
and said he'd get me the plane ticket and asked where I'd
like to go in America. Well, the only place I really cared
about was Nantucket, I suppose because we had such a
fine time there, so he did just that. Got us rooms and
took me there for three days at the end of my visit. I
remembered most of the streets and other places and it
was just the nicest time you can imagine. Jim and his wife
did everything I wanted and they really seemed glad to
be with me and to take me around."

"And Muskeget?"

Mrs. Stringfellow nodded. "Yes, I even went there
again, but only for a little while. They arranged for me
to fly in a seaplane from Nantucket back to Providence,
where I could get a train to New York and my plane
home. The pilot couldn't have been nicer about it. I told
him how I had been to Nantucket before the war and he
asked me if I'd seen everything and been everywhere I
wanted, just making conversation you know, and I said
everyplace but Muskeget Island. Well, we were going
over it anyway, I guess, but he just went right down and
landed in a little shallow harbor there. He said he
brought fishing people out there now and then and that
they would fish right from the plane. There were two
young men with us, and they helped me to get out on the
beach, off the pontoon, so I could walk around a little. It
was the kindest thing, what they did, and I loved being
there for a few minutes and thinking about Ben."

Eve leaned back in her chair and rubbed her hands

together. "Thomas Cope went to Muskeget"—she indicated the journal now lying on the table—"but he writes that he had no sense of anything odd or supernatural while he was there. No sense of magic, I think he says. When you and Ben went there, in 1939, what was it like? It must have meant something to you, for you to mention it after so many years to that pilot?"

Mrs. Stringfellow took a long drink of her bitter and nodded. "You Americans can't make bitter like that, Eve. I learned that. You do everything else wonderfully well, but not black bitter." She paused, then looked at Eve from alert, warm eyes. "Ben and I were on Nantucket for perhaps seven or eight days. We had a fine room in a big hotel that sat up high on a bluff to the north of the main town, overlooking the harbor and the little lighthouse at the entrance."

"The Sea Cliff Inn," said Eve at once. "It was torn down a while back."

"I guess that was it. It had the best views, I know that. Some days you could look out from the veranda off our corner room, it was right up under the roof, and see the whole island stretching out flat and yellow into the blue ocean. Well, when it seemed that we were going to have to leave because of the troubles in Europe, Ben decided to make a trip to Muskeget, just like Mr. Cope did. I remember when he told Miranda, she just smiled at us and wrote down something like, 'Pick a good day and a good captain,' and we did. I don't remember the old man's name who took us there, but he had an old sailboat with its mast cut to just a stump and a powerful engine. The captains would take you anyplace around those waters, and they brought a picnic that their wives fixed so you could have lunch on some deserted beach.

The old man rowed Ben and me ashore with a big hamper of lunch, and then went back to his boat for a nap."

Mrs. Stringfellow was now lost in the remembering. "It was a lovely, quiet day. The captain cautioned us, saying there might be flies on the island, but we weren't bothered by anything like that. The little old house where Miranda had been born was finally wrecked in the storm the year before, but they had built a new one on the old floor, for people who came to shoot ducks or to fish, I think, and we sat on the stone door stoop and ate our sandwiches. Nothing really happened that you could say was in any way strange or supernatural, but still . . ." Mrs. Stringfellow tried to find the words. "I can't really explain it. It was just a *nice* day, a wonderful day. Eve, have you ever just felt happy? I mean completely happy, for no reason that you can imagine?"

Eve shrugged. "When I was a little girl I think I felt like that sometimes. That's the sort of thing our wonderful schools manage to eliminate; joy for no reason, unearned happiness."

The old woman cocked her head, thinking. "Well, that's what the day was like, for Ben and for me. We were just happy to be together and at that place. After our picnic we walked along the beach in our bare feet and Ben rolled up his trousers. We went right around the island that afternoon, talking and laughing. The birds flew up ahead of us and swooped everywhere, but they didn't seem angry and they were beautiful.

"When we got back to the sailboat, the captain rowed in and picked us up and we put-putted back to Nantucket. We had a fine dinner at the hotel that evening, they had delicious fish all the time, and then . . ."

Eve smiled and took Mrs. Stringfellow's hand again. "And then, Rose?"

"I guess I said that Ben and I were never what you'd call passionate. I suppose that would seem almost worse than death to you younger women today, but it wasn't all that awful, really. Oh, we tried to have children. I've always missed that part of it, but we just never could. Well, that night when we went up to our room after that so-happy day, the moon was up and you could see silver views out in every direction. We went onto our little veranda to look out and my Ben became very warm and loving with me. I guess as much that way as he ever got. And I was the same way with him. It was the day that made us like that, such a wonderful happiness just had to spill over in some way at the end, and that is how it did. Days like that are important, especially to people who don't live very exciting lives. That's why I wanted to stop there last summer, to remember that day and how nicely it ended."

"I see," said Eve in a low voice, looking down at her lap. "You did find something on Muskeget then. Perhaps a reward for trying to understand it. For caring about it. Many people don't get that much, Rose."

Mrs. Stringfellow dabbed her eyes. "I really shouldn't cry over such a happy memory. You've been so interested and kind to hear all this. I don't get a chance to talk so much very often."

Eve bit her lip and then smiled and started asking Mrs. Stringfellow about her nephew's children and other pleasant, neutral things, until the time for the last train drew near.

Then, at the door, Eve suddenly remembered about

the other books and Ian's ideas. She turned to look down at Mrs. Stringfellow. "One more thing, Rose. Those other books you put in the auction later. Were those something your husband had, or . . . ?"

Mrs. Stringfellow frowned and narrowed her wrinkled lips. "Now that was an odd thing. A distant cousin of mine, an old man I hardly knew, had met maybe twice in my life, died a year ago. I never even knew it and, if the truth be told, didn't care all that much. Then this solicitor calls up and says he's left me some books. Well, I sent the list off to Mr. Ian, and he said they were well worth selling and I guess they were."

"But you were surprised that your cousin would leave you books?" said Eve.

"I was surprised that he left me anything," said Mrs. Stringfellow in a positive voice, "and what he was doing with those valuable, antique books I can't imagine. He worked in a metal shop, up in the midlands. I didn't know he ever read much of anything."

Eve leaned and gave Mrs. Stringfellow a kiss on the cheek and a long, firm hug. "This has been very interesting and exciting, dearest Rose. I'm going to write you when I get back to America. And you have my address there if anything else about Miranda should turn up."

Mrs. Stringfellow's shoulders drooped a bit then, but she stood up straighter in a moment and gave Eve a hug back. "Oh, do write me, Eve! I'll so love to hear from you," and she closed the door with a firm click as Eve turned to walk back to the station, the journal and the other book clutched tightly under her arm.

The railcar had a few more passengers for its final,

outbound trip of the day, but Eve found an isolated seat and eagerly opened the thick yellow book. She noted that it was published in 1934 by Cape Cod Printers of Chatham, Mass., and, from the penciled notation inside the cover, that it evidently cost Ben Stringfellow all of two dollars and a quarter.

·5·

"AN EVENING WITH 'SKIPPER' CHASE"

Everybody remembers the wonderful rescue of the crew of the *H. P. Kirkham* in '93 by "Skipper" Walter Chase and his "gold medal" Coskata lifesaving crew; how they were out on Rose and Crown shoal a whole day in a January storm, and finally brought seven men safely ashore at 'Sconset. A year or so before he passed away, I spent an evening with Skipper in his comfortable Nantucket home, sharing some mugs of warm "Nantucket cheer" and some of Skipper's yarns about the grand old days of storm and rescue.

But when I asked him which of his exciting experiences gave him the greatest satisfaction, he didn't talk about the famous *Kirkham* episode or some similar battle with the elements offshore in a surfboat.

Instead, Skipper gave me a big grin and shook his head in a cheerful way that I knew could only lead to one of his exciting yarns. "That's an easy one," he said at once. "It was when Horace Street went to save his ladylove, Miranda Macy, in a December blizzard." He took a pull on his mug of "something hot." "'Course he didn't know it was her till he got there in that awful snowstorm," he said, and I could see that he was thinking back to a long-ago moment that was really important to him.

"Horace was a strong, good-looking young feller, wanted to go to college and be an engineer. He was a Nantucketer and knew boats, helped his daddy go fishing for several years, so he joined the service. Pay was good, sixty a month, and you could keep most of it, so Horace figured he'd be a surfman for a year or so and save up for school. Being the youngest and rawest in my bunch at Coskata, he was number eight on the roster, but he was strong and could heft and pull as good as anyone.

"Now Horace had this here problem, namely, Miranda Macy. I can't say I blame Horace for getting fixed on that young woman. She was a humdinger, all right. Pretty as a picture, tough as a Boston banker, and she had money too. Miranda run one of them tourist hotels over in 'Sconset, the Ocean Breeze House it was, and she sailed a tight ship. There was money coming into 'Sconset then. Some New York theatrical people had, what they call, *discovered* 'Sconset and there was a lot of activity and building going on. Poor Horace would borrow the station hoss on his day off and ride over to court Miranda, but it appeared that she wouldn't give him the right time of day. I guess it's easy enough to see the thing from her side. She was busy running that big place, watching her help and all, and she was in no tremendous hurry to catch a man, even one as personable as Horace. And he didn't have, right then, what they called good prospects.

"Horace mooned around the station and wrote her plenty of letters. Some of them he delivered himself. Seems to me he even wrote some poetry to her, but of course he'd never show any of that to us. He knew the boys would make up some of their own poems, right quick!"

Skipper Chase gave me a big grin and poured a little more "flavoring" into our mugs. "Being in love is kinda like being seasick. It's plumb awful to the one actually doing it, but just a big joke for all the folks watching.

"Well, the summer before the rescue, Horace finally convinced Miranda to come to our end-of-July party at the station. During June and July, we had only one man at Coskata, a station watch, but when August came, we went back to full manning and regular patrols. To celebrate, we always had a party with catboat-loads of folks out from town, some music and refreshments. That was a big concession for Miranda, I suppose. It was her busiest time, and I imagine that afterward Horace surely wished she'd stayed in 'Sconset.

"Right at the noisiest and gayest part, with the fiddles sawing away and everybody stomping and laughing, I happened to look over at the big, open double door and there was Horace and Miranda, just standing alone. You didn't want to look at her too long, right then, 'cause you'd plumb freeze to death. She was pretty, right enough, but when she took a mind, she had a look that cut right through you like a knife.

"I suppose poor Horace had tried to take some of

them 'liberties' people was always talking about, and Miranda wasn't having any of it. Of course Horace looked like he'd been shot, stabbed, horsewhipped, and attacked by sharks. When he saw me staring at them, he excused himself from Miranda, she didn't even nod or look in his direction, and come over to where I was getting a bit of refreshment.

" 'Skipper,' he says in a low voice that might have come out of a fresh grave hole, 'can I borrow the sailing dory to take Miranda to town? She figures she better go back to see to her guests and I don't want to bother the rest of them.'

"Well, I never felt any sorrier for anyone than I did for Horace right then. It was a quiet night and the big dory was a good, steady sailer with just two people, so I nodded and said, 'Don't need to rush back, Horace. I'll switch your watch to tomorrow night,' and he looked mighty grateful at that. He went back to tell Miranda, and she just turned around without looking at anyone and walked out the door and down to the beach where we had a dock, with Horace kind of sleepwalking along behind, staring at his shoe tops.

"After that, Horace stopped riding over to 'Sconset, but he kept up with the letters, didn't really do much else but write to her, and he was so sad that even the worst kidders in the crew left him alone most of the time.

"That fall was pretty quiet, mostly calm weather and not much happening, but then in December we got a sudden blizzard and a mean one. We had two men out on beach patrol that night and the wind was really beginning to get its voice when they both come busting into the station yelling that two vessels had stranded on Point Rip, a bunch of bars that lay out to the east'ard of Great

Point. The bad thing about that spot is that you can come aground almost a mile out, and with the wind nor'east and picking up, I knew we probably wasn't going to launch a boat and row to them. Still, we had to take the surfboat in case, plus the Lyle gun, shore scissors, and rig, so we're all running around getting the oxen hitched to this great long kite tail of boat, gun cart, and God-knows-what-all, and in the midst of it, Horace comes down the stairs from the cupola lookout shouting that there's a wreck in Nantucket Sound about sou'west from us and he can see a signal light waving.

"Of course that was in the exact opposite direction from the two vessels aground on Point Rip, so I'm suddenly feeling kinda beset, but I run up those stairs after Horace and up the ladder to the cupola. By the time we got there, the snow had really started to come down and you couldn't see a mile in any direction. 'It's out there, Skipper,' Horace is yelling in my ear. 'I swear I saw it. Somebody was waving a lantern, honest to God!'

"I asked him if he got a good bearing on the light and he said he did. Right then I had to start making some choices."

Skipper Chase shook his head and his face was stern and set, remembering that moment. "Bill," he said to me, "it's one thing to get in a boat and just do your very best out in bad water, like that time with the *Kirkham*, but it's another thing entirely to decide something like that standing in a warm station. You know that if you guess wrong, people may get hurt bad or crews may not get to shore. But you *got* to guess 'cause there just ain't time for much else. Well, Horace suggested it. 'Let me go, Skipper,' he said right quick. 'I'll take the sailing dory. It's almost dead to leeward.'

"All of a sudden that idea seemed almost possible to me. We knew we had two crews out in a terrible, exposed place up off Great Point and we had to keep on with that, no matter what. The sound was going to get bad, but it wasn't as bad as the east side of the island yet. So I decided what to do, but I'll tell you, I didn't feel very good about it. 'Horace,' I says, 'get going now, afore the sound works up. Now you sail right down that bearing. If you get people off, just keep going to leeward. You'll hit Muskeget or Chappaquiddick, but for God's sake don't go betwixt them. We'll never get you back then.'

"I ran with him down to the water to help him get the dory rigged and in the water, and I almost stopped the whole thing right at that moment because that wind was working up fast. The snow was so thick by then you couldn't see fifty yards. But Horace wanted to do it real bad. His eyes were bright and his voice was fierce. 'I can do it, Skipper,' he says. 'I been out with Dad in some mean stuff.'

" 'Oh, God, Horace," I says to him, 'you got to take" care, boy! It's terrible, terrible bad, and I ain't just saying that!' I could see he was scared inside and trying to cover it up. Hell's delight! I was plumb scared to death and I wasn't even leaving the beach!

" 'I'm going to do it, Skipper. This is what we get our money for,' he says, then pushes the dory off and gets the sail up and in less than a minute he's gone into the snow. I didn't like it a bit but I sort of consoled myself with the idea that he probably would have gone anyway. As number eight on the roster, we were supposed to leave him as station watch when we went out, and thinking about the way he had talked and looked, I knew he wouldn't stay up in that cupola to answer the telephone.

"That was the awfullest night in just about every way you can imagine. The crew of one of the vessels got off in two rowing boats and they come ashore mostly sideways and swamped. We almost lost a couple of them in the surf and all my men got soaked. We got lines over the other one. She'd bumped along the bars and come hard on sand mebbe a quarter-mile offshore. We got across her on the first shot, but the lubbers rigged the lines wrong at the vessel end so we had a man half-in and half-out of the water for mebbe a half hour while we got the tangle sorted out.

"It was early in the morning by the time we got them all ashore and it was mighty lucky we had the light keeper's house at Great Point right close to put them in. Some of them were near dead from exposure. And all through that screaming blizzard and that screaming confusion, I'm thinking and worrying about Horace. Some of the time I'm thinking he might be all right, and the rest of the time I'm thinking it was plumb stupid to let him go when I could have just brought him along with us and left the damn station to go to hell.

"We finally got organized by four or so. The snow was still blowing hard from nor'east, and I sent three of my men back to the station with the oxen and gear and left the rest of them feeding rum into the fellers we'd rescued, and I climbed on the station hoss and went down the beach with the wind at my back heading for town. I figured I'd get Wallace Adams and his catboat with that big one-lunger in the well, and go looking for Horace. There wasn't no sense in going out with the surfboat. We couldn't row against the gale and I'd just be risking more of my men.

"It was a long cold ride and that hoss didn't like it any

better'n I did, I can tell you, but I finally came clattering
into town and headed for the telegraph office to see if
there was anything come in about the vessel that Horace
claimed to have seen.

"There was a message, all right, sent to the four
station keepers on Nantucket from Woods Hole. 'Had
we seen the schooner, *Joshua Billings?*' it asked. The
message went on to say the vessel had left the Hole just
before dark and carried a passenger, Miss Miranda
Macy. I guess you could say right then that my evening
had reached just about its lowest ebb. I went lickety-split
down Main Street to the wharves to look for the *Billings,*
but no such schooner was docked and there seemed no
sign of one anchored out in the harbor. So I finally went
to rouse up Wallace Adams and get started out into the
sound."

Skipper's eyes narrowed and he shook his head in
anger at the memory. "That was a real bad business with
the *Billings,* right enough. What had happened was that
this crew of thugs got the bright idea of unloading the
Billings into a barn over by Fairhaven, owned by a
crooked farmer they knew, and then wrecking her. She
carried a valuable cargo, and one easy to shift ashore,
mostly crates of tea and some logwood in five- and
six-foot lengths. Miranda had been in Boston seeing her
bankers and buying some fittings for her place in
'Sconset, when she got a telegram that claimed her
adopted mother, Joanna Macy, was real sick in the
hospital, but there was something funny about that
message, because only the first part of it got sent and
made the thing seem worse than it was.

"So Miranda offered these fellers on the schooner
twenty dollars in gold to get her to Nantucket that night.

The last ferry had left by the time she got to Woods Hole. That was money they couldn't resist and I suppose they were planning to wreck the vessel later, off Race Point or on Peaked Hill bars where she'd come apart easy, helped by some sawing and hole cutting, I imagine. But that storm really come up quick, and either they decided to use it, or else they really couldn't work their vessel to windward off the bars north of Tuckernuck. Anyway, they appear to have told Miranda she'd be safer below and when the *Billings* finally struck on a bar, Miranda found she was locked in a cabin. She broke out with a fire ax and discovered the crew had gone off in the only boat, leaving her on a listing, bilged schooner, coming apart in a nor'east gale that was just getting its strength. Right away she hoisted a lantern into the rigging, the light that Horace saw.

"I didn't know any of that then, but I sure got Wally out of bed fast, and pretty quick we had his catboat headed out past Brant Point. I've never been much of a praying man, Bill, but let me tell you, I was sure praying hard then."

Eve suddenly realized that the rattling railcar had become permanently silent and she looked up to see they were settled against the bumpers at the High Wycombe end of the line. She walked quickly across the pedestrian overpass to the up side of the platform and took a seat at the far end, away from the few waiting passengers near the ticket office, then plunged back into her book.

"By the time we cleared the Point, the sun was coming up and you could see for miles across the sound. I grabbed Wally's glasses and swept that whole horizon to

the north and west, back and forth, but there wasn't a
sign of any wreck, no masts, nothing big floating. 'Oh,
God, Wally,' I says, 'they've got to be at Muskeget.
Horace would have hit it dead center the way he was
headed.'

"It was cold but the storm was done with and there
was snow covering all the island. Pretty it was, and
different looking. Nantucket went by us white and shiny
and when we got closer I began to watch the Muskeget
beach with the glasses. There were snow mounds here
and there that might have been boats, but finally I saw
the black mast of the dory sticking out of a snowbank
and I says, 'The dory's there, Wally. Horace made it,' but
what I'm thinking is, what if he didn't find Miranda?
What if he missed her in that thick snow? And I'm
feeling worse and worse as we get closer and closer.

"Wally put the cat right up on the beach and I just
hopped off. I still had my high boots on, and I waded
ashore yelling for Horace. I started to run to the humane
house and the door opens and there's Horace waving at
me. I come up, huffing and puffing, and I says, 'Oh, God,
Horace. Did you find Miss Macy? Did you get Miranda,
boy?'

"Well, Horace has a kind of vague, happy look on his
face and he nods and grins, just as calm as can be. 'I got
her off the schooner, Skipper. The crew just deserted
her, locked her into a cabin to drown.'

"'And she's all right, Horace?' I says. 'She ain't hurt?'

"Horace grins harder. 'She's fine, Skipper. I got her
warm in here real quick.' But that didn't sound quite
right to him, so he shook his head and said, 'I mean, I
helped her to get warm real quick . . .' but by then he

was getting red in the face and he said, 'What I really mean, Skipper, is that she got *herself* warm real quick.'

"Now at that point there comes from inside that little house the sound of a young lady who's been trying to keep from laughing real hard and suddenly can't hold it in any longer, kind of a cheerful explosion, it was, and in a second she's standing there beside him with her arms tight around his shoulders. 'Thank you for sending Horace to save me, Skipper,' she says. Her cheeks have pink dimples and her eyes are brighter than that new snow. She turns and gives Horace a big, long kiss on the cheek. Horace, of course, is looking like a little boy on Christmas morning who's just gotten a Winchester, a hoss and saddle, a setter pup, and he's still got a dozen more big packages to open. As for me, I'm so dang relieved I'm just grinning like the village idiot, gawking at the pair of them."

At that pleasant juncture in the story, Skipper allowed that as the wind seemed to be getting up outside, we should take some slight, additional precautions against chill, and when that had been arranged I asked him, "Didn't Horace Street get a medal for that rescue?"

"Well, I guess he did," said Skipper with a big grin, "and quite an affair it was, too. They decided to get married that next month, end of January, and I wrote to a certain old congressman about the rescue and wedding, so as to try and hurry the medal business along. When we got them medals for the *Kirkham,* it took the govinmint a solid year to work it out."

Skipper gave me a wink and an apologetic smile. "I don't want you to think I messed with them miscreant congressmen all that much, Bill," he said seriously. "It's just that I'd given that particular old crook some dang good fishing whenever he was on the island and I thought, why not see if the old reprobate can't do something useful for once in his blasphemous life. I got to admit, he sure pushed the thing through. 'Course it was a pretty straightforward award, just one man, and the papers had made a big to-do over it, all the way to Philadelphia and Washington. You know, what with them getting married and all.

"I was Horace's best man and old Henry Macy gave his daughter away. I don't guess there's ever been a handsomer couple than that pair. Miranda was in a satin and lace getup that plumb took your breath away and Horace was in his dress whites, all pressed and sharp. The church was filled right up, with people looking in the windows and standing ten deep at the doors. Horace knew he was probably going to get a medal for the rescue, but we hadn't told him it was going to happen directly after the preacher tied the knot. Instead of instructing Horace to kiss Miranda then, the preacher turns to this feller from Boston, a chief inspector for the service, he was, and the man stands up and reads this long citation telling what a hero Horace was, then grins and hands the box with the medal to Miranda and tells her she's got to do the deed herself on her new husband."

Skipper really grinned himself, thinking about that moment. "I leaned over and whispered, 'Miranda, don't you stick him with that pin now. He's so proud of you, he'll just pop.'

"Miranda about popped herself then, but she got them sweet laughs under control and pinned the thing on Horace and then gave him a big kiss and everybody stood up and yelled and cheered so's I didn't think they would ever stop. Things in life don't often work out like that rescue did, and when they do, people like to make a fuss and act like that's the way the world really is, or mebbe should be."

Eve looked up startled to see the grumbling intercity express sitting with open doors, gaping in front of her. Holding a finger to mark her place in the book, she dashed into the nearest car and sat in the first empty seat that caught her eye. And as she stared down at the book again, her lips instinctively framed the name, "Miranda."

"Well, Horace stayed with the service till summer holiday, then went off to help Miranda with the hotel. In the fall, the two of them went off to college together. I suppose that Miranda paid for most of it, but she was a smart woman, could do about anything she wanted, and she finally got to be an engineer, a designer, and her husband, an electrical contractor. They worked together on electrical railways, you know, trolley cars, and made, I gather, considerable money over the years.

"Miranda sold the 'Sconset hotel when they got done with college and they didn't come back to Nantucket much after that, except maybe for quick visits. The Macys had died by then and Horace's father had moved someplace in California, so there wasn't much to bring them back here."

Skipper shook his head slowly, and I could see that the warm memory of that remarkable wedding day had slipped away from him. "The summer of seventeen was the first summer we was in the war, and they came back here for the last time. Horace was a major, in the transportation corps, I think, though he was old enough then so's he didn't have to go in the army at all. They were still a good-looking pair, but when they come to visit with me, they seemed, well kinda sad would be the best way to put it.

"Horace had the ribbon from the medal he'd won sewed on his uniform and a big, long bunch of dangling shooting bars he'd got when he was in the Connecticut National Guard. He and Miranda had worked in Connecticut some years back putting streetcars into all them little towns around Hartford and New Haven. I said it seemed to me he was getting a mite old to be shooting at Germans, but he just smiled a little and said he wasn't going to shoot nobody, but just help to get some electrical locomotives going, to pull them big cannon around in France.

"Miranda looked what you'd call right stylish, with a fur piece and a wide, fancy hat, and she gave me a big kiss on the cheek and a real hug. They'd traveled and worked in other states and countries, seen and done a bunch of things, but that real bright look, that happy look they'd both had after the rescue was gone. There weren't any children and I suppose that was part of it, but it seemed to me that maybe nothing could ever be quite as big as that moment when Horace come up to that listing, wrecked schooner and realized it was Miranda he was saving. I wonder, Bill, how do you go on past a thing like that, with all the wedding and medal to-do afterward? And what can you go on to?

"We had a pleasant visit, right enough, and Miranda asked me to suggest a captain to take them around the Nantucket waters. They'd been out to 'Sconset on the train and got quite a welcome, and now they wanted to make a trip to Coskata, the station was still active then, and do a day picnic to Muskeget. I walked with them over to Cap'n John R. Coffin's house and he was real happy to see them again and to be able to take them in his charter catboat to places that must have had some pretty powerful memories for both of them.

"Cap'n Coffin said later they'd had a fine couple of days sailing here and there with him, but I didn't see them again afore they left. I guess Horace got some hurry-up orders from the govinmint and they hopped on the *Sankaty* as soon as they got back from their day-sail to Muskeget."

Skipper shook his head and gave a sigh. "I don't know as he shot at any Germans, but Horace was killed in France a few months later. The *Inquirer and Mirror* made a big thing out of it, reprinted the medal citation and the story of the wedding and all, but Miranda never came back here after that, and I don't rightly know where she's at now."

It was getting late, and I stood up reluctantly to face the cold wind I could hear whistling around the windows. Skipper walked me to the front door and, until he unwound from his chair, I'd forgotten how tall he was. He had to duck a bit to even get through the doorways in his own house. I put my hand to open the front door and I could see that Skipper Chase was bothered by the ending of his story. He didn't want to send me out into the cold bluster with that kind of ending and when he shook my hand, his eyes lit up again.

"Bill," he said, "when we got that dory back in the water and tied astern, after ferrying them two on board Wally's catboat, it had turned into a fine, sunny, brisk day for the sail back to town. Wally was grinning at me hard and I sat looking at Miranda and Horace across from me. They were just staring at each other and saying quiet words, their heads close together, their arms tight around each other. I hadn't been in bed for a day and a night, but I didn't feel tired nor cold either. I looked over at Wally and I says, 'God, Wally, ain't this just the finest day you've ever seen in your whole life?' He nodded, still not saying anything but grinning something fierce, and we both just started to laugh and I guess I ain't never laughed like that, before or since. A man don't need many days like that one in a lifetime, Bill! Nossir!''

I left Skipper Walter Chase filling the doorway of his final, cozy "snug harbor" and waving after me, then set off along Main Street of Nantucket leaning against a sharp, cold fall wind. But as I walked by those old homes with their big fan windows that have looked out on so many remarkable events over the years, it seemed to me that Skipper had put his finger squarely on the meaning of those yarns we all love to tell and retell. They hold onto those days and those moments that illuminate all the rest of life. A man may not need many, but he would certainly never want to forget the ones he had.

And I guess that philosophical aside is probably as good a place as any to end this second volume of *Yankee Yarns.*

The End

Eve closed the book and stared out her window. The train was slowing down, coming through the North London yards, the tracks multiplying and fanning out as they ran past crowded tube-station platforms and lines of commuter cars heading north.

She shut her eyes and rested her forehead against the cool glass. Without really wanting to, she imagined the interior of the humane house, its dark, cozy warmth as the stove began to glow, and the two lovers, their meeting unexpected and beyond all coincidence, beyond all romance, undressed and discovered each other for the first time. Eve thought she had never been more lonely.

·6·

A MUCH-AWAITED PARTY

On the day of Eve Pennington's going-away party, Eve and Julia spent the entire morning buying the food, booze, and other necessities and the entire afternoon organizing them throughout the small flat. It would be a crowded, smoky, and noisy business and they stripped the flat to its barest furniture essentials, setting up one large folding table they had borrowed from a friend to hold the canapes, cold meats, and breads, and another to hold the mix and liquor. Julia had moved in with Eve for the final two weeks of Eve's stay in London, and would take over the flat for her remaining year when Eve left.

Eve fretted over the proper relationship between the number of gin and scotch bottles, but Julia just snorted, then pointed out that if the scotch ran out, the scotch freaks could make a foray downstairs to an off-license shop or else make do with something else. "They won't be tasting much by then, anyway," she said in a practical tone of voice.

By the time six o'clock arrived, they were more or less ready, the tiny fridge bulging with bags of ice and stacked plates of cold food. Droves of guests began to arrive moments after a nearby church bell bonged six times, and Julia whispered archly to Eve, "They don't know how well stocked we are and they're damned if they want to miss a single drink."

Still, it was a jovial and noisy start to the affair, pretty Eve greeting and kissing the men and women alike on their cheeks while they hugged her back and expressed their total desolation that she was, so soon, to head back to *dreadful* Boston, where, everyone knew, the police were prone to riot, the schools to shut at random times, and color wars to erupt without warning.

"Oh, dear, Noel," said Eve laughing merrily. "That doesn't happen in *Cambridge*, not across the Charles River. I mean, the universities wouldn't let it happen over there, you know?"

This was to Noel Fenwick, historian of science and a professor at Imperial. "After all, Noel," said Julia in a decidedly cool voice, "the angry young men from Brixton aren't out making rude gestures in Belgravia Square. Everything has its place."

Though almost fifty, Noel Fenwick had a smooth, round and unlined look, simultaneously weak and handsome, though if you looked closer his eyes showed a harder, sharper glitter. He gave Julia a sudden eyebrow lift. "I think we shall probably keep them out of Belgravia for about the same length of time you keep them out of Cambridge, Massachusetts," he said with almost a sweet smile. "Ah, at last here come some historians. I was afraid, Eve, that I would be sent off to sleep by astronomical gossip."

It was Forbish Wingate at the front door of the flat, accompanied by a tall, stocky, plain woman in her late fifties. Eve dashed over, gave him a peck on the cheek and shook his hand. The old man smiled faintly at the already-noisy room, and turned to his companion. "I hope it's all right, Eve. You said I might bring a friend and Dr. Hoerner expressed a desire to meet some science history and astronomical people. She's from Berkeley and in biology. Marta Hoerner, this is Eve Pennington."

The older woman inclined her head, then took Eve's offered hand in a firm grip. "I know of Dr. Pennington," said Marta Hoerner in a low, formal voice. "We are involved in something of the same search, I think. I am an exobiologist, Dr. Pennington, although whether such a field can really exist until someone finds us an exobiological specimen, I am not so sure."

Eve gave her a wide, red smile. "How nice that you could come. And we really are in the same sort of thing. Nobody knows if there are any extrasolar planets either."

A few moments later, while the noise level continued to climb, Ian McPherson, accompanied by the beautiful receptionist from Phillips, appeared at the door of the flat, and stood looking around bewildered as Eve pushed through her guests with a wave and a cry of welcome.

"I say," said a young historian in a scruffy turtleneck, "smashing!"

Julia, who was helping with the drinks, turned her head, blinked, and let out a whistle. "Well, I guess so," she breathed, staring at the new arrivals.

"Quite your type, dear," said Noel at Julia's elbow in a quiet voice, "the boy, I mean."

She turned to squint at his bright eyes peeping from under thick, black eyebrows. "Well, they're *both* your type, Noel," said Julia, also in a quiet voice, "and what fun *together*," but there was no smile in her voice.

Noel shook his head and his smooth forehead wrinkled only for a moment. "Tut-tut, Julia. I don't think you're being fair with me. Threesomes really aren't my style. And I don't remember ever subjecting you to anything like that."

But Julia was not placated. She shook her head and her lips were thin. "He *is* old for you, Noel, I suppose," her head indicating Ian. "We should have cleaned out the local boys' grammar school for this party."

And if Dr. Noel Fenwick winced inside at that cruelty, he concealed it with another round, cherubic smile and moved across the room, pushing between the groups to say "Hello," to Ian, whom he knew as "that Phillips' book fellow."

"How lovely you both could come," said Eve, squeezing one of the young lady's hands. "Alice Purley, is it? Please call me Eve."

The Phillips receptionist was dressed in a smooth, grey sheath of silk which her tall, perfect figure filled and shaped in different ways with each shift of her body. Her huge, clear eyes were darkly outlined and her smooth, lovely face had a serenity and innocence that had instantly caught the eye of every man at the party.

"You were so kind to think of me, Eve," said Alice Purley in a soft, diffident voice. "Ian said you suggested he ask me."

"Ian!" said Eve, waving a mock-angry finger in his face. "How ungallant to tell Alice that I suggested the invitation."

Ian smiled boyishly and peered at her through his thick lenses. "She wouldn't have come otherwise, Eve. Alice finds the excessively educated to be excessively awesome. I finally convinced her it was all just front."

"And he's right, Alice. Oh, my, how right he is," said Eve, squeezing the girl's hand again, but by then a phalanx of young astronomers and physicists had appeared with simultaneous requests that they might get Alice a drink and, after the introductions, she was whisked off to the liquor table with much laughing and chatter.

"She's really lovely," said Eve to Ian, who nodded ruefully, rubbing his chin.

"She doesn't like books much, Eve, but she is very kind for someone so pretty." He paused, then smiled at her. "You look very nice too, Eve."

Eve took his hand with an impulsive grasp. "I went to see Mrs. Stringfellow. I want to tell you about it," she said in a soft voice. Ian nodded, but there was no chance then for such a private discussion. Ice and mix were needed, then the plates came out to cover the food table, and the rising crescendo suddenly stilled as everyone sat down on a few chairs or on the floor to take in the welcome cold meats, cheeses and bread, washing it down with more drinks or beer. Since Julia's best black Leb had been going the rounds in her substantial hash pipe, many of the guests were beyond simple hunger and unable to talk for some time thereafter.

Julia and Eve almost bumped in the empty kitchen, now a shambles of residue, and grinned to each other over the gentle, lowing sounds coming from the living room. "Where is Noel?" said Eve to her friend. "I don't think he's gotten any food yet. I hid a plate for him behind the toaster."

Julia shrugged and curled her lip. "In the johnny, snorting up, I guess. He's coked to high heaven, Eve, look at his eyes. They're like gimlets."

Eve bit her lip. "Noel isn't that dreadful, Julia. He's trying to be nice to you. I know how you feel, but . . ."

Julia gave a great sigh, then slugged down her drink. "You're right. I shouldn't be so awful to Noel. We are supposed to all be adults. It's just that that nasty boy was so, well, *nasty*, Eve. I mean he was all muscles and stupidity, couldn't pronounce a word or say a sentence, just lay there gleaming with that dreadful oil all over him. Noel *knew* I was coming over . . ."

Eve nodded. "Noel has a problem. And he shouldn't have just hurt you like that. But he has good qualities too . . ."

At that moment the door from the living room swung open and Ian appeared, looking in owlishly and holding a half-empty plate. "I'm distraughtly missing the hostesses," he said brightly.

So Eve urged Julia out to check the booze and food, then beckoned Ian in and quickly told him about the day at Mrs. Stringfellow's house in Henley.

Ian nodded thoughtfully all through the account, asking a question now and then. "So," he said, "the Bion and that other stuff *were* planted. But I'll be damned if I can remember that second journal. She said it was attached to the other with a rubber band?"

Eve nodded. "She said she always kept them together since they were both about the same topic."

Ian shook his head in irritation. "I usually remember

things like that," he said, making a grimace. "Well, let me think about it. As to the rest of it . . ."

But at that moment a door opened behind them and Noel Fenwick's soft, round face appeared. He had come out of the tiny bathroom that had doors letting into both the small hall and the kitchen.

Eve started, then rose to get the plate hidden behind the toaster. "Luckily I saved you some food, Noel," said Eve cheerily, handing him the heaping plate. "The good things, like the shrimp, have been long-since vanished by munchie-madness."

"How nice of you, Eve," said Noel, and now his eyes turned fully upon her and Eve could see that Julia was right. Noel was flying a high kite, all right, and his glittery eyes were now large and very sharp, his pupils pinpointed, and they looked into hers with neither affection nor malice, Eve thought, but somehow with a sharp sadness.

Eve turned away and rubbed her cheeks in confusion, saying, "Oh, let's go in and see what's going on." Her speech was suddenly breathless and she felt a deep disquiet.

The food had mellowed the party, most people still lounging on the floor and against the walls, talking in low voices on various topics. But Noel sat down directly in the middle of the room and then turned to his hostesses with a large gesture of satisfaction. "Perfectly lovely food, Eve and Julia. I can't tell you how good it all tastes." He ate another mouthful, his plate still mostly full, then turned and looked again at Eve. "And how are the extrasolar sweepstakes, Eve dear? Any new excitements way out there in the distant dark?"

Eve grinned and sipped her gin and tonic. "Not much

seems to be happening, Noel," she said with a shrug. "Jack Goldman wrote and said some people at Palomar think they've got evidence of planet-driven perturbations involving Ceres and its little consort, but that little binary is so close and faint that the data suffers from all sorts of optical problems. Then there's Barnard's Star . . ."

Noel snorted loudly and waved his left hand in another large, vague gesture. "Ah yes, Barnard's Star. Two or three Jupiter-sized planets in orbit. Isn't that what some people are claiming?"

Eve shrugged again and pursed her lips. "It depends on who models the Barnard's orbit perturbation on which computer. Two big dark bodies will give a fit, maybe, but it could be almost any combination of from two to seven masses of various sizes and distances from the primary. I mean, you can fit an infinity of models to the kind of data we're getting."

Noel smiled and his round face had a benign, harmless appearance, belied only by frosty eyes that darted, almost commandingly, here and there. "It would be nice for NASA if you people happened to find some dark bodies around Barnard's, wouldn't it, Eve?" said Noel in a sharp voice.

"Come off it, Noel," said Julia, her own voice hard-edged. "You think NASA is going to build a star-going ship on the basis of artistic computer simulations that explain star perturbations measured in less than a second of arc? Even in Washington they wouldn't be that stupid."

Noel turned to stare at Julia. "Not a star vessel, dear Julia, but *maybe* an orbiting telescope?" He looked around the room. "Eh?"

Eve gave a bright laugh. "He's right, Julia. If we could definitely show there was something going around Barnard's, it would give the space shuttle something to take up and use that was exciting. He's right." She looked at Noel. "But nobody is claiming anything that can't be shown on the record. Certainly not me."

Noel rubbed his hands together and blinked several times. Then said in a loud, clear voice, "I know that, Eve, but there are other ways of finding what you seek, and other disciplines to lead you to an answer. The history of science and its scholarship, for example."

Julia gave a snort. "You mean that business of the pyramids being made by ancient astronauts as signals or something, Noel? I knew my hash was good, but I . . ."

Noel's voice frosted even more and his eyes narrowed at them all in the dark room, lit only by a few guttering candles on the two large tables. "Some people would never believe we have already been visited, even if the bug stepped up and said, 'Take me to your leader' in skin ridges on its chest. The fact is, we *have* been visited." He paused and looked fiercely around. "I have proof, far better and more direct than second-of-angle perturbations."

The room had grown progressively more silent, and all the guests looked in toward the center at the hunched, curly-haired man, his arms around his knees, who spoke now with a kind of steady coldness. A young astronomer grinned faintly at his friends and offered, "If not pyramids, flying saucers?"

"Beam me up, Scotty," said an American physicist and friend of Noel's. "There's a kook here that seems to know about us," and the moment's sharp edge was softened as the guests chuckled and smiled almost in relief at Noel's sudden, wide grin.

"All right," he said, "you flock of doubting Thomases. I'll convince you by the sheerest logic, step by step. Because when you think about the problem of interstellar trips, there really is only one way they can work and make sense. Now," and he stared around at them, "Barnard's is what, Eve, eight light-years out?"

"About six, Noel," said Eve at once, "but it's getting closer. It'll be inside four light-years by the year 2020."

Noel nodded. "But even with the most marvelous and yet-to-be-invented rocket toys, the so-called mass driver for example, we are unlikely to do better than one-tenth C, so the trip to or from Barnard's will take forty to sixty years, or more, and twice that if the mission requires a return. Could we do something like that, even if we had the treasure and the will to try it?" He looked around at them. "I think not, and for many reasons. But most obvious is the inherent undependability and weakness of inanimate machines that, no matter how redundantly and cleverly assembled, will fail, and stop, and misfunction if not tended by a human mind. There is no way that silicon, copper and steel can be assembled to meet the challenges of such a voyage."

Noel peered at his silent audience. "Okay, now postulate a race of creatures, on a world around Barnard's or somewhere else close by, that have developed in a slightly different technological direction than we have, driven perhaps by needs and problems we did not suffer. So these creatures discover the innermost secrets of biological engineering, just as we have always sought the innermost secrets of inanimate matter. And they gain a total, genetic control and manipulation ability that we are only beginning to imagine. If you could make a living, instructable organism small enough, you could send it into the germ plasm, the basic DNA itself, and have it do your bidding to change the characteristics of a plant or animal. Once you controlled that basic, blueprint system, the sky is truly the limit. Imagine telescopes in space constructed of billions of small creatures that give a signal when a photon of light strikes their surfaces, yet are so cunningly devised that they can live in open, airless space, indeed, delight to do so. No electronic computer is needed. The billion signals are sent to a central processing unit, an astronomical mind, that not only integrates the vast image, but draws conclusions about it, and instructs its many assistants where to focus, where to look. NASA could never put up anything remotely close to that telescope, and with such a tool, those biological engineers would know much more about our world and its immediate surroundings than we ever will about theirs."

The American physicist, his wrinkled face showing a thoughtful frown, nodded suddenly. "And such abilities would also make the crossing far simpler. Most of the ship would be simply put in a minimum metabolic condition."

Noel whirled and pointed a needle-sharp finger in his direction. "Exactly! Not only can such people see us much better, they can reach us with far greater ease than we can reach them. Who knows what physical ideas their living computational machines would discover, but even if it's only the old, tired mass driver, they could surely attempt the voyage. Furthermore, the creatures that you build to cross space can be made to *want* to cross space. They *want* to repair themselves, to complete the mission. Motivation and response could be *totally* controlled."

Julia shook her head. "Then why would they want to come, Noel, if they were so damned smart? Would we have *anything* they would care about?"

Noel nodded. "One sort of thing, certainly. Think about it! What would make us cross space, deeply depleting the world's store of wealth and treasure to mount an expedition that nobody living would be likely to see the end of? What would make us do such a mad thing?"

He stared around, his face fiercely questioning, and a young astronomer held up a finger and tentatively suggested, "A good aphrodisiac?"

"A *safe* aphrodisiac," the older physicist corrected him.

But Alice Purley had been prettily thinking about the question, and now she said suddenly in a simple voice, "Some sort of secret, like something that would let you live forever."

Noel nodded with sudden vigor. "You're close," he said. "That's a kind of metaphor of the answer." He smiled at the girl, then looked around the room. "Knowledge, truth, facts, those are the only possible rewards that could induce any rational race to become star travelers. Is there any element or compound, no matter how rare or difficult to get, that would pay us to seek it in a starward expedition, even if we could somehow miraculously determine that the rarity existed in another system?"

"What about ideology? What about religious drive?" asked Ian, standing against a wall, his face in shadow.

"Forty or more years in space to convert some large bugs to Christianity?" said Noel quickly. "And how would we know there were bugs there to convert?

Ian laughed back easily, but he spoke bluntly. "You know what I mean, Professor Fenwick, that old we'll-climb-it-if-it's-there business. The idea that the universe is daring us to do it and so we damned well will do it."

Noel shrugged. "A difficult motive to deny, I admit. My suggestion is that people who do things for those kinds of nonrational reasons will never achieve the planet-wide unity of purpose needed to launch a star-ship data-gathering campaign. I think our history will prove my contention, but of course we're directly in the middle of the critical period at this moment. Obviously, I hope I'm wrong."

"Do you mean, Noel," said Eve, "that you hope we do launch a star-ship or that we do things for sensible and useful reasons?"

"The latter, of course," said Noel dryly. "And anyway, why should every planetary civilization have to buzz around the galaxy? Also, we would not have as much to gain as they would. By the time we can even contemplate such a venture, our physics and metallurgy are going to be pretty damn good. What sort of new physics would we learn from looking at planets of another system, which if the projections for Barnard's are right, may seem an awful lot like Jupiter or Saturn? How many discoveries, new particles, new ways of doing things, are likely to result from such a voyage?"

He looked around at them. "Relatively few. You know that's true. Barnard's system and ours just won't be that different. But"—and he suddenly lifted a finger—"what if your whole economy, your whole sense of progress, the development of your society, were tied up in the continual alteration and design of self-reproducing, reasoning things. You turn your great, living telescopes flying around your world into that cold space on, eventually, our sun and its marvelous family of planets and moons. But most marvelous, most magnetic, and most beautiful in the most authentic sense of the word, is what you see of this world with its hazy mantle of atmosphere and its gentle greens and browns and blues, and its clouds, and maybe, even the lights of its great cities. For what those distant sights would say clearly and unmistakably is one, single thing, *here lies a cornucopia of treasure!*"

Eve started in the dim room as Noel sharply intoned this statement. Something of what he was really saying was beginning to speak inside her. The words had triggered an uneasy shiver. She shaded her eyes and tried to collect her thoughts.

Nobody was ready to interrupt Noel at this point, for they all saw the force of his argument. Noel turned again quite suddenly to where old Forbish Wingate and his guest, Marta Hoerner, of Berkeley, sat in small folding chairs, balancing almost-empty plates. "Dr. Hoerner," said Noel in neutral tones. "As an exobiologist, you know what a single, genuine biological specimen from beyond the earth would be worth to you. What would an entire world be worth, one that contains a half-million species of insects, untold millions of variations of smaller animals, biological adaptions to every manner of stress and danger, every kind of ingenious solution to multiple environmental problems, literally a billion bio-secrets of every imaginable kind? What would that be worth to a race capable of studying it, and probably duplicating it at the cellular level?"

The old woman sat in a shadow but her formal, stilted voice was clear. "It would represent many billions of years of biological experimentation, of success and failure." She paused, then, "Its value to them would be beyond calculation. It is a resource vast beyond our ability to even imagine its assimilation. And if they had the capacity to really synthesize such a knowledge store, they might well discover a number of ways to achieve virtually infinite life." She nodded, smiling coolly at Alice in her shining sheath. "At perhaps a dozen different levels of self-awareness. And who knows what more? They would seem as gods to us when they came, but they would leave as gods to their former selves. What our biosphere could show them would at least double their biological tool box!"

Julia stopped pulling on the bong that was passing around and gave a snort. There was a certain bullshit quality to Dr. Hoerner that bothered her, that smooth, weird way of talking. "So they wouldn't care about us poor lords of the earth even a little bit, eh, Noel?" she said in a disgusted tone.

Noel gave a short laugh. "On the contrary. They would find us of great interest, probably equal to that of the sperm whale. The pressure-withstanding ability of the sperm whale and its great, efficient size would certainly interest them just because of its obvious bioengineering uses in any deep ocean situation, but we would interest them because of our physical adaptions to intelligence and self-awareness . . . and a few other things, I suppose."

Eve looked piercingly at Noel and he suddenly seemed to her almost possessed by his theory, sure of its truth, speaking something dark and hidden, like that ancient mariner in the poem. My poor guests, thought Eve, are bewitched by his beady and coke-bright eyes. Still, she could not help but lead him on. "Do you think that such a zoological data-gathering system would have interests in strong human emotions; rage, love, sexual ecstasy?" said Eve.

Noel nodded in half-interest. "I suppose that sort of thing might be of interest to them. Such stimuli are sort of complicated since you need so much background to understand them, but they would be the sort of thing that might not be encountered on the home planet. In that sense, they might be interested, or, they might be unable to avoid them."

Ian spoke. "Do you see such organisms as having, let's say, power at a distance over living things?"

Noel hunched lower and hugged his legs tighter. "That would seem to me a very necessary ability to surmount the space journey, and equally essential in any data-gathering effort. It might be acoustic, optical, or electromagnetic. I don't know as it's essential to postulate some psychic force to make the things work."

"And what would they do, Noel?" said Eve, feeling breathless again. "Where would they go?"

Noel pursed his lips and the room waited. His heavy brows shrouded bright eyes as he looked around. "Dr. Hoerner," he said in an almost silky tone. "What would you say to that? Suppose you had their mission and their abilities. Where would you put down your probes?"

The room was silent as the old woman cleared her throat. "Oh, I think the obvious places are shallow estuaries. The ocean water would offer a great number of advantages that are lost in air. For example, any protection system based on acoustics or chemical release is far more effective under water. Temperature is more stable. The food supply comes in much higher density. If a fixed base of operations was to be set up, the best possible location would be where tidal currents give a good sweep, where the deep ocean lies not too far away so you can send scouts out to study the larger creatures."

Eve blinked, caught her breath, and stared at the floor. A light popped in her head. Was *that* what it was about? Had Thomas Cope gone hunting ghosts and found . . . something else? Something far more wonderful? She looked across the room at Ian and saw the same, sudden burst of comprehension, concealed but unmistakable, on his own face. She was suddenly filled by an excitement, a sense of promise, but when she then turned her head to look at Noel, her heart turned to ice. He was looking directly at her, noting in her the same stab of discovery that she had seen in Ian's face, but his expression was so bleak, so filled with a kind of dark compassion and darker dismay, that her party seemed turned to ashes and she looked down at the floor and felt suddenly dizzy from the liquor and the uncertainty.

Julia, annoyed that Noel had so successfully and completely absconded with the entire conversation, gave a loud and disgusted grumble. "Really, Noel, what are you smoking now?" she said in a bright, hostile voice. "You said you had proof that the space bugs were here, but this all sounds like fictional dream-stuff. Furthermore, your whole assumption on the driving purpose behind the flight is based on our psychology, not theirs. We might think it was swell to construct whales to flop around in alien oceans, but they might have utterly different imperatives."

Noel shrugged. "If their society developed without

the desires for safety, progress, and an improved life, they're probably not likely to be thinking very hard about star-ships, or to have the ability to make one."

"Unless, of course," Forbish Wingate blinked his pouched eyes and mildly interjected, "the thrust for safety, progress and an improved life happen to be the exactly wrong sort of impetus for the kind of organization it might take to mount such a project."

"Or," said Ian, "there are other and vaster rewards to be obtained from interstellar flight than anything we can conceive of, physical or biological. There may be whole new sciences about which we have no inkling."

"Well, now you're all in the who-can-be-cleverest-at-the-seminar groove," said Julia with almost a snarl. "You said *proof,* Noel. This sort of speculation wouldn't get by a referee in the *Journal of the Flat Earth Society.* All you're proving is that earthlings can spread more bullshit than any magic bugs in the entire star field."

Noel glared at her and Eve could see that Julia's needling and her sarcastic, sharp voice had finally roused his anger, for his bland, round face had turned a spotted pink and his eyes had lost that dismal compassion she had seen earlier, to be replaced by simple fury. He got to his feet, without the slightest trace of hesitation or unsteadiness, and walked into the bedroom where coats and umbrellas had been parked. "Don't go away, Julia," he said in a tight voice over his shoulder. "Proof is on the way."

In a moment he had returned to the room with a thin briefcase, from which he extracted a folder as he sat down, once more in the exact center of the room. "I'll pass these photos around as I describe them," he said coldly, "but I'll hold them up first."

He paused and turned to stare at Ian. "Mr. McPherson, you may well be able to guess the source of these photos and the home of the device they illustrate. Since I gave these people my word that they would not be publicly identified, I would appreciate it if you did not reveal the name of the family to the multitudes."

He paused again, looking down at the photos and organizing them in a sequence. "It is a family that once owned a very great library of scientific texts and other artifacts of sixteenth and seventeenth century scientific activity. Taxes and hard times have forced the dispersal of this valuable material, in discrete dribs and drabs, but a few good pieces have been retained, and the best of them is an orrery, among the finest ever built, and in my opinion, the most important artifact in the entire history of scientific thought."

He looked about the room, his eyes shifting and darting, as he held up the first picture, a photograph of a large, handsome brass and ivory orrery mounted on its own completely round table with drawers and adjusting fitments related to the operation of the device spaced around the edge.

Noel passed the first photo to Eve and held up the second. "As you'll see in that first photo going around, this device simulates the motion of the four inner planets, earth's moon, and the two moons of Mars. The gearing is excellent, the errors almost nonexistent, and the whole system is set in motion by that hand crank in the table. Alternatively, a clockwork drum can be hooked in to run the thing for twelve hours or so. It can run in real time, or about twelve times as fast, or whatever speed you want using the crank."

He handed off the second photo. "But that's only the

beginning of the story. In this second picture I show the orrery in its cometary configuration. In one of the drawers is a Halley's comet gearing outfit that lets you move a tiny Halley's comet through the system of the inner planets on its proper ellipse, and with an attached tail that always points outward on a comet-sun radius line, as it should. This system is good enough so that if you set the comet at the proper place in the model when you first spotted it in the sky, you could predict its entire passage, including times of best seeing, from the motion of the orrery.

"Halley predicted the return for 1756 and missed it by two years, so the construction of this device must predate that time by some amount. Even though he muffed on the return, Halley's orbital elements were plenty good to design this system and it was probably a useful tool when the comet was finally sighted."

Eve, though filled with a sense of dismay at Noel's strangely focused attentions, stared at the eight-by-ten glossy photos in fascination. "Who built this gorgeous thing, Noel?" she breathed, and when she saw the second picture gave a cry of amazement. "Why, there's nothing that good at South Kensington!"

Noel nodded. "You're right. There isn't anything that good at the Science Museum or the Smithsonian or anywhere else. I want to stress that I made a number of operating checks with this machine and the astronomical design is the equal of anything still in existence. It was built by Andrew MacInnison, an Edinburgh instrument maker and a sometime associate of Patrick Ferguson. But Ferguson didn't design this orrery. It was ordered and utilized by one Fergus Drummond, laird of Duinismere, a vast estate in northern Scotland, and an amateur stargazer completely besotted with the heavens. MacInnison probably worked for years on the orrery and its cost, in the context of the times, must have been truly astronomical."

Noel held up a third photo. "Another little kit that MacInnison worked out is shown in this picture. Four of the major asteroids can be set in motion along with and among the usual planetary models and will follow their proper orbits as the planets follow theirs. Again, this system is so accurate that if you once get them in the right places, you can use the device to predict their locations days or weeks later. Furthermore, their orbital angles to the plane of the ecliptic are exactly right."

Julia peered at a photo in the dim room. "So where are the extrasolar bugs," she said brightly, "living on the asteroids and eating meteors?"

"No, Julia," said Noel quietly. "They have their own vessel and their own module in the orrery too." He held up the last four photos. "In another drawer in the device's table base, I found the most remarkable, the most incredible device of all. These four shots show the overall assembly, then the earth-moon-something system in close-ups. The device fastens on the existing earth-moon model and is geared into it. When you turn the crank, a small sphere orbits the earth in a circular, transpolar orbit with a twelve-hour period. The orbit precesses from west to east, that is, in the same direction the earth is rotating, so that as it comes over the north pole it describes a diagonal, south-moving path, crossing the equator at an angle, and reaching the south pole when the earth has turned a quarter revolution. The precession rate is such that in thirty days, a little more than a lunar period, it will have passed over the entire earth's surface and will begin to make repeat crossings. Since it makes two orbital passes each day, the track is shifting eastward about six degrees on each orbit."

The room was very silent and many of the guests hunched or crawled forward along the floor to look at the pictures, not wanting to wait until they were passed around. An old, white-haired astronomer looked at Noel with a thin half-smile. "Something in an orbit of about fifteen thousand miles, then?" he suggested.

Noel nodded. "I realize that seems high for a reconnaissance mission, but remember that I'm assuming they have far better remote-sensing capabilities than we do. Also, they would probably want to minimize the chances of being seen by life-forms that might understand what they were looking at."

"Was this MacInnison's idea," asked Eve, "or the man who paid for it?"

"Oh, I think Lord Drummond's," said Noel at once. "MacInnison was not much of an observer, although he obviously had the ability to compute the gear trains and figure out the linkages. He was a wonderful artisan."

"So what you're suggesting, Noel," said Professor Wingate, "is that Drummond saw this thing in the sky, computed its orbit, and gave the elements to MacInnison, so that he could include this piece in the orrery?"

Noel nodded again. "Correct, but the model speaks more clearly to us than that. The comet and asteroid units were constructed at the same time as the basic planetary gearing system and fit right into it. This module was added afterward. The workmanship is slightly different and it is obvious when you study the mechanism that the thing was grafted onto the existing earth-moon system. It wasn't too difficult to do since the period was a simple multiple of the earth's spin rate, and the precession rate is close to that of the moon cycle."

The American physicist shook his head and grinned at Noel. "This Drummond knew something, all right, but are you sure it wasn't something to do with the consumption of scotch whiskey, Noel?"

Noel looked around the room and his fierce expression momentarily returned. "Look! Think about it and everything makes sense. Here's old Drummond peering up with his telescope, which by the way, was an excellent eight-inch refractor by Dollond, way in the north of Scotland, probably the northernmost large telescope in use at that time in the entire world. The orbiting star vessel comes over the pole, huge and way up, maybe in winter when the sun is south. Drummond's observatory is in darkness most of the time and somehow he sees it, moving south like hell over him against the fixed stars. If he can hold it for even a minute, he can get a rough shot at the orbit. So the next night he has a good idea where to look and he sees it again! Now he can really pin down the elements and from then on, he can find it every night. Eventually, in a few days, the orbit precession has moved the track away from Scotland, but by then he can compute when it will be back."

Noel waved a hand in his excitement, telling the story in a loud, positive voice, and the room was perfectly quiet, other than the slight rustling of people looking at the photos. "But," he almost shouted, "this isn't a few nights of wonder and then it's gone away forever. This orrery was built by Drummond as an analog computing device, to assist him in making sightings. That is perfectly obvious from the entire layout of the machine. For example, when searching for asteroids, he would be able to get the declination and hour angle of the target body by simply setting the device to his day and time of observation and measuring the angle from his observing point on the miniature earth to the asteroid sphere. One drawer contained a device that fits on the earth sphere to directly give the two sighting angles on scales, so there is no doubt about the machine's purpose or use."

He waved his hand again, peering at an astronomy professor. "Obviously that target body appeared often enough and over a long enough period to induce Drummond to add its motion to his computing device. Well, think about it! It's 1760 in the north of Scotland. Either parts of the orrery have to go down by horseback and stage to Edinburgh, or MacInnison, if he built the module, has to ride north with his supplies and kit and do the job at Duinismere. The whole episode would have to involve a year or so of time, and presumably the thing keeps showing up now and then, plus some unknown length of time thereafter."

Eve shook her head. "It couldn't have been too long thereafter, Noel," she said positively. "Somebody else would have certainly picked it up eventually. The rate of increase in telescope use for that period is very high. Every year there were more and more snoopers peering up. And didn't Drummond write to anyone about this?"

Noel gave them all an unexpected grin. "He was an irascible old gentleman, decidedly a recluse. He seems to have hated everybody and apparently never wrote down a word. While I was studying this orrery, I also went over the complete sale and auction catalogues of the family's collection of scientific books, since they had conveniently kept all this stuff, but there wasn't a single suggestion of anything there from or about Drummond. Did you ever hear of him, Eve?"

Eve was frowning and thinking hard. "Wasn't there something in one of the later printings of Ferguson's *Astronomy* that referred to a Drummond Tidal Predictor? I think Ferguson had not actually seen it and sort of dumped on the thing."

Noel's eyes widened in interest. "Listen, if you can find that reference, I'd love to have it. The trouble is that *Astronomy* appears in about a million different versions.

"But consider," said Noel to Eve, "it may be that this vessel was so well concealed that Drummond's spotting it was simply a moment of good luck, a perfectly chance matter."

"And what albedo for the object are you estimating, Noel?" said an astronomer.

"Possibly zero," said Noel with a shrug, and when several of the astronomers snorted, Noel gave them a superior smile. "If you coated the outside of your star-ship with an organism that was programmed to reflect all solar photons at an angle away from the earth, wherever the earth happened to be overhead, that entire, so-coated structure would have an albedo of zero to an earth observer."

"But what about moonshine, Noel?" asked Eve.

Noel smiled at her and then clapped his hands in applause. "That idea would fit Drummond's location around the winter solstice quite well. There might well be some moon angles when the thing would be illuminated during the almost perpetual winter nights. If he didn't pick it up by moonshine, then it might have been by occultation of the background stars, but to be able to *follow* an orbiting body by that method would mean that the thing was huge indeed.''

The room became silent as the party goers, half-drunk, besotted with food and dope, imagined a vast, dark vessel moving in its great arc south over sleepy, frozen Scotland, through the winter blackness, while an eccentric old man followed its path, the ice-cold Scottish air caught by his chest in a gasp of astonishment. Yet his eye remained intent at the eyepiece, watching, watching *something* pass across the great spangle of star fields.

"Drummond died in 1778 and never communicated this to anyone," said Noel, "at least, as far as I can tell, but it does seem a bit unreasonable that nobody else even had a look."

Eve shrugged. "Such as MacInnison," she suggested. "Didn't he think it was kind of an odd addition to Laird Drummond's lovely toy?"

Noel shook his head. "MacInnison died before Drummond, in 1771, so it's possible the star-ship device was added afterward. Perhaps Drummond made it himself."

Julia found herself reluctantly admitting that Noel had, perhaps, found something quite extraordinary. "Even if it was up there for ten years," she said in a slightly more friendly voice, "could the bugs possibly get what they wanted in that time?"

Noel gave Julia a smile. "I don't think anyone here can judge that, knowing as little about them as we do, but there are a couple of mission profiles, as NASA would call them, that make sense with a two-, five-, even ten-year orbiting period. One is that they can get what data they need out of our biosphere in that period and leave. The other is that they simply use the time to decide where to set down their scouts, then put them in place and go off to, maybe, the next star. There is something to be said for a sort of circular, multiple-star mission. You drop off your people, then circle again and pick them up."

"Which," said Professor Wingate in an amused voice, "would essentially imply that they are still around and about, since any such circle might require hundreds of years to complete and, anyway, if the vessel had returned in the nineteenth century, it would surely have been spotted."

Noel shrugged. "Perhaps it would have been spotted in, say, nineteen-hundred, but then again, perhaps not. But I have to admit that what you're saying is reasonable. Either they came and went around the time old Drummond watched, or they're still around."

"Noel," said Eve, "what do you think Drummond thought it was? Could he have realized it might be an alien vessel?"

Noel shook his head. "I doubt if that idea crossed his mind. He probably thought it was a small satellite that had been recently caught by the earth and set into orbit. He would see it as a relatively tiny and very close second moon. If it went away while he was still watching it, that would have puzzled the hell out of him, but if it was there when he died, he would never have known that it didn't remain in orbit."

"And which theory do you subscribe to, Noel?" said Eve in a low voice.

"I happen to think that at least some of them might still be around," he said to her, "but not necessarily because their transportation is returning here at some future time. There has to be some practical time limit beyond which leaving your scouts to their own devices on an alien world is certain to result in attrition of said scouts. Two hundred years is just too long, in my opinion. They must have realized that this world was in an explosive development phase, involving an active and rapacious life-form. No sane mission commander would have left them here for more than fifty or a hundred years at most, even in the most isolated places. In my opinion, something happened to the mission, at some other place beyond here, and they never returned for their data-gathering brood."

"This data-gathering brood might be, then, immortal?" said Ian suddenly.

"Not necessarily immortal, but probably quite persistent, equipped with a variety of solutions, countermeasures, tricks, alternate modes, fallbacks, redundancies and every other necessary thing to allow them to roll with whatever punch the strange world threw at them."

He looked around the room thoughtfully. "Yet they would eventually realize that they were marooned in a way no earthly mariner ever faced. And if they had the intellectual capacity to accomplish tasks that now lie far beyond our intelligence, it seems to me that eventually they would see and face the truth of their meaningless activities. Yet their discretion to date, if my theories make any sense, seems to have been total."

Marta Hoerner cleared her throat. "Yet you speak quite positively of their psychological reactions to, as you put it, being marooned. Surely, sentient beings that have spent fifty or more years in space are not likely to become discouraged at the failure of a planned rendezvous? Surely they would be instructed, or conditioned, to expect rescue, backup or redundant missions to arrive in due time?"

Noel looked steadily at her and the room was silent. "On a primitive world, this world a million years ago for example, what you say would obviously be the case. An understanding of despair would be anathema to the success of the mission. The creatures would not learn that existential vision from, say, a trilobite or, later, from the great lizards with their tiny heads, and so they would remain what we might call programmed optimists."

His eyes were no longer sharp but now distant and thoughtful. "But what about when they contacted us, in ways so deep that we probably cannot use them to contact each other? Now that programmed biological machine might learn more than its masters would wish. Now it might learn, too well, about pain and despair and failure."

"Well, Noel," said Julia, but now not with that sharp sarcasm but with more of a sense of resigned wonder, "if there has to be a shrink for abandoned, unloved, alien space pilots, it might as well be you!"

And that almost-affectionate quip somehow produced a round of laughs and comments and the informal lecture broke up into several, contiguous groups, drinking their last drinks and peering at Noel's pictures with many a shake of the head and an argumentative "Yes, but . . ." until the guests managed to get to their feet and thank their hostesses for such a "spacey" evening, in every sense of the word.

Eve warmly kissed both Ian and Alice and whispered in Ian's ear, "Call me tomorrow, please?" to which he gave her a single, sober nod.

Professor Wingate and his guest from Berkeley

thanked Eve profusely, if coolly, at the door and as soon as they had gone down the stairs, Eve turned to find herself alone with Noel, in the foyer, and once again his face wore that sharp, pained look that had so disturbed her earlier. He glanced back over his shoulder, then seized her hand in a large hand as cold as ice, making Eve shudder as she stared into his masklike face. "Eve, you must not trust them!" he said in a hissing, quiet voice. "That bitch Hoerner is in it with the Americans, and old Wingate is as bent as an Italian customs official. God knows whose shit bucket he's carrying."

"What is *it*, Noel?" asked Eve in a thin, frightened voice.

"Don't dissemble to me, Eve! Don't balk me on this!" he said fiercely, his breath hissing in her face. "*You* have been drawn in by that thing, that immensely sad, immensely powerful thing, perhaps the last of its kind, lost, forgotten, abandoned, yet competent and dangerous beyond imagination . . ."

And when her face still blinked in bewilderment he put his face even closer to hers and spoke in a hissing whisper, tense with fright, "That thing at Muskeget Island, Eve! It has chosen you for some inscrutable purpose, some unimaginable need. Yes, *you*, Eve, and now they are all watching you, that scum of science, those pimps and whores of natural philosophy who do the bidding and the filthy, workaday abominations of their political masters. Listen, Eve! You lived, worked with, a young hypnotist and magician, the Great Calivari, when you went to graduate school at Columbia. You often assisted him during his Park Avenue duplex magic shows, the rich people in evening dress barking like dogs. You know the genuine power of posthypnotic suggestion, how readily a person can be made to do something nonlogical and . . ."

Eve stared, still bewildered but now angry, at Noel. "How did you know all that, Noel? Johnny Finn, the Great Calivari to you, was my dearest lover and my intended husband. He died when a swivel broke while he was hanging upside down, getting out of a new kind of straitjacket at a county fair in Katonah, but what right do you, or anyone, have to all that personal information?"

His cold hand squeezed her harder. "The moment that creature identified you as important to its plans, no part of your life could be hidden from them, from us, for I am one of those despicable scientific whores as well."

"You keep saying I've been identified," said Eve in a whisper. "How can that be? When did it happen?"

"When you bought the book at Phillips, of course."

Eve shook her head. "Impossible. That was an essentially random chance."

"You and Jack Goldman have cruised in Nantucket Sound almost every summer for years," said Noel intently. "When you get close to Muskeget, the thing's power to force future events, to regulate your future behavior, are immense, and it can deal with complex alternatives."

"Then what about the Bion and the other books at the auction?" said Eve. "I suppose this alien swam the ocean and plopped the things onto Mrs. Stringfellow's doorstep?"

"No," said Noel coolly, "I arranged for those books to go to Mrs. Stringfellow so that somebody, you as it happened, would be certain to be decoyed into attending that auction."

Eve felt dizzy with surprise. "You did that? You, Noel? But why?"

"It told me to," said Noel in a low, serious voice and that suddenly sounded so funny to both of them that they laughed and Eve felt his hand was warmer and gave it a squeeze back.

"A little voice?" she said. "In your head?"

"Okay," he said, now laughing easily. "Maybe that's enough to say for tonight. You're leaving when? In three days? Let me call you when I get to Boston this summer and see if we can't go further on this. Meanwhile, don't trust a soul."

Eve thought for a moment of asking about Ian, but then realized that if Ian were her enemy too, the world had turned upside down and to hell with it. Better not to know. "Good night, Noel," she said, leaning to kiss his cold cheek.

"Good night, Iphigenia," he said with a grim smile.

·7·

A
REMEMBERED
VISIT TO
MUSKEGET

And then he called you Iphigenia?" said Ian, looking at her from concerned eyes.

Eve nodded. "When he said good night. He'd waited until most of the rest of you had left before he gave me that warning. Ian, who the hell was Iphigenia? I'm a supposed Doctor of Philosophy and I haven't the foggiest remembrance. Was she a Greek goddess?"

Ian got up from his chair in Eve's living room and walked over to look out the window, down the wide street at the tall, expensive, old brick homes of Hampstead, now turned into more-expensive and trendy flats.

He sighed and shook his head. "I'm afraid not. She was Agamemnon's youngest daughter. The Greek military establishment decided she had to be sacrificed to the gods so that they could get a decent wind to blow them to Troy. Partly because of that dreadful butchery, Agamemnon's wife, Clytemnestra, eventually killed the bastard and was killed, in turn, by her other children, Electra and Orestes. A nasty, bloody-minded bunch. No wonder any decent British schoolboy always prefers the Trojans, even though they lose, to those filthy Greeks."

"Dear me," said Eve. "Why should he have called me that, I wonder?"

Ian looked across the room at her with a set face. "You can't see it? Suppose that visitor at Muskeget Island offered them, Noel's people, or somebody else's people, or all of them together, part or all of what it knew? Wouldn't that be a gigantic first step toward the crossing of deep space? Wouldn't that eventually enable us to set sail, not for Troy, but for Barnard's Star or Ceres? And if the thing will do this favor as part of a bargain in which you prominently figure, then what Noel said was an exact metaphor of the situation. You must see that, Eve? That *must* be what he was saying to you!"

Eve sipped her drink, shaking her head slowly. "Then you really think he wasn't just having a cocaine fit, I mean, seeing things? You believe that something, an alien, is really there on that island?"

Ian shook his head in angry frustration. "The thing is, Eve, if somebody said to John Watson, there's an otherworldly thing on an American island that can influence what people do in London or anywhere else by some sort of superhypnotic power, Holmes would imme-diately ask the doctor whether the teller of the story was offering to sell shares in the 'secrets of the alien.' In other words, he wouldn't believe a word of it!"

Ian clenched his fist, striding back and forth. "But,

damn it, Fenwick, Professor Wingate, that Hoerner woman from California, are plainly not just an imaginative extortion team. And what about the Macy stories? Has that stuff all been cooked up or fabricated? I wish we had Miranda Macy's interview with Ben Stringfellow! Of all of them, she had the closest link with that damn island. What did Rose Stringfellow say to you, that Miranda went back to Muskeget to join her dead husband?"

"To see her lover, Rose said," answered Eve, watching him stride back and forth, but continuing to shake her head in slow arcs. "Ian, the idea that something never seen or sensed, by its simple proximity months or years earlier, could implant some instructions in my head so that I lifted up that book at Phillips and opened it as the result of such implanted instructions, defies all belief. Okay, Noel was right. I've seen dear, lost Johnny Finn take an especially good subject and implant a posthypnotic suggestion so that they are suddenly perched on a chair and crowing like a chicken, ten or twenty minutes after they were awakened and sent back into the audience, but, Ian, to hold that power over someone for years is not possible. Johnny claimed he could make almost any girl call him up the next day by posthypnotic command, but beyond that length of time it all slipped away."

Ian mixed himself a drink and suddenly flopped into a low chair across from Eve. "All very well, but let's assume that Noel is right, completely right. What powers and abilities does the thing have?" He held up one finger. "It can make human beings hallucinate. See Henry Macy and the humane house vision." He held up a second finger. "It can control, somewhat, both muscular and glandular activity, namely, the woman in labor, the fish, the sudden milk in Mrs. Macy's bosom."

He stuck out a thumb. "It must have a posthypnotic or postvisit sort of ability. Mrs. Stringfellow went to Muskeget last summer and the pilot landed her there, 'just to be nice.' Then later, she decides to sell her library that contains the crucial stories." Ian shook his head. "Too coincidental. It's easier to think that one act leads to the next one. And if the alien can manipulate behavior over an interim period of months, why not over a year or more? Who knows how many trigger words or key visual symbols it could implant, with a whole matrix of possible behavior outputs."

Eve got up to splash a bit more gin into her drink and wrinkled her nose at Ian. "If the thing has psychic powers, why not assume it can control us anyplace? Why not by direct wire, Muskeget–London. Who knows, it may be monitoring us right now." She tried to give him a bright smile.

Ian shook his head. "It can't do that or it wouldn't be working in such indirect ways. If it could control you here, it wouldn't need to mess with any of the rest of this, or involve anyone else. Also, there is no account we have seen involving Muskeget and the people associated with it, where there is any direct, immediate intervention at more than a few miles away. If we assume that the alien helped Horace to see Miranda's light, then it has a range of maybe eight miles, covering most of Nantucket, I would think. But I don't believe its methods involve any undiscovered or psychic forces. The fact that there is a range on its activities suggests some kind of electromagnetic ability that allows it, when near a target, to read out stored nervous system memories and to implant a variety of commands and suggestions. I'll bet you some sort of electronic instruments could pick up the signals. Maybe that's how Noel got orders from the thing."

Eve shook her head so hard her thin hair flew in all directions. "Orders! Do you really believe that Noel *talked* to the damn thing? I mean, why Noel, Ian? There's no suggestion in any of the stories of any direct communication. Not with Henry Macy, or his wife, or with Miranda and Horace. And I sure as hell never had any extrasolar conversations on Muskeget. Noel is a highly educated, highly imaginative druggie. God only knows what imaginary beings he's talked to over the years!"

Ian's face was serious and thoughtful. "The baby talked to Mrs. Macy. The Nantucket telegrapher was balked during a transmission. Horace went haring off on a suicide mission . . . just because he saw a distant light? There's really all sorts of communication going on in the stories, Eve. The difference, the new thing, is that Noel knows, or claims to know, where it's all coming from."

"And," said Eve with a sigh, "all those earlier people would have been totally freaked out by the truth, assuming what Noel is saying is the truth. The Yoho, a hundred years ago, could do what it wanted in those isolated locations and people either said spooks, rum, or some of each. And the wonderful thing about spooks, then and now, is that they don't have to follow any rules. But now we're so smart and overeducated and ready to go out and nuke the universe, it doesn't need the Yoho anymore. The truth, or something closer to the truth, serves its needs better . . . and what needs, Ian?" Eve turned to peer directly at him.

Ian rubbed his face in exasperation. "This is really

crazy! Why the hell would something of this sort pick out
Dr. Eve Pennington, astronomer and scholar in ancient
science?" He grinned at her, then leaned to seize her
hand. "I don't mean that you aren't somebody that
plenty of people would greatly wish to cherish. I think
you are very attractive, a fine person. I just can't picture
you as the bride of Frankenstein."

Eve gave a shriek of laughter, then lifted his hand and
put it warmly to her cheek. "You mean I have to get into
a white bathrobe and a fright hairdo like Elsa Lanchester
when I meet the monster of Muskeget?"

Ian kissed her hand, then leaned closer and put an arm
around her shoulders. "Dear Eve. I am very attracted to
you. I admire you in every possible way."

Eve put both her hands around Ian's neck and pulled
him gently toward her. "Kiss me, Ian, until I stop
believing in this crazy stuff. Then we'll go out for
supper," she said, closing her eyes.

The little pub at the top of the Heath was mostly
empty and they took a tiny table alone in the back,
ordered the house specialty, fish and chips, and warmly
held hands under the table. "I wish we had met or gotten
together sooner, Ian," said a smiling Eve. "Day after
tomorrow, I'm gone away."

"You'll be back," said Ian, "or I'll be over before long.
Phillips has a place in New York, you know, and they're
talking about starting one or two book auctions a year
over there."

Eve watched his clouded, handsome face, his magnified eyes. "Ian, could it *make* me go there, to that island,
do you think?" she said in a low voice. "Could there be
some command hidden in my head, waiting for some
sort of signal? I think that would be scary."

Ian shook his head. "That seems sort of unlikely, under the circumstances as we know them. If you didn't suspect you were involved with this supposed alien, then you might find yourself there for any of a dozen reasons or under any of a dozen arrangements. Somebody might ask you to visit them at Nantucket, or to cruise on their sailboat. But now that you're alerted, I doubt if it could simply override your natural caution. None of the stories suggest any such absolute power, or at least, the application of such a direct kind of control. Remember, the thing didn't simply use Joanna Macy's hand to cut that woman's body. It had the baby ask Joanna to do it."

Ian looked at her steadily and continued. "Eve, maybe you're a replacement for Miranda Macy. If we knew what she intended to do when she went back to Muskeget in 1938, I think we'd know much more about why you seem to have become part of this."

He paused and rubbed his cheeks in embarrassment. "Eve, did you ever, uh, go to Muskeget with a boy, maybe just the two of you, during that summer you spent on Nantucket?"

Eve gave him a warm, but slightly rueful smile. "I've never been a tremendously sexy person, Ian. I was just fourteen that summer, and I didn't even go out with boys then. Neither did my sister. My defloration, which is an awful big word for something so short and quick, came in a college dorm room years later."

She squeezed his hand. "I was really an innocent little wimp. I never went to Muskeget with any big, strong Horace Streets. I would have been scared out of my wits to do something like that. Also, there were only a few boys at Madaket and on Tuckernuck Island right across the harbor from us, and they were just as shy and wimpy as I was. No, it was my sister, Priscilla, with whom I usually went to Muskeget for picnics and exploring."

"And you don't remember anything unusual, anything special about any of the visits? Nothing, say, involving your father, perhaps?" Ian said this in a low, halting and distressed voice, but Eve just looked at him from loving eyes.

"My father was a bastard, but not that kind of a bastard. He was too weak to have a try at incest, if that's what you're looking for. This morning I talked to Julia about what Noel said to me, and I tried to think about those Muskeget times. I guess we did make several trips there during the summer, maybe six or seven, but they all sort of blend into the whole, happy time."

"It couldn't just be that you went there several times. Hell, some people have lived on that island for years, a caretaker, some fishing sports and shooters who spent months there in the summer and fall, a lifesaving crew employed by your government. I've been doing some research on the place. Three American academics did a book-length ecological study of Muskeget in the sixties and included a short history of the place."

"If only we knew what it wanted, assuming it really is there. Could it be that I'm an astronomer, Ian?" said Eve. "I guess it is sort of an astronomical matter?"

Ian shrugged as he chewed thoughtfully on some hot, fried fish. "Miranda was a hotelier and an engineer, probably had no interest in the stars whatever."

"But she was actually born there and lived on nearby Tuckernuck for years. The alien would have a tremendous grip on her after all of that."

"That still doesn't tell us what it wanted from her," said Ian. "It all comes down to that. What was, or is, its purpose?"

Eve ate in thoughtful silence, nodding her head in a faint motion. "That's what Joanna Macy said, way back when Miranda was born. Who can tell about the true purposes of anyone?"

Ian scratched his head. "All right. What about the whole chronology? Let's think about that. Noel's orrery sets the arrival of these things in the third quarter of the seventeen-hundreds. So what is happening at Muskeget then?" He peered at her, then suddenly lifted an excited finger. "The smallpox hospital, right? Noel implied, both in his lecture and when he spoke to you at the end of the evening, that the thing might be somehow injured in an emotional sense, by pain and whatever, right? Even the Macys had a sense of that, way back when."

Eve nodded. "Noel used the word 'sad' when talking about it."

Ian rubbed his hands excitedly. "Noel felt these scouts would not be left here for more than fifty years or so, but that wouldn't be long enough for the mother ship to go to another star system and return. But look! Suppose the mission put down investigators on this world, then went to have a look at the much less promising worlds that still might have some marginal life. They surely would be interested in anything on Mars or maybe Titan, even though there might be only a very few species. Those would be very tough species indeed. So they drop off their main force here to poke around the seas, and explore outward, figuring to return and recover all the scouts in, who knows, twenty, forty, years?"

Ian put down his fork to gesture excitedly. "Something happens. The mother ship never gets back here. So by the eighteen-sixties, at least one alien scout is getting restless. Not only is the mother ship late, and perhaps no longer in communication, but the Muskeget scout has had opportunities to sift the emotional content, the raw despair and pain, of the smallpox victims at a distance of no more than a few yards."

Ian squeezed her hand. "And that makes the wonderful biological machine sad, and perhaps a bit more like us and less of a machine."

Eve's face was thoughtful. Her eyes softened and her cheeks flushed. "Then perhaps Miranda gave the alien the opposite, gave it a taste of joy. Is that all it wanted, Ian? God, think about crossing space, such a vast, unimaginable effort, all the intellectual accomplishment, the deep purposes, all aimed at a tiny moment of passionate joy!"

Ian smiled warmly and for the first time touched Eve's knee, gently cupping it in his hand. "I think you are a very passionate person, Eve," he said in a soft voice. "But if that alien thing wanted passion, I should think it could have attracted any number of couples any number of times to Muskeget."

Eve nodded. "I guess that's true. Yet it didn't seem to have quite that big an effect on Rose Stringfellow and Ben. They didn't make love until they got back to Nantucket, back to the Sea Cliff Inn."

"Its control must be variable, depending on how receptive a person is. Perhaps Miranda was tuned right in to the thing, but Rose wasn't," suggested Ian.

"And also, Rose and Ben Stringfellow wouldn't have made mad, sudden love on Muskeget, no matter what," said Eve. "They didn't know what it was they were feeling. It just seemed like a general happiness, but once they got back to their room-with-a-view at a resort hotel, where people are supposed to make love, they understood their feelings."

Eve took her hand from on top of Ian's and reached to touch his knee, then stroke his leg while gently leaning forward. She took a deep breath, staring into her lap as she spoke. "Ian, Julia is in Manchester for the weekend. If you could spend the night, I would like that very much." Her voice became very small and faint as she said the "very much."

A delighted Ian pressed her hand against his leg. "I think I love you, Eve," he said softly. "I . . . I want to protect you, to keep you safe."

Eve caressed his cheek. "I haven't loved anybody in a long time, Ian. I guess I loved Johnny Finn. He was a gallant, brave person, full of confidence and fun, and we were young in New York City when it was still a neat place to be. But after he fell, I never could get that kind of feeling again. But Ian, I need your strength and your tenderness. Things can grow between us, even if I am half a generation older."

"You will always be young and bright to me. Let's get back to your flat. I desire you so much."

"As I desire you," said Eve, bringing his hand back firmly and warmly to a brief, intimate touch. "I'm ready."

They fell asleep later in each other's arms, their faces in repose and their bodies twined together, but in the early morning after they had rolled apart, Eve began to gasp and then whimper and as her motion became more agitated, Ian woke up and turned on the reading light over the bed, leaning to caress and comfort her as he did so. "Eve, wake up, Eve. Don't dream," he whispered as she desperately clutched him and her eyes flew open, staring at him.

"Oh, how lovely that you're here, Ian," she said with a gasp of fright. "Oh, my, how awful it is to dream like that!"

"What is it? Were you chased?"

Eve clung to him, shaking her head. "No, it's never that obvious. It's just a growing sense of menace, of terror. And I know it's going to get worse, so I try to wake myself, to do something, anything to wake up."

"How often do you have bad dreams?" he asked.

Eve lay back, pulling him down with her, kissing his ear and cheek. "Not very often. I never had them until after Johnny was killed. I never get them when I drink a lot at night. Today, with you here, I didn't want to vague out at the end of the evening so I went easy on the gin."

"You were *perfect* with me!" said Ian passionately, holding her tightly. "Oh, dearest Eve, how can I stop your trembling?"

Eve grit her teeth and hugged him tightly. "It'll stop in a minute. Talk to me, Ian. Tell me what's happening to me."

Ian raised himself on an elbow and looked into Eve's white, pinched face. "Eve, did you and Johnny Finn ever hypnotize each other, by yourselves when you were alone?"

Eve brushed his hair back, looking up at him. "Sometimes we tried it making love, but it wasn't especially good for that, at least I didn't think so."

Ian nodded, then hugged her tightly as she gave an

involuntary shudder. "Did he ever try to hypnotize you to go back to when you were a child? I saw it done at a party once with a middle-aged woman. She remembered, under hypnosis, her sixth birthday party, in Mexico City. More than remembered, she relived it! She spoke and acted like a six-year-old child."

Eve pressed her lips against his cheek. "Johnny didn't like to do that sort of thing in a big show. He said you never knew what might turn up, and sometimes it was embarrassing. But now and then, at small parties where it was all one family or good friends, he would lead someone back to a childhood event. It worked best when you picked something that the subject acknowledged as memorable, like a party or a trip, so you have a tie-in at both the conscious and unconscious levels. Also, you need to kind of guess your way along, to lead the subject through the event."

Ian caressed her shoulders and kissed her gently. "Could you show me how to do it to you, or could you do it to yourself, with me asking the questions?"

Eve sighed and released him to lie back on her pillow. "You mean to go back to Muskeget, that summer?" she said in a small voice.

Ian nodded. "Everything that's happening, your whole relationship to this, perhaps even your nightmares, must be connected with that summer."

Eve nodded, then took a deep breath. "Okay, let's try it. The way Johnny used to put me under was with reflected light off his eyeglass lenses. He had thick ones like you wear and he often used them to put people under hypnosis without appearing to the audience to do a thing. Actually, he was nodding slightly so as to flicker a reflection off his eyeglasses into their eyes and whispering while holding his lips still. He used ventriloquism in some of his acts."

Eve reached over to her bed stand and picked up Ian's glasses, then handed them to him. "Reflect that bed light into my eyes," she said, "and jiggle the glasses just enough to give some flicker. That's it. Now talk me down, just like you've seen it done. You know, your eyes are getting heavy, you are sleepy, all that stuff."

Ian, now up on one elbow and holding the glasses in his other hand, looked down at Eve's drawn face and said awkwardly, "Your eyelids are getting heavy . . ."

But Eve gave a sudden giggle and raised up to kiss his cheek. "It's got to be authoritative, deep and confident. You don't really believe it will work and your voice shows it. Say whatever words you're comfortable with, but speak slowly, deep, calm voice, plenty of command and assurance."

Ian nodded, grinning ruefully, and began again. "You will sleep deeply, deeply," he said in a slow voice. "Deeply, deeply. Close your eyes, deeply, slowly, close, deeply . . ."

And Eve closed her eyes, nodding, whispering, "Yes, yes, deeply . . ."

"When I count to three, to three, to three," said Ian, "you will be asleep. I count, one. Heavy eyes, deep, deep, deep, going to sleep. Two. Deeper, deeper, sleepy eyes, deeper. Three! You are deeply, soundly asleep, but you still hear me. Can you hear me, Eve?"

"Yes, I can hear you," came the little answer, but he saw with hope and excitement that she was breathing in full, regular inspirations.

"Eve, you are fourteen. It is a warm, quiet summer day at Madaket. You love summer on Nantucket, don't you, Eve?"

"Yes, I love summer."

"You are in your little sailboat. Who is with you?"

"Prissy."

"And what does Prissy call you?"

"Evie."

"You and Prissy are wonderful friends, aren't you, Evie? You love Prissy very much?"

"Yes, very much. She is my dearest Prissy."

"You are sailing to Muskeget, the nearby little island. Is it hard to sail there?"

"Not in good weather. The other islands protect you from the waves the whole way."

"Are you sailing, Evie?"

"Yes, I'll sail. Oh, Prissy, you made so many sandwiches. We'll just eat and eat."

"We always have lots of sandwiches, Evie," said Ian quietly, but his mind was racing, his whole body intent on focusing the flickering light on Eve's eyes and listening to her soft, girlish speech.

"We'll pull it right up on the cove beach, Prissy," said Eve, and she smiled widely, her eyes almost closed. The flicker, flicker, flicker played against her eyelids.

"Where shall we eat our lunch, Evie?" said Ian, trying desperately to keep his voice soft and calm.

"Oh, let's go to the little house. There usually aren't many bugs there. How the gulls scream, Prissy."

"They think we'll bother their babies," said Ian. "What fun! The whole island is ours. We will be the two queens of Muskeget."

It was an inspired shot in the dark. Eve smiled with a

sweetness that made Ian catch his breath. "And the little house will be our castle. And the birds our subjects and courtiers. See! They go to announce our return." And Eve lifted her right arm and, turning her palm up, made the gesture of a ruler acknowledging the cheers of her subjects. "At our castle we'll set out our wedding feast."

Ian stared down at her and his hand holding the glasses shook. "Let's have the wedding feast inside our castle, Evie," he said.

"And then we'll skinny-dip and get the jam off our hands!" said Eve in a young, sweet voice, bright with delight, and brought her hands together in a very quiet clap.

"The sandwiches are yummy, aren't they, Evie?"

Eve licked her lips. "Ummmm, I'll say! Oooh, I got a huge gobbet of jam on my shorts."

"I'll brush it off," said Ian, lightly brushing her thigh. "Is a swim what queens do after a wedding feast, I wonder?"

Eve laughed merrily. "Since it's our very own island kingdom, we can decide what rituals are right, anytime we choose. I'm going to save my sandwiches and go for a swim now. Let's get undressed."

Ian saw her hand make an almost instinctive gesture to her right breast and he immediately and very softly touched her there. "You're really getting big up there, Evie," he said in a low, tense voice.

Eve smiled and seemed to caress the air. "So are you, Prissy." She paused and her hand moved to touch an edge of hair on Ian's groin. "We're both getting to be women, Prissy. Oh, how beautiful you are!"

"And you too!" said Ian breathlessly. "We are beautiful, naked pagan queens. And it is our wedding night."

Ian took a very deep breath, and, dropping the glasses, touched Eve now with his other hand, very softly but very personally.

"I've never felt like this, Prissy, have you?" Eve smiled and gave a great sigh. "So *happy!* So beautifully happy! Ah, your touch is sweet, my darling sister."

Eve was starting to twist and rise to him. "Something lovely is going to happen to me, dear Evie," Ian said in a passionate tone.

"Ohhh, and to me too," said Eve at once, her head rolling back and forth. "Kiss me, my beloved Prissy."

Ian lifted Eve with one arm, catching her head in his hand, and kissed her as gently as possible, and at that moment she gave a deep gasp and pressed up tautly against him, her lips falling away, and as she clenched, gripping him fiercely, she said in a small, gasping voice, "When we grow up and get married to husbands and have babies and all that stuff, we'll still be queens together, won't we? This little kingdom will be just ours? We two. Oh say that it will, Prissy!"

Ian, now feeling the tears running down her cheeks, and his own tears beginning, answered in a choked voice, "Always!" and with that word, Eve awoke and clung to Ian, even as her spasms subsided, while a slow, steady flood of tears drenched the pillow under her head.

They dozed, holding each other tightly, for an hour or so, but the early daylight and the bird chirps outside made Eve restive and she lightly pressed her lips to Ian's neck. When she felt him turn and kiss her back, she drew away and asked in a tired yet steady voice, "You figured out it was something like that, didn't you, something between me and Prissy?"

Ian nodded, his eyes soft with compassion and love. "It

had to be that. And there was every reason for you to put it out of your mind. You may have actually blamed yourself for sexually awakening Prissy so she went on that date when she was killed."

Eve nodded and her face was sober. "I might have felt that way, Ian. I think, remembering now what happened, that day on Muskeget made Prissy's death the next winter very much more terrible for me. Yet we never did that together again."

"Do you think that you forgot it soon after the day on Muskeget, or later, after Prissy died that next winter?" said Ian.

Eve released him and lay back. "After Prissy was killed, my father left home. I guess he had a woman someplace, he was a salesman, and when my mother started to drink and cry every day, he disappeared. Later, Johnny Finn told me fifty thousand men do that in the U.S. every year. Sometimes, at his mentalism shows where he read questions from sealed envelopes, a woman would ask where her husband had gone."

"And what did he tell them?" asked Ian, trying to smile and speak lightly.

Eve shrugged and smiled back. "He never messed with that kind of question. Johnny was very ethical. He really didn't want to hurt anybody. His idea was to con the quidnuncs, as he called them, beyond what anyone had done before. If he had lived, he would have eventually been the very best."

Eve squinted, trying to remember. "That next spring, when I was fifteen, my mother fell down in the supermarket and broke her arm. She was a complete drunk by then. My aunt, father's sister, came and took me to her house in Connecticut. I went through what I guess they call now a severe depression, but my aunt wasn't a big believer in pills, or shock treatments. Instead, she did exactly the right, sensible thing; bought me some good-looking clothes, paid to have my hair fixed up, and got me dates with attractive boys."

Eve shook her head. "I was never much of a real charmer, but more of a pretty tease, I guess, and I remained a virgin until college in only the most technical sense, but it was fun and superficial and dumb and got me through somehow. I don't think that I actually forgot that day with Prissy so much as that I sort of agreed with myself never to think about things like that, things to do with Prissy."

Ian leaned to kiss her tired, yet he thought beautiful, face. "Did you and Prissy ever talk about that Muskeget day the fall before she died?" he asked.

Eve thought deeply and blinked back a few more tears. "I don't think we did, but it was a bond between us, something special. I never felt ashamed of doing that with her. I'm sure she didn't either. I think we both knew that some sort of lovely, special thing had happened to us. I don't know if we might have done it again if she had lived, but I suppose we might have had to go back to the island to make it happen."

Ian frowned and shook his head. "I was dead wrong last night, when I said that thing could attract any couples it wanted to Muskeget if it wanted passion. What it needed, or needs, first from Miranda and then from you, must be rare indeed. In some ways its powers are immense, as Noel said, but in other ways, it must depend, as we do, on luck and chance."

"Depend on luck for what, Ian?" said Eve.

"To find or attract a person, perhaps specifically a

woman, with a special and intense sensitivity." Ian blushed and took a breath, then said in a low voice, "Eve, uh, I'm no expert on this subject, and I haven't had a whole lot of experience in it, but . . . well, was that time on Muskeget . . . with Prissy . . . somehow different from, uh, other times?"

Eve grinned and warmly kissed him. "You really are a shy person, aren't you? I don't meet many nowadays, especially at the university. You've never discussed this subject with a woman before?"

Ian gulped and shook his head. "The force, the influence, on that island must have gotten you and your sister going. But was there more to it than that? I mean . . . was it better . . . different . . . ?" He was red-faced and unable to say more.

"You are a dear, dear man," sighed Eve. "To answer your question, I guess women are a little different than men when their sweet moment arrives, Ian. Sometimes the moment is more friendly than physical, and sometimes it's so physical you even forget whom you're being friendly with. In fact, you kind of lose everything for a bit. You don't see very well, and your mind sort of focuses inside yourself, down there where it's all going on. That sort of thing never happened to me very often, but I really like the friendly part better, anyhow."

Ian peered at her and he felt almost overwhelmed by his affection for her. Yet they had to go forward, to discover and learn more. "That time with Prissy, the time just now when I tried to take Prissy's place, can you remember those with any special intensity?"

Eve nodded and her eyes were sober and thoughtful. "What happened tonight, when you made me remember about Prissy, that was just wrenching, Ian. It was an agony because it was so intense, yet remembering brought me such grief at the same time. That first time with her on Muskeget was very different."

Eve wiped her eyes and tried to smile. "We were very close, Ian. We shared a room, went to the same school, talked late into the night about boys and other things. But when that alien started us kissing and caressing, it was like a whole new dimension. It was as though we had stepped into another world, a fairyland of joy. Our lives seemed utterly transformed and, and . . ." Eve lay back then and put her hands up to her eyes, "that thing made us *see,* see and feel what was inside the other and it made everything go very slow, *beautifully* slow, so that when that first great bubble of joy began to expand and get ready to burst inside me, I saw the same thing happening inside Prissy. And I also sensed how she sensed it happening inside me, so it was like facing mirrors that reflect and reflect, forever, deeper and deeper, and when that lovely bubble burst, in me and in Prissy, I saw it in her face and I saw my face in her mind, and the joy went on and on, growing and reflecting. Oh, God, Ian, why did she have to get killed like that? Why?"

"If she had lived, she would be one year younger than you are and probably as slim and beautiful." Ian looked at her and his face reddened again. "Would . . . would . . . ?"

"Would we be lovers now, are you asking?" Eve took a deep, thoughtful breath. "I don't think so. I think we would have led our own lives, meeting often, as close as close sisters can be. Yet perhaps now and then, if we were alone together, we might have tried to return to that moment. Ian, that time with Prissy was beyond lust, beyond what any coarse and stupid interpretations some dumb shrink would glibly spout. My sister and I shared a moment of total love, love acting at every level of consciousness, of physical contact and emotional connection. Oh, Ian, if she had lived, we would never have escaped that day and I would never have wished to escape it. Who would ever want to escape from paradise, from joy and love utterly unconfined and without guilt or cant or selfishness? Oh, poor Prissy," and the name was a long sigh.

Ian nodded, then sat up and rubbed his palms together. "You and Prissy must have qualified with it the same way Miranda did. After whatever it had organized with Miranda failed, maybe because of the storm, it searched for somebody new. It didn't have the time or luck or ability to start completely over, so it must have tried its influences out in more random situations. The fact that it seems to have taken such time and care organizing Miranda shows that whatever it sought, some sort of emotional resonance effect from the sound of it, isn't easy to achieve. I should have seen that point earlier." He turned and pointed a finger at her. "The Stringfellows were influenced, but their passions were either too weak or the sexual resonance between them was impossible to get going in the time available. It must have tried it with other couples in the forty or so years since Miranda's death, but only with you and Prissy did it get the effect it wanted, or needed."

"Needed for what? That's the big question," said Eve, looking up at his serious, concerned face.

"Exactly! Needed for what? Think we could have a try at talking to Miranda Street with one of Ben Stringfellow's Ouija boards? We've got to figure this out, somehow or other."

Eve reached up and stroked his chest and shoulders. "We can't do everything at once. Ian, I would like very much to make love with you again," and she grinned at his sudden flush of embarrassed pleasure. "Something down there, which isn't exactly a little bird, tells me you would like to do that too," and she caressed him and pulled him down to her.

And as her tired yet open body began to delight in his strength and passion, she whispered breathlessly in his ear, "What a strange, sweet gift to bring us, all that distance across such cold, black space."

·8·

FLYING TO AMERICA

On the next day, Ian had an auction to deal with, so Eve did not see him until evening. They had supper together at a West End restaurant and went back to Eve's flat to make love, but they both faced an early day and Ian left her at midnight. "My beloved, I will be in America by fall at least," he said to her, kissing her neck and cheek. "Have a good flight."

Eve was sad to see him go, but she was also filled with a certain anticipation at flying to America the next morning. It seemed to her that her life was in a sudden flux, approaching a change of profound significance, and she was filled with unfocused expectations.

She had sent most of her things home by mail in the past weeks, and so kissed Julia at the flat door and went off to Heathrow on the tube, lugging only two small bags and a huge purse.

She checked through the airline counter and entered the vast departure lounge to wait for her flight call.

Restless, she decided to give Ian a call at Phillips, and
dialed the number in a booth. When "Phillips, heaah,"
came in her ear she asked for Ian, but the voice paused,
then said much more quietly, "Is this Eve?"

"Yes. Alice?"

"Eve, give me your number and I'll get right back. We,
uh, aren't supposed to take personal calls on this line."

Eve read her the number and pushed down the
receiver hook with her finger, while still holding the
receiver to her ear. Three minutes later the phone rang
and Eve let up the hook.

"Yes?"

"Eve?"

"Yes. Still here."

"Ian said I shouldn't talk with you on a Phillips phone,
so I zipped out to a booth. He said to say that if you
called, I was to tell you that something important has
happened and that he has decided to start on his
vacation a bit early to see about some of the things that
you and he had talked about." There was a pause. "Is
this making any sense, luv? I'm trying to repeat what 'e
said to me."

"Yes," said Eve. "It's making sense."

"Well, then the last thing 'e said was that 'e would
contact you about writing back and forth to America.
Before 'e does, 'e said not to write anything to him. Does
that sound right?"

"Yes, tell him I understand, Alice, and thank you."

There was a pause, then, "Eve, be careful," she said.
"Ian seemed worried about you."

"I'll be careful," said Eve. "I'm a big girl, Alice. At
some point we ladies have to start looking out for
ourselves."

"Oh, that's true, luv, but, oh, be careful anyway. Well, 'bye now."

"Good-bye, luv," said Eve. She left the booth and stared around the long, busy departure hall. There might be a dozen of them watching her out in this mob, she thought. No point in even being concerned about it.

The plane left the terminal late and then sat on the runway approach ramp in a line of planes, for almost an hour. A stewardess came by with an armful of newspapers and Eve idly selected an *International Herald Tribune,* and then idly looked over its front page as the big jumbo turned, finally, into the wind for takeoff.

As they accelerated, Eve folded open the paper to the next two pages and scanned them. The story caught her eye instantly.

Five Yachtsmen Dead in Western Isles Storm
United Press International

PORTPATRICK, U.K.–Coast Guard authorities here announced that a large charter sailboat, the *North Star II,* was washed ashore and broken up yesterday on the western side of the island of Barra, one of the southernmost islands of the Outer Hebrides group. Although no bodies were found on or near the remains of the forty-foot ketch, Coast Guard officials at the scene stated that the vessel apparently came ashore partly inverted, and suggested that the crew were lost overboard during a knockdown and overturn. Winds in the area have reached eighty to ninety miles per hour during the past two days as a northwest gale struck viciously at the western Scottish coast.

The yacht owners, Skye Cruising Ltd. of Glasgow,

named the charterer as Dr. Noel Fenwick, a Professor of the History of Science at Imperial College, London. Dr. Wilbur Barden, Dean of Engineering at Imperial, confirmed that Professor Fenwick had intended a two-week cruise of the Western Isles, in part to further his research into early Scottish astronomical activities. He named the other members of Dr. Fenwick's party as: Dr. Arthur Bedford, a neurological physician, employed as a research fellow at Southampton University, and three Americans, Drs. Jacob Hirshfeld and Timothy Fogarty, respectively Professors of Medicine and Electrical Engineering at the California Institute of Technology, and Mr. Frank Mitchell, described as a professional yacht captain residing in Miami, Florida.

Dr. Barden noted that Professor Fenwick was an enthusiastic yachtsman who had chartered in many waters, including New England, the Caribbean, Hawaii, and the barrier reefs of Australia. He had been twice before to the Hebrides, Dr. Barden stated. American Embassy spokesperson Phyllis Gold described Dr. Hirshfeld as "a distinguished neurologist who was combining high-speed computer technology and high-sensitivity brain monitoring." Ms. Gold described his loss and that of Dr. Fogarty, who was assisting Dr. Hirshfeld in his research, as "tragic for their university, for their country, and for the world of science."

The island of Barra is a remote and rocky part of the Hebrides group and has only two harbors of refuge, both on the eastern side of the island. Coast Guard authorities speculated that the *North Star II* was heading east for a passage at the north end of Barra, leading into the protected Sound of Barra, when they were overtaken by a wave or wind gust and swamped or overturned.

Since the disabled yacht would be driven more to the south in a northwest blast, they noted, it would have eventually struck where it did on the Barra west coast. So remote and desolate is this location, that after Coast Guard patrol aircraft spotted the wreck, it was necessary to use helicopters from the airfield at Tragh More at the southern end of Barra to reach the rocky beach where the remains were strewn. Coast Guards who had been at the scene stated that it was unlikely that any bodies would be found.

Although the summer storm disabled several other yachts and resulted in three busy days for the Coast Guards and lifesaving crews, only the *North Star II* wreck resulted in loss of life.

The jet rotated its nose upward for takeoff and Eve dropped the paper into her lap and let her head sink back into the chair cushion. Noel dead, just three days after her party and his wild lecturing. What was he doing in the Hebrides? Were there other alien scouts scattered about the world and had Noel found some way to locate them? Was that where it was all headed? Each nasty country out to force or extract what secrets it could from abandoned, lonely interstellar visitors? Eve smiled grimly to herself, in spite of her dismay at Noel's loss. Whatever values they brought across the void to us, she thought, they surely must be learning something about rapacity, greed and viciousness. Would such creatures be stupid enough to trade their vital abilities to a quarreling, demoralized race that might easily use those very secrets to fly to the aliens' own home system, with God-knows-what appalling results? Eve shook her head. Unlikely. If they were programmed to accomplish anything, at the core of the instructions would be a home-world protection imperative.

Eve stared at the news story again, feeling a sense of fright and dismay rise within her. Even though the creatures give us nothing really valuable, she knew, they would probably have some petty trade goods, beads and bright things, biotechnical toys to swap off for whatever favors an alien wanted from the ruling race. Me, for instance, said Eve to herself. And *anything* might have happened to Noel. It might have been a real accident. A local alien might have intervened, feeling the deal was going sour. One of the other human groups might have done Noel and his friends in. They didn't find bodies, only the boat.

And Ian was now in Scotland. If murder was, in fact, afoot, they would not waste a second on him, a totally extraneous meddler whose only loyalty in the matter lay in his passionate attachment to Iphigenia. If they eliminated Noel, who was obviously a principal in the thing, Ian was as good as dead.

Eve blinked, breathing deeply and looking out of her window, when the stewardess intruded on her racing thoughts with a, "Would you care for a drink, madam?"

Eve snapped her head around, trying to keep an impassive expression. "Two double gin and tonics, please," she said in a rush, and as the woman turned to prepare these at the booze cart, a small and ancient man who, Eve realized for the first time, was sitting in the aisle seat in her three-seat row said in an amused, if creaky voice, "Double, double, toil and trouble . . ."

Eve set her teeth and turned to stare directly at him. With the plane not even a quarter full, she wondered, why do *I* have to be exactly one seat away from a foxy grandpa with eight hours to indulge his decrepit and horny fantasies? "Sir," she said in a firm, cold voice, "if you're afraid that this aircraft's gin supply may become depleted, I suggest you do as I did and lay in a small store. In any case, I'd appreciate it if from now on you kept your opinions of my drinking habits entirely to yourself!"

The perky little wizened face turned from pink to a modest red and when the stewardess asked what he would like, he responded in a now sad and quavery voice, "A Bloody Mary, please." Then, pausing to try and recover some of the bright little smile he had shown earlier, muttered under his breath, "Under the fell clutch of circumstance, my head is Bloody-Maryed but unbowed."

Eve took down a full half of one of her drinks and began to grin. He was a spunky old cuss, give him that. She turned and sent him a wide smile. "Sir, I'm sorry I spoke out at you. I know you meant no harm. It's just that I've been reading about the unexpected death of a colleague in a great storm and it disturbed me deeply. I hope you'll forgive my hard words to you."

The small, beady eyes turned up and down the aisle and, noting that the liquor cart was now several rows ahead, turned on her. He spoke softly but with a steadiness that Eve had not noted before. "Also, Dr. Pennington, do you fear that Ian may be caught up in this great storm as well?"

Eve blinked at him and took another drink. "You are . . . who?" she asked, but as she spoke he pulled out a calling card and presented it to her.

Ed C. Berry
Antiquarian Bookseller
Telephone (617) 524-5830
131B Joy Street, Boston, MA 02114

"Put that in a secure place, Dr. Pennington," he said in a soft voice, his glass held to mask his lips. "On the back is written my second, unlisted phone number. As to Ian's safety, he understands the risks as well as you or I do, and I know he will be careful."

Eve gave him a warm smile and leaned to pat his hand. "Should I talk so that somebody can't read my lips too?" she said, speaking clearly, but with only the barest lip motion.

Ed Berry's beady, small eyes now sparkled like black garnets, almost hidden in fleshy eye wrinkles. "The Great Calivari taught you to do that! Ah, this is a deep, enthralling business, Dr. Pennington! How glad I am that Ian called me last night. All my life I've waited for that call!"

"Ian called you last night?" said Eve in a startled voice. "But he was with me."

Berry shook his tufted, white head thoughtfully. "Actually, it was at two this morning, after he heard about Professor Fenwick's death on the radio news." He took another long and casual look around. "I had planned to go back to Boston on Friday, but Ian came to my hotel room in the wee hours and explained this whole, amazing business so that I agreed to go on this flight and to try to talk with, and help, you." He sighed, sipping from his drink. "I should have just given you my card and introduced myself, but I stupidly tried to play at being a secret agent. I hope you'll forgive my foolishness. I was never a success as a masher, even in my greenest salad days, Dr. Pennington."

"Ed, call me Eve. And you made a lovely recovery with the Bloody-Maryed-but-unbowed thing. You made me feel perfectly awful for being so nasty to you. I don't think James Bond could have done it a *bit* better."

That seemed to make him much more cheerful and when the stewardess came to ask about wine with dinner, he expansively ordered a bottle of champagne for them both. "I'm glad to hear you say that, Eve. Actually, I would prefer to be more of the Richard Hannay sort of undercover gentleman, but even he had to introduce himself to strange ladies now and then. Reading about it isn't adequate, I see that, even when you've been reading for sixty or seventy years. I don't have the courage or temperament to *really* do it, I suppose. Look at George Smiley in the le Carré novels. I could never be that cold and withdrawn."

Eve was now squeezing his small, wrinkled hand warmly. "Ed," she said from an impassive face, "you don't read science fiction too, do you?"

Ed Berry shook his head in disgust. "Absolutely not! It has no rules at all, that I can see, and so it's mostly confusing trash. Thrillers, spy stories, and detectives are my meat. Ratiocination and logic, intricate double and triple dealing . . ."

But then he blushed modestly as he realized what she was getting at and he peered at her, his old lips pursing. "Eve, this affair you are in, this strange game they are playing, is no different than all the other games in which valuable information is the treasure, and economic and military gain, the thrusting motive. That creature will not give them the Norden bombsight in return for you, but the results of what it hands over will, no doubt, be distressingly similar. This is not fantastic science, Eve, this is human duplicity and greed, center stage once again."

Eve nodded with a thoughtful expression. "Yet, there is one difference between the alien and the adversaries of Richard Hannay or Smiley. This game player is nonhuman. Its psychology derives from an extrasolar world. Furthermore, it may be a constructed artifact. How is an earth-conditioned detective or spy master to deal with such an antagonist, although I personally don't believe the alien intends to be the antagonist of anyone?"

Ed Berry pinched his cheek, so as to mask his mouth from the aisle, and said, "Like Ian, I am a Baker Street Irregular, indeed, the present vice-president of the society. All the Holmes stories, brilliant in their variety of activity, setting, and character, nevertheless derive from only a few basic human emotions and drives. That star-traveling thing is living on *our* world and dealing, in obvious purposefulness, with human beings to accomplish certain ends. In the final completion, its purpose will be no different from those, good and evil, of the men and women in the Holmes stories. If we can study its track, follow what has happened, we can learn its aims, just as surely as any capable fictional detective derives a solution from the disparate rubbish of many seemingly random events. That's what Ian is up to now."

Eve brushed away a single, smiling tear. "I am surrounded by bold and capable champions. No damsel ever set out so finely escorted."

He turned his hand over and squeezed her palm against his. "I wish that was true, my dear. We are, alas, raw amateurs in all of this, taking our cues from books written by other men and women as amateur as we. I fear Ian may be your Quixote, Eve, while I stand trembling by, an ancient Sancho Panza."

Eve remembered the time at Phillips when Ian had called her Doctor Watson. She smiled at Ed Berry and leaned suddenly to kiss his wrinkled cheek. "Sancho Panza had his qualities, Ed. I think almost anyone would select him for a squire. I'm *more* than satisfied with mine!"

At that point the dinner and champagne arrived and they abandoned the more sensitive subjects and chatted about what any two strangers discovering a mutual friend on a long flight might talk about over dinner.

"Ian worked for me in London, at a West End bookstore, and eventually we were partners," said Ed Berry, "but Ian soon outstripped the old master, and the quiet life of an antiquarian book cave didn't satisfy his interests. He saw the auction business as the best possible way to handle, learn about, and understand rare books, and he's been hard at it ever since, perhaps five years."

"When did you go back to America?" said Eve after toasting Ed in thanks with her full, plastic, champagne glass.

"Four years ago, after my wife died," he said. "She was English and preferred London, but when she was gone, I decided to come back to Boston. I bought in with old Simeon Greenberg but he died last year and so it's just my business now." Ed shrugged. "I deal in early science and technology, sport fishing, weapons, topography, most of the usual stuff. Old Greenberg, he was in his eighties, had a lot of good contacts all over the world, and I've tried to keep them up. When a very valuable book is moved by its owner in a suitcase across national borders, its later sale has to be undertaken with the utmost discretion. Thus I have my unlisted number and several postboxes under, uh, slightly dummy firm names. I've never knowingly dealt with a stolen book, but when it comes to outwitting tax authorities, I'm afraid we all take a rather, uh, *international* outlook." His eyes twinkled and he winked.

"How *kind* you are to offer to help me," said Eve, sighing, but he held up his palm and his face was now flushed, intent, his black eyes filled with a passionate sincerity.

"I am seventy-four and Ian, now you, have involved me in something beyond all romance, beyond all imagination. When I say that I will give the tag end of my life to protect you, such a beautiful, vibrant, intellectual woman, I mean that absolutely and without reservation!"

Eve blinked back some more tears and nodded at him. "This extraterrestrial thing can't be all evil or strangeness. It seems to bring out the very nicest behavior in us. Or maybe it attracts nice people."

They chatted on about Boston and the rare book business until the last champagne was drunk and the trays were taken away and the plane settled down to a truncated and mindless movie having something to do with a girls' Little League team. As the lights were dimmed, Eve leaned across and said in a low voice, "Ed, did Ian think that Noel was killed by human agents?"

"No, nor do I think that," he answered quietly. "That would make no sense, especially since Noel is apparently the only one we know about who claims to have actually communicated with the thing. Even an adversary to Noel's group wouldn't just kill such a vital asset. They would be much more likely to capture or suborn him."

"Another alien, then?"

"No again, Eve. Ian believes the only living alien on our world is now at Muskeget. I agree. After all, why would Thomas Cope come to a small island in America to find his most important story if the same sort of thing was going on only as far as the Hebrides? Yet it is possible that some accounts of legends out of the Western Isles might have set Cope to looking around at other places. One of the many things Ian wants to follow up in Scotland are any Macy-type stories from those islands. Can you see these things killing five men?"

Eve shook her head emphatically. "I can't, based on what I've read, but we have no idea what type of defenses they may have against self-aware and dangerous creatures. I mean, human beings. At some point they might well kill five or five hundred. After all, Ed, if that Muskeget thing went through the smallpox hospital and a variety of wrecks like the one described by Henry Macy, plus any sensing of conditions on some of the ships that passed nearby, it well knows we don't put much stock in human life."

Ed Berry shook his head and made a suspicious frown. "Two neurologists and an electrical engineer with Fenwick. And the paper says they're up there researching Scottish astronomical history!" He snorted. "I wonder what that yacht carried in the way of electronics in addition to the usual yachting toys?"

Eve nodded soberly. "The presence of those people does suggest that they were up there looking for something. Maybe the Hebrides alien was so quiet that its neighbor, Tom Cope, just never heard about it at all?"

As the movie wore on, Ed Berry and Eve earnestly discussed the possible sources of Noel Fenwick's disaster, but they could only seem to circle around the event, poking and prying at it, but not opening any large vision. Finally they fell silent in the dark cabin and Eve looked over to see Ed busily writing a note on a bit of paper taken from his wallet. He soon passed it secretively to her and got up to make his way to the rest rooms at the rear of the plane.

Eve,

Ian has some messages he said should only be spoken in a rest room. He thinks they may be able to bug specific seats. In a couple of minutes, go to the rear of the plane and into the most rearward rest room with an 'unoccupied' showing. Don't come in too quickly. They aren't very big.

Ed

Eve shook her head and looked at her watch, then stretched and sighed. What if Noel was simply crazy and had a yachting accident and there is nothing whatever to any of this, she thought in sudden dismay. A lonely Ph.D. in astronomy, a geriatric Galahad, and a dear, overwrought book nut produce their very own extrasolar extravaganza. She checked her watch and squeezed out of her seat row. At the rear of the plane, all the rest rooms showed "unoccupied" and Eve carefully edged into the furthest one at the rear and squeezed by thin, little Ed who was half-perched on the basin. "Sit down, Eve," he whispered and Eve did, after some knee fitting.

Eve gave him a bright wink. "I've seen two different movies in which couples have mad sex in one of these, but how is it possible? They really seem so tiny!" And when she saw his blush she seized his hand. "Oh, I didn't mean to say that and embarrass you, Ed."

"That flush was from sheer pleasure and not embarrassment, Eve. You said exactly the right thing, and if I were forty years younger and as handsome as Ian, I would bow, not far I confess and only as a gesture of worldliness in these cramped circumstances, and say in deep, modulated tones, 'Madam, we have important concerns to discuss. Afterward, we might think about the delightful, technical difficulties in certain of your favorite movie scenes.' But given the actual facts which are that you came along far too late and that I could never say that anyway, or do anything if I did, I can only respond, madam, we have important concerns to discuss."

Eve kept his hand in hers and nodded. "We're all of us a little bit displaced in time, Ed. Ian is lost up here from the coal fogs of Baker Street; me, from some convent astronomical observatory in seventeen-ten and you from the yacht in the *Riddle of the Sands,* stopping the Kaiser and saving that nice young lady with the father who was a traitor."

He beamed from a golden-edged smile and his white tufts of hair had a rakish spikiness. "You *knew* that would be one of my favorite books. But now listen." He produced another calling card. "On the back of this card is a box address in Boston. When you are settled, go rent a box somewhere nearby in another name. Send the address in a letter to this box. Ian will write you two kinds of letters. Some will come to you at your apartment and will deal with subjects that he knows they also know about. There is no need to conceal the general idea that Ian is pursuing the Scottish threads such as Cope and Fergus Drummond, and no way to prevent anyone else from knowing what he is doing. Anything that he thinks they don't know or any questions that he would not want them to read, he will send to me disguised to arrive in my usual mass of morning mail. I will contact you, either by phone or by postbox, to come and get them. Is this all clear, Eve?"

Eve nodded. "Completely, and Holmes himself could have done no better. You think we should not talk in an open fashion, even on your unlisted line?"

He pondered her question, his eyes bright slits. "Let's say this; only in a real emergency, when time is too short for you to come over to Boston, or a call for help. Otherwise, I think we should meet."

He took a deep breath, propped himself a bit more securely on the narrow basin, and lowered his voice further. "Eve, when we get back to our seats, I don't think we should discuss this any more, and what I say to you now, Ian said must be protected from them above all."

Eve nodded.

"Ian asked me what was the best way in Boston for you to keep track of tropical storms forming in the Caribbean. I said a weather radio was the easiest thing."

Eve nodded. "Jack had that squawking thing turned on most of the time we cruised."

"Ian said this to you, 'Get the best one you can, so you can always receive the stations at any time, day or night.

Immediately start listening morning and night, say when you get up for breakfast and then after supper, but definitely before you go to bed.' "

Eve listened carefully, nodding and watching his wrinkled, alert face. "And what, exactly, am I listening for?"

"For information on the formation, growth and position of tropical storms in the Caribbean area. If a storm is beginning anywhere down there, start listening more often. The advisories come out about every four to six hours, so you should keep track of each new one. The moment that the weather service projects any possible effects *anywhere* along the Atlantic coast north of Florida you should come at once to my house on Joy Street. The first thing you will receive when I obtain your box number will be two keys and instructions for getting into my house. When that weather advisory is heard by you, don't bother to call me or anything else. Just come at once by the safest, most open way possible, a cab might not be a good idea, to my place, day or night."

Eve nodded, her face set and serious. "Now he thinks the storm and Miranda's attempted end were connected?"

Ed gave another big smile. "He told me you'd ask that. He said he'd thought about it and it was purely a binary question. There are only two conclusions possible. One is that whatever Miranda and the alien worked out was interrupted by the storm and the other is that the storm was part of what they worked out but that it, or some other chance factor, intervened in some unexpected way. Since he had absolutely no evidence to choose either one, he chose both, for the moment, and assumes there is a fifty percent chance that tropical storms and the alien's need for you are connected."

Eve pursed her lips. "You're right. There is no reason for choosing either one that I can see. I'll obviously do what you say, get the radio and do the rest of it."

Ed was momentarily silent. "I guess that's about all there is to say right now. Oh, yes. Julia Stetson is working for you too, you know?" he said finally.

Eve blinked. "Doing what?"

"Finding out at Imperial what Noel Fenwick was doing with those people in Scotland and who they really are." He gave Eve a slightly raffish wink. "Ian said on the phone this morning that she had a serious date with the other professor in Fenwick's department no later than tomorrow night."

"Good old Julia," said Eve with a grin and a sigh. "I do hope he's halfway nice. Ed, is it right that Julia should give some English academic toad the best night of his life in my service?"

"As a minor espionage official, also in your service, madam, I can only say that with operatives as loyal and ingenious as now surround you, your cause is certain to be triumphant."

"I'm feeling quite triumphant now, but my knees are awful cramped. Can you think of anything else?"

"The four great Cape Cod hurricanes of this century occurred on August 26, September 21, that was Miranda's storm, September 14, and August 31. Those dates define our most dangerous period, but hurricanes can come earlier, even in June, and you should get in the habit of listening now." He pulled back against the wall further. "You go out first and I'll follow in a couple of minutes."

He squeezed to let her inch by and she whispered,

"I'm sorry we couldn't get to those movie scenes, Ed, but I don't know if Ian would die for that."

And he, giving her a peck on the cheek as she opened the door, murmured, "Oh, those scenes will be played out, beautiful Eve, but at the only place now possible, inside my head."

·9·

BOSTON
SUMMER
AND A
DOWN-EAST
CRUISE

The plane got to Boston about an hour late, but they went through customs rapidly, there being only a few passengers in each customs line. Eve watched the young, black agent flip through his thick book of computer sheets, while holding her passport in his right hand, but his face remained, as far as she could tell, totally impassive. He gave her back the passport, smiled briefly, and nodded at her three bags. "That's all right. Go ahead," he said and signed her declaration form.

Eve pushed through the swinging doors into the main foyer of the international terminal building and saw big Jack Goldman behind the ropes, waving and grinning at her. Eve smiled back and walked rapidly over to greet Jack, then dropped her bags and gave him a brief kiss on his wide, smiling mouth, one hand up to prevent too tight an embrace, as Jack's strong arm swept her to him. "Oh, Eve! Hi!" he said, looking into her face.

"Hi, Jack," said Eve, patting his cheek. "You're sweet to meet me, dear."

Jack looked at her red lips, then her large, dark eyes. "Listen, you're lovelier than ever and dead beat, too. Let me take you to dinner and you spend the night at my place. Why fight the tenant-abandoned mess in your apartment?"

Eve stepped back a pace and cocked her head. "Jack, I'd love to have dinner with you and stay over, but I've got to sleep in your study. I just don't want to make love tonight, with you or anybody else." She took a deep breath but still looked steadily into his eyes. "I've got some emotional problems, Jack. I've got to work them out myself. I've missed you and thought about you, but right now, I've got to be by myself. If it bothers you, let's split after dinner. I can find a bed at my place to flop on, with or without sheets for one night."

Jack took her hand in his big grasp and gave her a tender, lengthy squeeze. "I won't bug you, Eve. Of course you can sleep in the study bed." He rubbed his cheek with her hand and his large, expressive lips gave her a small, intense smile. "I've missed you, Eve. Seeing you, I miss you all the more."

She squeezed him back. "I know that, dear Jack. I'm not what I was last year. Maybe I can be that again and maybe not, but right now, I need breathing room."

"Sure you do," said Jack in a large, hearty voice.

"Let's go hoist a couple of cool, tall ones in some dark bistro."

They spent the rest of the afternoon in a small, dim bar near Harvard Square, talking amiably and impersonally about their lives over the past year, then walked to supper at a nearby Chinese restaurant, where, as Jack explained, they used almost no celery.

Finally, as they sipped their final bowls of Chinese tea, Jack bit his lip and gave Eve another small but passionate smile. "Have you got an English fellow, Eve?" he asked quietly.

Eve nodded immediately. "Sort of. I probably won't see him till fall but I'm very fond of him. He's a rare book person, works for Phillips, the auction house."

Jack rubbed his big face and pinched his hawk nose. "Eve, you and I . . ." He took a breath and started over. "When you left, I said anytime you wanted it to just be us, we two together any way you wanted, I'd be ready. I'm still ready."

Eve nodded and tried to smile. "Jack, I'm forty-three. I'm not sure there's ever going to be just one person, and for all of the time. I'm kind of set in my ways, but I have a good, warm feeling about you, Jack. We've had some nice, happy times over the last eight years or so."

Jack's deep, brown eyes peered steadily at her. "I love you, Eve. Nobody else in my life has half the elegance or a quarter of the sweetness that you do. Nobody ever had."

"Thanks for saying that, but let's not get too heavy. I'm really pooped. All I can think about is bed. It's way after midnight in my head, Jack."

Jack's apartment occupied the entire second floor of an old, once-luxurious Cambridge mansion and the study was a small sun porch that stuck out over the first-floor kitchen and had continuous windows on three sides, so that even on that hot, stuffy Cambridge night, a tree-cooled breeze blew across the daybed. Eve relaxed in the dark, little room, drawing deep breaths and listening to Jack prowl around his bedroom, opening windows and dropping shoes, until the light showing under the adjoining door went out and the apartment became silent.

Eve had a sudden, strong sense of what Jack was doing by himself in the next room. After probably abstaining for some time to be ready for a supper performance at their first lovemaking, he now had only one immediate solution to his urgent needs. That thought brought quite a large lump to Eve's throat. She dearly hoped that he would catch at least a tiny nugget of sweetness when his solitary moment came. Perhaps he would be visualizing one of their good times, when, at his touch, her body arched and her face became a mask of pleasure to feed his own deep lust. Thinking that made her feel better and she slipped away into a deep, dreamless sleep.

At breakfast the next morning, Jack raised the possibility of a two-week yacht charter with two other couples, something Eve and Jack had done during several past summers. Eve shook her head sadly. "You'd really have more fun with some other lady, Jack," she said. "It just couldn't be like the other times, not for me, anyhow."

"Look," said Jack in a practical voice, "if you're doing without it, I can sure do without it. I don't want some other lady. I want gorgeous Eve Pennington at my side. I thought about it last night. Suppose we ask Katie Rusk, you know, that photo lady over in my department. She's a hell of a good sport. And your boss, Doc Fred Sykes, and then Chuck and Carol to hustle around sheeting in the number-two gennie and to recover the anchor. That way, you and Katie will share a space with me and Doc Sykes bunking together, so there won't be any big rape scenes if I get horny with too much booze under my belt."

Eve patted his arm. "Let me think about it a bit, Jack. I really need a little time to get back into things, okay?"

"Sure, but don't take too long. If we're going to hit the first week in August for a start, we've got to get some money down someplace or wind up with a clunky boat."

Jack drove Eve to her apartment, where she found her tenants had actually swept up and washed the sheets, though the stove was still a fairly gummy mess. By that afternoon she had organized her place, gone through a year's worth of less than first class mail, and was off to the nearby postal substation to rent a box in the name, "Antiquarian Science Search Co." She sent the address to Ed with a note.

> Ed,
> Here's the box number and phony name. As soon as you get back to me, I think I'd like to come and see you. The main question that's come up is this; should I go with Jack Goldman and some other people on a two-weeks yacht cruise in early August? You can be thinking about it.
> Love,
> Eve

Eve got a note the next Tuesday, including keys and directions,

Eve,

Don't use these keys except when you come in an emergency or at a late hour. Otherwise, just come to my front entrance and if the door on the second floor is locked, ring the buzzer two quick buzzes. Come over anytime this week about the cruise problem.

Love,
Ed

Eve went to Boston that afternoon and walked from the Charles Street T station to Joy Street. Ed's building had an open front door that led to a first-floor entrance labeled Muriel's Dance Academy next to a set of narrow stairs that led to another door at the top with "Ed C. Berry, Antiquarian Books" painted in gilt letters. A rough sign hanging on the knob announced, "Out to lunch, back at 2 P.M.," but Eve gave the buzzer two quick pushes and had barely taken her thumb away when the door popped open and a beaming Ed Berry ushered her into his store.

He checked the sign, shut the door, and directed her into a small back office, lying beyond several rooms filled floor-to-ceiling with shelves of books. "Nothing from Ian as yet," he said quickly, "but a couple of other things have come along. How about some toasted bagels and tea?"

"With strawberry jam, please," said Eve, noticing he had a large pot of it on his desk.

Ed busied himself at a toaster and hot plate next to his overloaded desk and chattered on as he sliced the bagels. "The first, and I guess most important, piece of news is that the Island of Muskeget is now a restricted area patrolled by the Coast Guard."

Eve gave a long sigh. "Well, I suppose that had to come if the truth is anything like we've been assuming."

Ed nodded, his white, spiky hair falling in several directions. "There was something of a stink about it on Nantucket, and a couple of public meetings, but the Coast Guard appeared and said there would be no bombing or shell fire using Muskeget as a target. They announced, in fact, that the government had decided to completely isolate Muskeget as a kind of test-tube, ecology project to determine just how severely all of society's environmental inputs were damaging an isolated and natural ecosystem."

Ed grinned in tribute. "Quite a clever cover, really. After all, nobody lives there so they weren't goring any private-property oxen, and with that kind of press output, they soon had the ecology fans on their side, figuring that Muskeget would be as good a predictor of future disaster as any other small, remote place that was still near population centers."

Ed shrugged. "Apparently, Defense and NASA are jointly managing the thing through the screen of a sometime Maryland ecological think tank, Ecofunctions Incorporated."

"So what else is new?" said Eve disgustedly. "They always front things that way, with an airline, student organization, phony publication, or a foundation think tank."

"True," said Ed, "and probably most of the so-called think tanks are in their pocket already. Anyway, I have a good book friend and client on Nantucket, and he gave me the background. He said that if you attempt to sail directly to Muskeget, either from the open sea or Nantucket Sound, a permanently stationed patrol boat will intercept you and explain the restrictions."

Ed sighed deeply and his eyes were somber. "Eve, as much fun as this has been already, in my heart I hoped we were all mad and that somehow a totally safe and prosaic explanation would leap upon us and our madness would fall away like a cloak. Alas, I do not think they would so closely patrol that modest island strand unless there is some truth in all of this."

He paused, staring at her from beady, alert eyes. "And furthermore, that whatever momentum has dogged you from the start is surely quickening. If the star vessel came when Professor Fenwick suggested, then this visitor has been on the planet over two hundred years without revealing itself . . . until now."

He held up his hand as Eve started to speak. "Let me give you my second piece of data, for it relates to the first, I think. In the past week I have called a few associates on Cape Cod and Nantucket with regard to particularities about Miranda Street, née Macy. This morning I received a call from a very old book collector in Truro and I found his story, in some ways, rather extraordinary. It seems that he plays bingo at a senior citizen get-together every Monday night and always sits with this very old woman, with whom he apparently discusses whatever either of them happens to think about."

Ed waved his hand excitedly. "Once, some time ago, she told him something about Miranda, about the rescue and how she had been a nurse in the Nantucket hospital when Miranda died there. Well, yesterday, he got her going on Miranda again. She said that Miranda had been dying of throat cancer before the storm, and decided to go to Muskeget to end her life. At that time, the spring of 1938, the doctors figured she couldn't possibly get through the summer. Yet she was saved after the hurricane in September and brought back to live almost another year. Furthermore, Miranda didn't die from cancer but from a stroke. Her cancer was evidently in remission.''

Eve nodded. "Well, the thing has its little goodies to give, doesn't it? Cures for cancer, herding of fish, making people act nice with each other."

"Plus," said Ed, suddenly holding up his hand, "an apparent ability to make weather predictions that far exceed our own. The point is, Miranda went to Muskeget in May or June, and the storm came in September. You started your current involvement with this business at the auction in June, so . . ." He paused and held his palms up, staring at her.

"You're betting on a hurricane this fall, I gather?" said Eve.

"A reasonable expectation," said Ed at once, "but there is one problem. You've been out of the hemisphere for almost a year, yet we have to believe that this creature set in motion a particular chain of events before you left. Did you and Jack Goldman cruise in Nantucket Sound that previous summer, Eve, the summer before you went to England?"

Eve nodded. "For two weeks. In early August."

"And did you go to, or near, Muskeget?"

Eve thought for a moment. "Really, I don't particularly remember. But we were on or around Nantucket for several days of the charter."

"Okay," said Ed, "let's assume you were close enough

for it to do its implanting stuff. That would imply that it knew over a year ahead of time that a hurricane was coming, assuming that the hurricane and you together are needed for its schemes. The next question is, when did Miranda return to Nantucket and for what reason?"

But Eve had been thinking. "What about her particular cancer? Is a one-year remission unusual? Was it a miracle, or what?"

Ed's spiky white head nodded excitedly. "*Very* good! And my own thought as well, though it took me longer to get to it than it took you. I discussed this on the phone with a medical neighbor and, of course, book collector, here on the Hill, and he said that while it was highly unusual, it was by no means unknown. Furthermore, the drastic change of going from a semi-invalid state in town to living alone in an island shack, even in the summer, might very well have some sort of shock-type, therapeutic effect."

"So it wasn't quite a miracle?"

"No, but certainly a suggestive event. Clearly, if Miranda had died in August, when the doctors predicted, she would have been of no use on September 21."

"So," said Eve at once, "that's a piece of evidence slanting us toward the storm being some part of what was intended for Miranda?"

"I think so. If Miranda's death was all that the thing needed, why not let her die during the easy times of summer? But if some particular date has to be kept, then the intervention to cause cancer remission makes sense. Also, Miranda left Muskeget after the storm and apparently never returned." He shrugged. "We must go where the trail leads us, Eve.

"Tell me," he said suddenly, "is there any way you can

get from Professor Goldman, without rousing suspicions, some details on your cruise last summer?"

Eve peered at him. "You don't think I should say anything about this to Jack?"

Ed Berry lifted his white eyebrows in a question. "I know nothing about him. But he is getting NASA money."

"So am I," said Eve. "So is everybody."

They sat silent for a moment, then Eve spoke soberly. "The best way to find out about that cruise is to look at Jack's logbook."

"Logbook?" said Ed.

"Jack has a regulation ship's logbook that he brings on every cruise. He starts the new entries with stuff about the boat, the cost, who is aboard, with phony nautical ranks and all that sort of joking, and then keeps a day-by-day account of our trip."

Eve smiled cheerfully. "It got to be quite fun on some of the cruises. Jack, as captain, would dutifully fill in the log at sunset, and then we made him read it to us so that we could decide if we accepted it or not. If we voted against him, he had to write in corrections and addenda." Eve shrugged. "It was just something to do and kid about while we drank in the evening, I guess, but anyway the log is sometimes pretty detailed."

"Totally detailed?" asked Ed in a careful, neutral voice.

Eve gave him an open grin. "Nothing, I'm afraid, about whether Jack and I made mad, passionate love on Muskeget. Once, one of our younger and peppier crew objected to the cocktail hour logbook ritual and said the thing could never be properly completed until just before sleep, but Jack just laughed and said logbooks were about sailing and not screwing."

Eve leaned across the desk and gave Ed's arm a pat.
"Ed, since we have sort of a client and detective relationship, I think I should pretty well tell you the whole
business." She paused. "So I want to tell you, and you
don't have to write it to Ian since I've done it already
myself, that I'm not sleeping with Jack, and that I won't
make love with him on the cruise. I told Jack that and I
think he understands it. I'll be in a cabin with a nice lady,
a sixty-year-old Ph.D. in photographic science, Katie
Rusk, and poor, horny Jack will be baching it with
jabbering Doc Sykes, professional Yankee character and
the chairman of my department. The question is, do you
think I ought to do this?"

Ed drew his old lips together until his cheeks were a
mass of wrinkles. "Only if you charter north of Boston,
preferably in Maine, and the farther north, the better."

"Farther from Muskeget, you mean?"

Ed nodded. "Boats can be blown places, even over
large distances, and fogs can bewilder navigators. And
Jack Goldman, perhaps others in your crew, have been
near Muskeget frequently."

They sat silently while Eve pondered his words. She
began to nod. "Okay. We did Maine twice before and it
was mostly fun. I'm sure I can get Jack to go along with
that idea. I'll try to get him interested in some real
remote gunkholing, going east beyond Bar Harbor. Old
Doc Sykes is a 'Mainiac' so he'll probably be for it too."

"Then I suggest you make the cruise, Eve," said Ed
Berry. "It will give us breathing space before the real
time of danger arrives. Perhaps I can get to Cape Cod
and do a bit of snooping on my own while you're gone.
You can consult the logbook and maybe talk with
Goldman casually about those other cruises. And getting

you back from some distant corner of Maine scenery in the event of a sudden need, might not be so easy for them. Yes, I would definitely go, but only north and east."

"And what if an early hurricane appears?"

"Hide in some tiny, forgotten harbor," said Ed Berry solemnly, "and pray like hell!"

Eve saw Jack Goldman at the university that next morning and he readily agreed to the Maine idea. "The Cape's getting so damn crowded in the middle of the summer you can't anchor in some harbors after two in the afternoon," he said at once. "Let's see what we can charter out of Casco Bay and then really head way down east."

Ian wrote her several letters during July, only one through Ed Berry's address, the rest coming directly to her apartment, and these were filled with a passionate intensity. Eve wrote back, not with quite the same extravagant cries of love, but affectionately and warmly, trying to recall Ian's earnest, nearsighted look as she did so. She sometimes found it easier to recall his touch and his urgent, hard strength and she said so, smiling as she imagined his happy flush as he read her frank and loving words. She had never had a really shy man as a lover. Johnny Finn had many superior and fine qualities, but shyness was certainly not one of them. And Jack, after all, simply liked to fuck, and was good at it, and perfectly willing to lecture his lady friends on the subject anytime.

Ian's single letter on sensitive matters gave Eve and Ed little new information. There were some vague hints at something like the Macy business occurring in the Hebrides and concerning legends of the "seal people," seals with the souls of islanders who were supposed to provide food and assistance to mariners and fishermen lost on the bare rock islands of the Hebrides. Yet these yarns seemed to be only hearsay, collected by folklorists years ago, and no longer in any oral traditions of Hebrides residents. There was no suggestion of any such influences acting over the last hundred years in the Western Isles, Ian stated.

Ian had been on Skye and Barra and was now back on the Scottish mainland to search for connections between Fergus Drummond, Thomas Cope, and the owners of the remarkable orrery, since all of them had resided on the northwestern part of Scotland. "When I finish going through the stuff at the orrery house," wrote Ian, "I'm heading south to talk with Mrs. Stringfellow. I want to take her through two question sessions, one about what her husband and Cope talked about that one night she had dinner at Cope's house, and the other, what Miranda really said to them in the hospital. We now know enough, Eve, so I have plenty of things to ask that would never have occurred to you on your visit. Eve and Ed, take care! September is coming. Pay attention to the weather!"

On the first Friday of August, Eve, Jack, and their four crew members flew in a small plane from Boston to a grass-strip airport near Woldoboro, Maine, where the yacht charterer met them in a station wagon and took them to their sloop, a broad, sturdy, thirty-seven footer. By next Tuesday, they were ghosting among the spectacular, rocky seascapes of Mount Desert Island in perfect sunny weather with a mild south wind driving them along the coast. They swam, usually quite briefly in the frigid water, ate boiled lobsters at night, and drank a great deal, and as they saw fewer and fewer boats and fewer houses ashore, Eve had a sense of going backward, to a sanctuary that was still safe and undiscovered, a kind of northern-Maine womb where not even a stern Joanna Macy could force her into the subtle, disturbing storms of the present.

But before Mount Desert was even reached, Eve had determined that she would see what was in Jack's logbook, so after the first day's run and after Jack had completed the evening ritual of log approval, first dealing with complaints about his uncomplimentary description of the setting and recovery of a spinnaker, Eve picked up the book from the cockpit seat and began to idly leaf through it. She showed what seemed to be only the most casual interest, but paid particular attention to days on which they were in Nantucket Sound and near Muskeget.

The cocktail conversation swirled on around her and she went deeper into the logbook, trying to remember specific days and specific events as she came upon them. Year by year she went through the entries, but though they had often passed near Muskeget, going on the direct but rather shoal route between the Vineyard and Nantucket, they never seemed to stop and go ashore. Once, five years ago, they had anchored for lunch just north of the island, but there was no mention of any expeditions ashore or even any swimming.

Eve had reached the previous summer's cruise in the log entries and now she read more carefully. On the entry for the sixth day she found the following in Jack's slanty but readable handwriting.

Sunday, Aug. 6: Captain, mates and crew returned from raucous night ashore in Oak Bluff's hotel and mates served breakfast. Vessel left Oak Bluffs at about nine A.M. under power. Wind SW and a steady twelve knots. Hoisted main and big gennie off Oak Bluffs and squared away for Nantucket, course due east magnetic. Off Cape Pogue before noon and at Muskeget about fourteen hundred hours. Wind dropping, so decided to swim ashore and explore the island. Some of crew and officers wore bathing suits, some did not, since island is deserted. Two small houses in decrepit shape ashore and every kind of biting insect. Water very warm and pleasant and crew carried out substantial treasure-hunting and moon-cussing activities on beaches and interior parts of island. Clear winner of scavenger hunt was First Mate Pennington who unearthed an antique (well, old) military medal in one of the collapsing shacks. Other contestants had (2) a quite decent mooring buoy, (3) one half of a mahogany boat hook, unfortunately not the hook half, (4) a great mass of lobster line which none in our party had the energy or coordination to untangle, and (5) an empty, plastic twelve-pack condom box labeled, Natural Goat Skin, which Apprentice Seaman F. Perry claimed had once been used by Black Bellamy when he raped the goatherd witch-girl Maria Hallett in 1715. When asked why Maria soon had a bastard son, Perry retorted with his usual coarseness that 'the damn, feeble things were no better then than they are now.' Wind picked up at about sixteen-thirty hours and crew managed to return to vessel before it dragged onto Muskeget Bank. Good, swift run to Nantucket Harbor under working sails with stiff, evening wind, backing a bit east of south as it does in these waters in August. On YC mooring and soon ashore for credit card spree in bars and expensive eating spots. Must sleep aboard, since no-rooms-at-the-inn in Nantucket in August. A quiet, dropping south wind and a fine sunset behind handsome Nantucket town ends this day.

"Refreshing some old memories, Eve?" said Jack quietly.

With a start, Eve realized that the cocktail chatter had fallen away and that Doc Sykes and Katie were finally silenced by the gin and the spectacular crimson sunset spreading behind the jagged rock bluffs that now stood almost black in stark silhouette. Chuck Woodruff and Carol Fine, two large and healthy assistant professors in the Computer Science Department, had moved forward of the deckhouse where a bit of kissing, touching, and dope would prepare them for the lobster glut to come, after the sky turned grey and the sun was really gone.

Eve nodded, then turned to smile at Jack. "Yeah, I guess I am. They really all run together don't they, the memories? You kind of put different places and years together, to edit and remake what really happened."

Jack nodded back, his big face impassive in the fading light. "We had some good old times, Eve. Whatever happens, we had those, anyway." He made a small shrug.

Eve put her hand on his arm and shook her head. "I can't even remember half those good old times. Like this entry, for example. What the hell is this about? I found a medal or something?"

"Let me see," said Jack, taking the book from her and starting to read the entry. As he went through it he began to smile and then finally looked at her with a big grin. "I can well believe you can't remember *that* day. That was one of the wilder ones."

Eve looked at him and her mouth was a line. "I was really drunk, huh?"

Jack nodded happily. "Exquisitely, extravagantly drunk. God, you were great!"

"And," said Eve in an even voice, "I suppose I was one of the crew who dispensed with bathing suits?"

"You were the leader of that clique, and I was your most devoted follower, and I mean I followed and I looked. Buddy, you were brown and sleek and yummy! That cutie from the spectro lab twitched out of her bikini and joined us au naturel and finally, fat, dirty Freddy who was floating in the surge with his hairy belly awash, blowing on a big reefer dropped off his pants. Then you suggested that the nudies and the straights should compete in a scavenger hunt and we all went prowling around the place, with, uh, some distractions, but I've got to admit, you absolutely won it fair and square."

Eve squinted at him, trying to remember any part of it. "With exactly what?"

"The Eve Pennington Dock-Shooting-Medal." Jack turned the book over and opened the back to where an envelope was taped inside the back cover. He lifted out a dangling, bronze medal from the paper holder and dropped it in Eve's hand. "While the rest of us went messing around the shores of the island, you went right to this shack in the middle and started to poke around there. When we all got together where we'd beached the tender, people had discovered that stuff I listed in the log, but it was unanimous that you had much the best find."

Eve studied the dull, bronze medal, its lower pendant made of crossed rifles behind a bull's-eye of concentric blue enamel rings suspended from a chain of five bars bearing dates between 1906 and 1911 and each showing the word *Marksman, Sharpshooter* or in one case, *First-Class Marksman.* She held it closer to the binnacle light and Jack leaned to study it. "It's certainly a shooting medal. Initials 'C.N.C.' around the rifles. Wonder what they stand for?"

Eve looked closer. "That last initial is a 'G,' not a 'C,' Jack," she said quietly. "I think they stand for the Connecticut National Guard."

Jack nodded excitedly. "I'll bet you're right! What else could it be but that?" Eve knew that she was right. This was Horace Street's shooting medal, mentioned in the Cape Cod yarn of Skipper Chase. Somehow, during a drunken, forgetful spasm, that thing had put her hand on it. Horace must have lost it through a floor crack on the 1917 visit, before he was killed in France and probably when he undressed in that earlier shack to make love. She felt a sudden empty ache that she and Prissy would never return to that little place where, in his passionate haste, about-to-die Major Street lost his shooting medal as he disrobed to caress his wife. There was no shame in her longing, only the huge, great longing itself.

Jack lifted the medal and let it dangle from its pin in the ruddy sun flash off the water. "We only kept the medal, the mooring buoy, and Freddy's condom box, which was awarded fifth prize. We used the box for matches and that night at supper you proposed that the medal be awarded each year on the last day of cruising to whichever helmsman made the best dead-shot landing."

Jack was thoughtful for a moment. "As I remember, we actually didn't get it awarded last summer because there was so much disagreement about just what constituted a good landing. For example, you claimed that your landing in Edgartown was actually perfect until Fat Freddy threw all the line ashore without keeping hold of one end, and so the boat was carried off by the current. Others had similar complaints about nonhelm failures in the docking situations."

Eve shook her head in disgust. "Drunk again. I do remember some of those arguments now, but I don't think I ever realized we were arguing about an award I had suggested."

She took the medal back from Jack, letting it lie in her palm. "Jack, since I found this, can I keep it? We can do the award on the last day if you want, and write it up in the log, but I'd like to keep this." She closed her fist around it. "It's time I started remembering things, I think."

As one bright, summer day followed another, Eve began to feel more guilty about her cool treatment of Jack. She had somewhat dreaded the cruise, thinking that as Jack got more hard up, he might also get meaner, but instead he remained attentive yet entirely proper, constantly praising her tan and looks, chattering along about almost anything as though they had only just been introduced. At a cocktail party in a huge house near Bar Harbor, he escorted her with the same pleasure and pride he had shown in those days when he knew that afterward, they would share some sort of intimate and passionate episode.

So as they sailed lazily northeast, deeper into the

wilder, coastal regions of Maine, Eve thought about what she might do for Jack that would be both friendly and better than what she was doing now.

On Saturday, halfway through the cruise, they had reached their farthest point north, a tiny, secluded and pine-bound hole that they guessed was Moose Pond Harbor, somewhere east of Jonesport. It was a quiet ending to a fine day, the stiff westerly wind falling to gentle puffs and the sun coming down into some low but handsome clouds. Katie Rusk and Doc Sykes, cooks for the day and dismayed at discovering only beans and chili for supper, went off in the tender, put-putting around the west point of the little harbor to a dock they had seen in the next cove. "There are lobster pots," said Katie in a practical voice. "Somewhere is a man who will take our money."

Eve sat in her bikini on the cabin top, her smooth, long legs dangling and a gin and tonic resting coolly on her brown knee. Big, hearty Chuck looked up from the cockpit and sighed. "Eve, you're sitting there defining the good life, absolutely making it live. Isn't she gorgeous, Carol?"

Large and somewhat chubby Carol Fine sighed and nodded. "Boy, I guess! Well, some people have it and some don't."

Eve grinned down at them and swung her legs. "Phooey, Carol. Skinniness just happens to be in style. You've got a nice small waist. You'd be number one if this were nineteen-oh-five." She gave Chuck a wink. "Don't you think Carol has an especially graceful tummy?"

Chuck nodded enthusiastically and put a hand gently on the object of the discussion. "Some days I think her belly button is her finest part. Then, other days, her butt. Of course, when you look at her totally . . ."

"That's enough!" said Carol in mock anger. "Eve, why do you get him going on this chauvinist stuff? Women are *not* objects, dammit!" She got to her feet and leaned to seize Chuck's hand. "Come on, famous fan of belly buttons. We said we were going to row and explore that east point. Let's do it before they come back with the lobsters."

Chuck grinned and stretched lazily, but he soon had the rubber boat off the deckhouse and into the water. Carol threw in some beach towels. "In case we stick a piggy in the ice water," she said, grinning back at them, but all four friends knew well enough that Chuck and Carol did not want to wait for a late dinner of lobsters not yet even found and an even later bedtime before they were alone. On the open, breezy, and probably bug-free point there would doubtless be a soft place where the towels could be spread.

As Chuck pulled away from the yacht, Jack gave them a lopsided grin and a sudden victory V sign with his fingers. "Let me know if you two discover anything more about belly buttons," he said in pretend seriousness. "For example: shape, flexibility, possible uses, relative sensitivity. Quite a deep subject when you start to think about it."

"Particularly when you have a dirty, male mind," shouted Carol stoutly back, then turned, immediately forgetting them, to stroke Chuck's leg as he rowed strongly toward the distant point.

Eve took a deep breath and jumped off the cabin top to sit with Jack in the stern. "Jack?" she said tentatively.

He turned and smiled at her, scratching the greying thatch on his wide, brown chest. "Yeah?" His expression seemed mild, accepting, and she leaned to take his hand.

"You've been very nice . . . no, nice is a dumb word. You've been *kind* to me on this cruise. I appreciate it."

He turned and leaned toward her, stroking her forearm. "What good would it do to be bitter? Nothing could possibly come out of that. But I do desire you, Eve." He stared at her from deep, soft eyes. "I remembered how you looked that day you found the medal, how we made love in the grass there, after we talked about it. You were a queen of love that day, a queen of desire!"

She touched his cheek. "Jack, I just am not going to give myself to you like I used to, but . . . but, perhaps I can go some of the way with you. Right now, here, if you'd like it."

Jack peered at her, his face impassive. "What do you mean?"

Eve moved closer until their legs touched. "Sometimes, when I was incapacitated for the usual reason, I did you that other, friendly way. I know how you like it done and I'll do that for you now, if you want."

Jack looked down from her face, down at her body. "Can I touch you? What are the ground rules?" he said in a slow, thick voice.

Eve smiled and leaned to kiss his cheek. "You can touch me up above," she said, reaching behind her back to undo her bikini top and let it fall across her legs. "And you can kiss as much as you want to," she added softly, touching him through his bathing suit.

"Okay," he said in a suddenly breathless voice, and arched above the seat to strip off his trunks, his eyes never leaving her breasts.

"Dear, horny Jack," said Eve in his ear. "You're gigantically big and excited. I'll go as slow as I can with you to make it last and be sweet."

She drew him close to her as he cupped her breasts in his two, large hands. As he caressed her, she kissed his lips and face, but she knew that no matter how slow she went, it was still very fast for trembling, intent Jack. She held him tight against her and whispered, "Tell me just what to do when it gets close . . . like you used to," and Jack immediately whispered a few words of instruction, gave a huge gasp, then turned to kiss her deeply and passionately.

For a moment, Eve felt only warm satisfaction that she had helped Jack to this reward, but only for a moment. Some perverse and, she knew, unwise compulsion forced her to draw her head back, back from his passionate lips and busy tongue, to look at his big, dark face, distorted and made heavy with joy. But she did not see Jack Goldman, as she had seen him at other times and on other cruises. Instead, it was Prissy's face. Her sister's lips were soft and slackly open, and her bright teeth were parted to show her pink tongue. In Prissy's eyes, Eve saw a total, overwhelming love, a sweetness too large to ever be contained.

Jack urgently pressed a hand over her back and drew her mouth again to his, but this time, he was the one who drew his face back from Eve, for his cheek and chin were wet from her tears. He stared at her in angry bewilderment, still breathing heavily. "Eve, it was nice. It was very good. What's the matter? What did I do?"

Eve pressed her dry hand open and tightly against her eyes, shaking her head. "Jack, it's nothing to do with you! Truly! I promise! It's in my head, Jack. I'm . . . well, remembering things, from way back, long before I met you. I have a problem, Jack." She shut her eyes tightly, forcing her hand against them, and breathed deeply, trying to stop the tears.

Jack said nothing, and they sat silently that way, sitting upright, their legs pressed lightly together, until the distant sound of an outboard sounded off to the west. Eve blinked hard and wiped her eyes on her thin bikini top. She tried to smile, looking at his expressionless face, and to make her voice sound cheerful and warm. "You'll need a giant towel to mop up, powerful Jack. My goodness!" and she patted his thigh and leaned to kiss him.

But Jack did not kiss her back. He picked his swimming trunks off the cockpit floor and stood up, then looked down at her drawn and ravaged face. "Yeah, I guess we both need big towels," he said in a thin voice, then quickly went down the companionway ladder into the main cabin.

Eve bit her lip and her heart shrank to a point. "I tried to do my best for you, Jack," she said in a small, tight voice. "I'm sorry." But all she heard was the whine of the electric pump below and the splash of water as Jack washed himself. She knew he could not hear her.

If Jack had asked for that service again, Eve had decided she would help him, even if it meant getting drunk and maybe sitting with him in the dark, but he never gave the slightest suggestion of desire or need to her during the final week of cruising. As often happens with six people on a thirty-seven-foot sailboat, small attitudes and habits began to poison the day-to-day living. Doc Sykes became more and more garrulous and opinionated, or seemed to, while Katie, nursing a tough sunburn, became progressively quieter and almost sullen. Chuck and Carol had a couple of sharp fights over the cooking and washing dishes, but Eve knew that the true viper in their midst was Jack's skillful, yet unmistakable attention to Carol Fine. Jack was too smooth and sensible to try something on the boat, but Eve knew that Carol could expect some heavy courting back at the school. And poor, young, rather awkward Chuck knew his wagon train was being raided, but was never quite able to see a single Indian.

Eve, feeling miserably guilty and responsible for all of this, tried to be at her prettiest and sunniest, but when the weather turned blustery, wet, and northeast on Wednesday, they all began to visualize the end of it with both hope and impatience. Jack was still friendly with her, but the warmth and the occasional close intensity of the first week were over and done.

Better a buxom and uncomplicated Carol, Eve thought, than a scrawny, sick, and neurotic me. The easterly blast drove rain behind the reefed, hurrying yacht, and Eve sat steering, bundled in her slicker outfit, staring at the distant dark shore as the heavy yacht plunged along, driving into large, steep seas.

Aside from an occasional, impressive broadside of spunk, Eve wondered, what would Carol Fine really get from Jack? Help if she has a drinking problem? Steadfastness if some new secretary puts her hand on Jack's cock in the dimness of the mail room? Understanding if she goes crazy? The yacht hammered along, rising readily to the big swells, smashing through the chop that rode these larger hills, while the rain drove down on Eve's wide slicker hat. Julia had said Jack was a wimp, yet he must not seem that to Carol. Just the opposite, in fact.

Large and powerful in every sense; the large, distinguished reputation, the large, strong body, the large urge to use the large cock. But what he did best, of course, was writing phony, funny, nautical flourishes in the log and running a fun-filled, floating, drunken whorehouse where everybody gets a chance to see just how big a man, or maybe how small a boy, Jack really is.

But the sturdy, onward plunge of the yacht and the cleansing blast of rain and wind drove these bitter thoughts from Eve's head, and by the end of her wheel watch she was exhilarated, her cheeks bright with warm life and her eyes sparkling so that, for a moment, Jack turned from shouting a joke into the cabin at Carol to stare at her face, perhaps for the last time, with wistful and hungry eyes. And Eve, seeing that momentary sweet look, smiled warmly at Jack and hoped, perhaps believed at that instant, that young, round, cheerful Carol would somehow end his endless childhood.

By the final day, as they drove west in a dry but still brisk southeast wind, Jack had completely forgotten the Eve Pennington dock-shooting award, but there was one final moment of magic. As they moved swiftly offshore past Vinalhaven in the deep water, they were joined by two big humpbacks, one on each side of the yacht, which ran along with them for almost forty minutes, holding the steady eight-plus knots with no apparent effort, their shiny black backs seeming to almost skim across the sea surface. That moment almost redeemed the entire, contentious, stormy week. The sun conveniently came out and dozens of photographs were taken from every imaginable perch on the boat, including Chuck at the masthead. Katie ranged along the sides, three cameras dangling and bumping from her neck, and constant cheers, suggestions, and expressions of delight flowed about the yacht. The big, dark mammals held their steady course, each about twenty feet out, and Eve had a dizzy, icy thought that she was being escorted back, back from the distant, isolated waters of northern Maine. The two whales ran steadily, implacably along with them in perfect formation. Then, in less than an eye blink, they dropped away and disappeared.

·10·

AN
UNEXPECTED
VISIT

Ed Berry peered intently at the shooting medal through a large magnifying glass while shaking his head. "Perfectly extraordinary, Eve," he said finally. "In no possible way could you have found that in an hour or so of searching without that thing's help. Why, Miranda herself lived on that floor, or its predecessor, for over three months in 1938. Many other explorers, like you and your sister, like your yachting party last year, must have poked around that shack location. Why in heaven's name did it do that, I wonder?"

Eve looked at Ed from thoughtful eyes. "To send me a message, a sign." She rubbed her cheeks. "Ed, everybody has always sort of assumed that visiting life-forms, being defined as damn smart by simply being able to get here, would deal in all kinds of high-level, abstract, language-type concepts. But if Noel is right, this thing is geared to manipulate and study mostly zoological, I mean simple, instinctive sorts of intelligences. All the episodes we connect with it, the Macy stuff, Miranda and Horace, my sister and I, now this finding of the medal, involve human reactions at the glandular or instinctive levels."

"The babbling baby?" asked Ed.

"*Cut* isn't a very hard word to form," said Eve at once, "but Joanna was a kind of supernatural believer, Miranda told Cope, and probably Mrs. Pease too. So maybe they had a vision, an auditory vision instead of Henry Macy's visual vision of the humane house."

"Okay, I'm with you, but what about Noel Fenwick's claim that he actually got orders from the thing?"

Eve shrugged. "I wish he'd said more, although at the time I only wished he would get the hell out of my flat instead of scaring me to death. But look, Ed, suppose it can't deal in concepts and ideas quite the way we do? Joanna describes the Yoho in terms of moods, impressions, visions. Nobody claims it ever spoke directly. Think about the vast amount of essentially verbal integration that would be needed just to introduce ourselves to each other. Suppose also, it isn't all that good at overtly manipulating creatures at our self-awareness level without simply driving them gaga. Look at the stories. You can pull almost anything off during a big storm emergency with a pregnant woman, with a man weeping over a frozen captain and his frozen son, or in the warm aftermath of a totally heroic, totally unlikely rescue."

Eve shook her head and her voice showed disgust. "Of course Eve Pennington made her most recent contact with the alien a little differently than those good people, by being stupidly drunk and stupidly egocentric about her *stupid* body! It only needed to do two things with me, suggest the scavenger hunt, then lead me to the medal. I was so bombed it could have had me standing on my head and chanting mantras.

"But," said Eve, waving a sudden finger at Ed, "however contacted, the contact is unmistakable and the thing is making a whole lot of complicated points in the simplest possible way. Most obvious is that Horace and Miranda must have undressed, and no doubt made love, in the house in 1917. It must have helped them. Read the account again, Ed. They weren't all that chummy then." Eve gestured at the *More Yankee Yarns* book lying open next to the medal. "Perhaps the thing did that to show Miranda something. What? Could it be that if Miranda came back, when it needed her, something like that would happen again?"

Eve rubbed her cheek excitedly. "Now it leads *me* to the medal. What is it saying to me? Maybe that whatever deal it had with Miranda is now on with me. And of course, while I was there last year, it did the deeper stuff, concerning the books, the long-term suggestions, just as it did with Mrs. Stringfellow when that pilot landed her there."

Ed blew out a breath and an *"Harrrumph!"* at the same time. "Well, you're running way ahead of me on all of that. I guess I might agree that the medal is a message that links you and Miranda. As to the rest . . . ?" He shrugged. "Anything more turn up on your cruise?"

Eve was thoughtful for a moment. "Ed, without going into detail, I had a somewhat tender moment with Jack, and at its tenderest—tenderest for Jack, not for me—I looked into his face and saw my sister's face for an instant, instead. Quite distinctly. I wrote all about it to Ian." She handed a sealed envelope to Ed. "Last week, after we got back to Boston. I'd appreciate it if you sent it along sealed. There are some quite personal things in it."

Ed smiled at her but he spoke in a low, direct voice. "Did you 'see' your sister's face as it was on that particular visit you two made to Muskeget?"

Eve sighed and stared at the floor. "Yes, I did. You've mentioned my sister a couple of times. Did Ian tell you about that particular day, the one that I finally remembered under hypnotism?"

Ed nodded at her. "He felt, and I agree, that within that day lies the core of all of this. He told me that if I was tortured," Ed's eyes twinkled at her, "I was to hold that back to the end. Only you, Ian, and I know about that."

"Plus our friend on Muskeget," said Eve slowly, but then she sat up and smiled at him again. "Okay, what's your news?"

Ed threw a sheaf of several papers across the desk to her. "You can read Ian's stuff when we get done talking. He's obviously connected Fergus Drummond and Cope, which means that Cope may have had more than an inkling of what was happening on Muskeget. Again, the coincidences are just too pointed to admit much else."

Ed rubbed his chin. "But only Mrs. Stringfellow might possibly confirm that, and she's apparently visiting relatives. Ian can't seem to locate her. I don't like the sound of that."

Eve frowned and her face suddenly seemed old and drawn. "They wouldn't hurt that old lady, Ed. Nobody would do that, would they?"

Ed shook his head. "There's no reason or indication why they should. But they might have taken her someplace to get her out of the way, and away from questioning by whomever."

Eve shook her head and her face was set. "You're right. I don't like the sound of that either."

"As far as my own studies," said Ed, "I got to Nantucket while you were away and managed to look at Miranda's medical records. Never mind exactly how, although if you promise people their names will appear in a book, you can accomplish quite a bit. My Truro friend's report was correct. Miranda was in the hospital in 1939 for her heart condition, not her cancer. The Stringfellows probably didn't realize that, since part of Miranda's throat had been taken out two years earlier. They just figured she was dying of cancer."

Ed formed his fingers into a steeple. "Miranda returned to Nantucket three years before the storm, four years before her death. I felt it important to try and discover why she came back, what exactly called her, and a day poking in the newspaper files gave the answer." He handed her a copied *Nantucket Inquirer and Mirror* news clip dated in the summer of 1935.

LIFESAVER'S DAY RECALLS FAMOUS BLIZZARD RESCUE

Miranda Street Returns to Accept Tributes to Her Husband's Courage in Plucking Her from Sinking Schooner

Standing with several men who had participated in Nantucket rescues during the nineteenth century and who received honors on Lifesavers Day, was Mrs. Miranda Street, widow of Major Horace Street, formerly of Nantucket and killed in action in France in 1918. Mrs. Street, the former Miranda Macy also of Nantucket, returned here from her home in California at the personal request of John Coffin, Jr., organizer of the lifesaving memorial celebration.

The rescue of Miranda Macy by young Surfman Street remains one of the most stirring, and yet tender, stories in the history of the island. Horace Street, described by his mentor and superior, the great hero Skipper Walter Chase, keeper of the Coskata Station, as "the greenest in our crew, but he could pull as good as anybody," went out alone in a sailing dory, a blizzard wind at his back . . .

And Eve read to the end, noting that the copywriter owed much of his material to *More Yankee Yarns,* a book she suspected might well remain a well-thumbed source at the *Inquirer and Mirror* today.

When she looked up from the article, Ed continued. "I tried to find somebody connected with John Coffin, Jr., and soon located Mr. Coffin's widow, Hester Coffin. We had a reasonably companionable afternoon, considering that she can't hear much and tries to pretend that she can. I finally got her to understand that I wanted to know why her husband had come up with this Lifesavers Day idea. Had it been some kind of anniversary of something? I yelled at her. She thought about that and said, no, her husband just got the idea one day when he took a fishing party out to Tuckernuck, then on to Muskeget, and noticed that the shack where the rescue happened was kind of falling over. He suddenly felt there should be some sort of get-together of those people involved in the old rescues before they all died.

And . . ." Ed shrugged, "things weren't so hot with the summer vacation business then, she told me, so it wasn't hard to convince the town fathers to help the thing along. Miranda stayed at Coffin's house."

"Why didn't she go back to California afterward?" said Eve.

"Mrs. Coffin wasn't exactly sure about that. Seemed to think she didn't have anything much back there. Miranda had money and she paid the Coffins room and board for about six months, then rented a cottage for a year and a half. The next February she went to Boston for her throat thing, and came back to Nantucket to arrange going to Muskeget for the summer. There was a caretaker on Muskeget then, looking after some shooting-club property, and Coffin arranged with him to fix the little house up so she could cook, and to look in on her. He's long gone, unfortunately, especially since he was one of the men who got Miranda off Muskeget during the storm."

Eve considered, then spoke. "So the thing's early-warning system gave it a three-year head start on the storm with Miranda. But my dreadful little episode on Muskeget was only one year ago?" She looked at him with raised eyebrows.

"True," said Ed in a thoughtful voice, "but we have a sample of one, single event, Miranda's, from which to predict. I think it is much more significant that she was essentially attracted to the island in the late spring of the year, and your attraction, if the auction business can be called that, began in June."

"Why did Mrs. Coffin feel Miranda went to Muskeget? Didn't she think it was a strange action for an invalid?"

Ed shook his head. "Not a bit. Any more than I would

have, if I knew only what Hester Coffin knew. The Coffins had heard of Miranda's strange arrival at Muskeget and they would have had to be fairly stupid not to have some sense of what the night in the humane house involved after the rescue. Any of them might have gone back to die there as she did. New Englanders, Cape Codders especially, have a great longing for symmetry. It is, in some ways, our curse. We really believe in an ordered cosmos. We believe, as the Shaker tune puts it, that 'to turn, to turn, will be our delight, until by turning we come around right.'"

"Rose Stringfellow could comment on this," said Eve, her eyes bleak. "Oh, Ed, pray that she is safe and happy."

Eve read soberly through Ian's accounts, then looked up in grim surprise at Ed. "So two of the people on Noel's yacht were associates of Marta Hoerner, that witchy academic from California who was at my party? That's certainly suggestive."

Ed nodded. "That came from Julia, but her Imperial friend seemed to know nothing about their purposes. I think it's clear that the cruise was an exobiological mission of some sort. It sounds as though your man, Noel, was playing all the sides of the street. When I read that, I tried to find out on Nantucket if there was a Dr. Hoerner on the ecological team working on Muskeget, but the project seems to be running out of a secured location on Martha's Vineyard. Nobody knows much about it. I called her at Berkeley, claiming to be the editor of a Pergamon anthology, *Modern Biological Developments,* but all they would say was that she was on leave, and that I should send her a letter, which would be forwarded."

Eve frowned and continued to read through Ian's

findings and ideas, though she only half took in the words, diverted as she was by a nagging concern over Rose Stringfellow.

Yet, two days later, Eve's concerns were set to rest by the appearance of Mrs. Stringfellow herself, all gotten up in a bright, print dress, fancy hat, and stylish, if flat, shoes, in front of Eve's office door. The old woman knocked lightly and heard a terse, "Yes, come in," then slowly opened the door to peek around its edge.

"Hello? Eve Pennington?" she offered tentatively.

What happened next thoroughly astonished Mrs. Stringfellow, for though she had expected a cordial and warm welcome from Eve, if she had managed to connect with her, the actual event went far beyond what she might ever have imagined. In an instant she was seized in a hug tighter, she felt, than she had ever been given. "Oh, Rose! Oh, it *is* you! How lovely! I've been so . . ." and Eve finally drew back from her, her eyes filled with happy tears. "But what are you doing here! Why didn't you tell me you were coming?"

Rose Stringfellow caught her breath and set down her airline tote bag. Her cheeks were pink from the vigor of the welcome and she reached to adjust her skewed hat. "My goodness," she said unsteadily, beaming at Eve, "I hope the rest of my trip is as nice as this part. Well, my nephew and his wife and children were traveling around in Britain in a van and they took me along, and we had such a nice time. Well, I do know how things work in small towns so I could help them with finding rooms and friendly pubs. So they got me a ticket to, *think* of it, California! And I'm on my way there now. It all happened so quickly, they only got back there themselves two days ago, that I just didn't have time to call you. How

I prayed you wouldn't be on vacation." She put out both hands and seized Eve's, feeling suddenly that she might be a bit more demonstrative herself.

"Dear friend, Rose," said Eve in a voice warm with delight, "when do you have to leave for California?"

"Oh, not till ten tonight. My baggage got sent over."

Eve squeezed both her hands. "How does this sound, Rose? We'll go right now to a little, dark place and have one drink to toast your arrival. Although there's no black bitter anywhere in dreadful Cambridge, America, I'm afraid."

"Vodka will be just fine," said Rose Stringfellow in a practical tone.

"Then we'll go to my place and you can take a long bath and unwind from that cattle-car ride coming over."

"Well, it wasn't all that awful, Eve," said Rose thoughtfully. "When I was a girl I had to go third class on the Great Western a few times. Those were true cattle cars, let me tell you that."

"Anyway," said Eve laughing, "you can relax and then we'll go and have a yummy dinner, and I'll pop you on your ten o'clock flight at Logan."

"It sounds just too nice to believe," said a beaming Rose, and they were soon off in a cab to the same, small, dark place that Eve had gone with Jack her first afternoon in Boston.

As Rose sipped her vodka and orange juice and chattered on about her trip with her relatives through England and Wales, Eve marshaled the questions she wished to put to Rose in her mind, then responded briefly to Rose's polite questions about her own summer, and finally leaned forward to look carefully at the older woman. "Rose, remember when I asked you about that visit years ago to see Thomas Cope. You know, you and your . . ."

But Rose had suddenly given her a rueful smile and was digging into her tote bag. "If that isn't something. I brought you a present and I was all set to give it to you in your office, and that lovely welcome of yours just drove it right out of my head. Anyway, here it is," and she handed over to Eve a thin, rectangular package wrapped in shiny paper.

Eve took it from her and as she did, she felt a sudden dismay at the inexorable pattern of her life. She sensed at once what was in the package and she looked carefully about the dusky bar to see who was there and where they were sitting. "What is it, dear Rose?" she said in a quiet voice, putting her hand on it and taking a drink as she spoke.

Rose Stringfellow smiled in further embarrassment. "Not much of a gift, is it, when I never told you what it was? Well, Eve, it's that book you so wanted from the auction, Miranda Street's interviews with Ben. It was the funniest thing—"

But Eve put a quick, nervous hand on Rose's arm. "Rose, we have tons of time, but since you've finished your drink, why don't we zip to my place so you can just luxuriate in my tub for as long as you want."

Rose was relaxed by the vodka, and the thought of the warm tub seemed attractive indeed. As she got to her feet, Eve put the book back in Rose's tote bag and then took the bag from Rose. "Let me carry it," she said. "You'll have lugged it long enough by the time you hit Los Angeles." She swept Rose ahead of her, out through the small bar, and her eyes darted over the half-dozen customers sitting up front. Any of them could have seen the book when Rose took it out of the bag.

"Cab!" shouted Eve, and opened the door to urge Rose in ahead of her. She gave the driver the address and settled back to pat Rose's arm, trying not to breathe too hard or tremble, and said in a chatty voice, "What does your nephew do in California . . . ?"

But once inside her apartment, Eve felt better, and she soon had Rose happily immersed in a fragrant bath. With the door ajar, Eve sat on a chair outside the bathroom. "Can we talk while you soak, Rose? Or would you rather just doze in there?"

"Let's talk, Eve. I love to talk."

"Then tell me where you found this journal," said Eve, holding the still-wrapped book in her hand. "I'm *so* grateful that you brought it to me."

"When I knew my nephew and his family were coming to see me in Henley," came the voice, "I decided to really clean the place up. Well, I worked along, but you remember that great big bookcase in my parlor . . . ?"

"Yes."

"Well, I suddenly thought that I hadn't moved it in years, to clean behind, because it was just too heavy for me to move. So I asked a nice young man who lives down the street and he came and pulled it out for me. I was so embarrassed that he saw the terrible, dusty mess back there."

"And in the dust," said Eve, "was this journal?"

"There were three thin books back there and some other things, pens, letters, but the moment I saw that book, I knew what it was. Thinking back, I guess it happened when Mr. Ian from Phillips was there. We had my books stacked all over the room, sorted into piles, and that journal must have fallen down behind while we were figuring things out. The broken rubber band was down there too."

Eve leaned intently forward. "Rose, try to think back to when you decided to move that bookcase. Was there any exact moment or thing that got you thinking about doing it?"

Rose was silent for so long then that Eve thought she had dozed off in the warm water, but when her voice finally came, it was both thoughtful and alert. "You know, it's odd you would ask me that so pointedly, Eve. Because there *was* a very strange thing that happened, and it involved you. When I knew my nephew and his family were coming to visit, I rushed around and got the place cleaned up, but to tell the truth, I wasn't going to worry about the dust behind that bookcase when they were only going to be in Henley for a day or two. Well, while I was cleaning, I got your letter. I guess it was your second one, where you just said at the end that if I ran on to anything more about Miranda, to keep you in mind." Her voice paused until Eve said, "Yes, I remember writing that."

"Well, I finished reading your letter. I was sitting in that same chair I was in the day you visited, and I sort of turned to look at the other chair, the one you sat in, and, my goodness! There you were, all of a sudden!"

"Was I . . . solid?" asked Eve.

"Oh, yes, completely there. Not in any way faint or ghostlike." Rose paused a moment and then went on speaking thoughtfully. "Eve, what happened to Ben, that thing I told you about in the army hospital when he saw his friend's image at the same time the friend died, that kind of occurrence is the commonest of all the occult stories."

"You mean a hallucinatory visitation or dream brought on by some crisis or need?"

"That's right," said Mrs. Stringfellow. "One of the psychic-study societies that Ben joined especially collected stories about that sort of thing, and they insisted on all kinds of proof and sworn statements. They had, oh I don't know, perhaps a dozen accounts of people who had not gone on the *Titanic* or the *Lusitania* because they got warnings, from relatives, strangers, or their own nightmares. In one or two cases, the warnings came from people who themselves went on the ships and died. But there are hundreds of stories like that. The railway men have theirs, and so do the seafarers. My goodness, I think Ben interviewed at least three old sea captains who had been roused from their bunks by a dream, of a mother or wife crying out, and got up on deck just in time to turn the ship from rocks."

"Yo, ho, ho, and a bottle of rum, gin, or whiskey," said Eve in a cheerful voice.

Rose Stringfellow gave a chuckle. "That's what I always thought, that they were drunk and at the last minute had to think up a story as to why they weren't properly on duty or paying attention. Well, nothing like that ever happened to me, Eve, even though I did hear an awful lot of stories from people who had it happen to them. But then, last month, there you were!"

"What did I do?" said Eve.

"Smiled at me, not excited, but just interested and friendly, just like you always are, and then you said in a very natural voice, 'Did you look behind the bookcase for the book, Rose?'"

There was another long pause and finally Eve said, "Would someone else in the room have seen or heard me, do you think?"

Rose answered in an uncertain tone. "I guess not, but I'm only saying that since I knew then, and know now, that you weren't really there."

"What happened then?"

"I guess I blinked, or perhaps shut my eyes, and you were gone. It was very quick. But then I just got up off that chair, pulled on a scarf and walked four doors down the street to get young Mr. Bristol. He runs a bookstore in Henley and sometimes stops in to chat. He'd just finished his lunch but he came right up and pulled that great thing out from the wall, and I cleared everything from behind it, swept, and he pushed it in again. I gave him a glass of bitter for his help, but you know, I don't think I would have ever done that except for my psychic moment, or whatever it was."

"Did you know then that you were coming to America?"

"No, that all came up after my nephew arrived. I was going to mail it off to you, but when the American trip came along, I thought I would keep it and bring it to you myself."

"That was wonderful of you, Rose. I can copy it and send it back, if you like?"

"No, I thought before that I'd sent it to the sale. I'm glad you have it since it means so much to you. I suppose you don't have any memory of dreaming about telling me to look behind the bookcase, do you, Eve?"

"I'm afraid I don't," said Eve at once, "but they say you don't remember many of your dreams."

Mrs. Stringfellow splashed for a while and her voice

was warm and thoughtful when she answered. "The kind of stories that Ben liked best were the ones where somebody got a message and could testify to it, and where somebody else sent the message, and there was independent testimony to that too. And, of course, the times had to fit. Like the railway engineer who goes into a siding because he sees his wife in the cab urging him to do so. Of course there's a runaway engine coming along the main line. At the same time, the wife is awakened by a nightmare and screams to her children that their father is in danger. The psychic societies made all kinds of studies of things like that."

"That's one of the few data-transmission systems yet to be harnessed by our wonderful science establishment," said Eve with a grin. "Rose, you were reading my letter, thinking about the lost book, sitting in the same chair, and maybe way down in your subconscious, something put it all together and produced me for a second."

"It was still a very real experience," said Rose. She paused then, and spoke in a slower voice. "And I suppose if I were ever to have one, a psychic event I mean, it would be connected with that island." She spoke more slowly. "Ben had a sense of that, after we went to see Miranda. All the rest of his life, when we talked together or with other people about the occult, Ben just laughed and joked about his studies . . . except Miranda." And the voice had become very slow and very thoughtful.

"Well," said Eve, suddenly brisk, "you soak away, Rose, and I'll get my clothes organized. A quick shower is my thing before dinner and I can do that while you're dressing."

Eve had selected a restaurant where large, widely spaced booths gave them privacy. Since she had the actual interview, she had decided not to question Rose any more about Miranda, especially after her very thoughtful words from the tub, but she kept her hand always on her bag and the book contained inside it.

Rose had another vodka and Eve had a double gin and tonic and they chatted along, but when the personal news began to get used up, Eve, remembering Ian's intent to question Mrs. Stringfellow, smiled at Rose in the dim light and said, "Rose, when we talked at your place, you told me about going to see old Mr. Cope with Ben and you said he, Mr. Cope I mean, had some interesting ideas, I think you said. Do you remember any of those ideas?"

Mrs. Stringfellow drew her lips together and lifted an eyebrow. "Well, one thing he and Ben talked about was trying to get all the psychic stories sorted out into groups. I guess several of the members of the societies had been trying to do that."

Eve thought hard for a moment. "Okay, but once they were all classified into groups, did Cope think they were all caused by the same basic phenomenon?"

Mrs. Stringfellow beamed in pleasure as a second vodka arrived, then shook her head. "No, the opposite, as I remember. Mr. Cope, and I guess Ben too, thought that there were all sorts of causes, only some of which were psychic. I remember Mr. Cope saying that there was probably no real difference between the pigeon that finds its way home and the dog on the lawn that howls the moment its master stops breathing inside the house."

"I've heard the howling-dog story," said Eve in complete interest. "Did it happen regardless of where the dog was in relation to the dying master, or did the dog have to be close?"

"Well," said Mrs. Stringfellow, "that was the point that Mr. Cope was trying to make, I think. The pigeons, he said, were responding to tiny magnetic and radio signals sent out from the earth to find their way home. The dog, he said, was responding to tiny radio signals from the master. When the signal stopped, the dog cried."

"Amazing!" said Eve. "And old Tom Cope was saying this in the nineteen-twenties? So that dog had to be close to the dying master, otherwise it would lose the weak signal. And then what about those stories of animals that find people who move, after they've been left behind? A dear friend of mine from long ago, Johnny Finn, was interested in that sort of thing. But if the animal was really sensitive and just started running, maybe it could stay within the electromagnetic field generated by its master? Yet, what a weak field the brain and nervous system must set up." Eve's voice trailed away in her concentration.

The vodkas had stimulated Rose Stringfellow and she nodded in sudden agreement. "Mr. Cope told Ben that evolution, that business that Mr. Darwin started, might have produced creatures on other worlds that could receive those radio waves and send other waves back, much better than even the most sensitive animals."

Eve dropped her eyes, clasped her hands in her lap, and took a deep breath. Their time was growing shorter. "Rose, let me ask you a direct and simple question. Did Mr. Cope, or your Ben, suggest or believe that some sort of thing from another world might have taken residence on Muskeget Island?"

The lobsters arrived just then in a rush. Eve offered assistance to Rose, but the old woman snapped off the lobster's body expertly, shaking her head. "My goodness, Ben and I had these delicious things lots of times. And I ate them twice when I was on Nantucket last year." She broke away the tail, expelled the meat from the body, and opened the back to remove the intestine.

Soon, both women were enjoying their buttery lobster meat, so it was some time before Rose spoke. But when she did, her voice was quiet and serious. "To answer your question, Eve, about there being a star visitor on Muskeget, I'm sure Mr. Cope believed that and so did Ben. Now, I do too. When we saw Mr. Cope that one time, he didn't mention the island especially, until the end, but he told Ben that some episodes we call psychic come from what he called 'star visitors.' He told us both that, when we came to see him again, he would take us on a short carriage ride and show us proof that other people had visited our world, but of course we never went back up there to see him."

"And why do *you* think he's right, Rose?" said Eve in a breathless voice, not wanting to draw Mrs. Stringfellow any further into it, yet still driven to probe and poke.

Rose stared across at her, and the old face was shrewd and solemn. "I read Ben's journal on the flight over," she said slowly. "I'd forgotten most of what Miranda said and what Ben asked her. It's a very strange story."

Rose Stringfellow gave a deep sigh. "Eve, do you remember when I told you about that day with Ben on Muskeget, that day we were so happy?"

"Yes," said Eve. "I remember."

"Well, going back there a year ago and then telling you about it in June has made me really think about it and remember it, much better, I guess, than I did even right after Ben and I were there."

Eve nodded. "Yes, I understand. I believe that whatever, uh, force is there can make you do that, if you go near enough to it. I mean, it can make you remember things that happened near or on the island. It must have a way of accumulating such memories."

"So," said Rose, "when I read in Ben's journal how being on that island had done sort of the same thing to Miranda and Horace Street that it did, though not as strongly, to Ben and me, I began to see that what Mr. Cope suggested is possibly true. And now I think that you being an astronomer and being so interested in these stories and all, it really is true. Is it, Eve?"

Eve nodded, her voice shaken by the rapidity with which Mrs. Stringfellow had reached her conclusion. "Yes, Rose, I think it must be true, but it's a story beyond all the other stories of the world, and you and Ben have played crucial parts, dear, dear Rose. Oh, you *must* be careful and not talk about this with anyone, not even your nephew. I'm not with any government or anything like that. I stand only for myself and a few friends, but who can turn away from something like this? Who?"

"Ben and I are really part of something so important, so wonderful . . . ?"

"And so horribly dangerous," finished Eve. "Yes, you are links in an amazing chain of people, starting with an old Scotsman named Fergus Drummond who saw them arrive in their huge, dark ship, then leading to Thomas Cope, who, when he saw Drummond's wonderful model of the orbiting object, must have guessed the truth and sought for the visitors it had left here. The stories led Cope to Miranda, who had been, and was still, deeply involved with one of the creatures. Finally, Cope passed the idea on to Ben Stringfellow and Ben made his own studies. Then you retained the essential books for years until, once again, you were influenced during that visit last summer and passed the material to me, both through the auction and directly."

But Rose was now fiercely shaking her head and her expression was sober. "It's impossible, that's what it is. People like Ben and Rose Stringfellow could never be part of anything like this. We come and we go, but it's a completely different sort of smart, powerful, rich person who would speak with a star visitor. That's the way the world *is,* Eve! It's impossible. I was crazy to think it."

Eve covered Rose's hand with her own and leaned intently toward her. "The world is that way, Rose. You're right. But this thing is from outside the world. What do we know about what or who counts out in that great glitter of worlds and suns? Think about how it spoke, to Miranda, to you and Ben, and to me too, because I had a sweet, sweet moment on that island. It spoke of joy and desire. Is that the language of presidents and parliaments and prime ministers? Just the opposite, I think. Yet I still don't know what it wants or why it does these things," and Eve shook her head in exasperated puzzlement.

Rose Stringfellow sighed again, and her eyes were filled with sadness. "Miranda thought she knew that, Eve. It's in the book and it's very melancholy. The star visitor wanted to die. That's all it wanted, just to die."

Eve suddenly shut her eyes tightly and took a very deep breath. "I see, I see," she whispered, "I . . . I thought it might be that," but then she caught herself and gave Rose's hand a warm squeeze. "Let's not be melancholy, Rose. Let's talk about where you're going, to California," and she said this in a bright, cheerful voice.

But on the way to the airport in a cab, Eve again whispered to Rose about the danger of discussing the Muskeget theories with anyone, then watched her go off, smiling and waving, down the ramp to her plane. Eve had a large lump in her throat as she waved back. I could get a ticket to California . . . or to Hong Kong, she thought. I've got a ton of credit cards. But instead, she took a cab back to her Cambridge apartment.

·11·

MIRANDA'S STORY

When she got into her warm, muggy apartment, Eve quickly undressed and lay down on her dusky bed with only a pinpoint reading lamp focused on Ben Stringfellow's journal. Next to her hand was a gin and tonic, and she opened the cover to find, "With love for Eve from her dear friend, Rose," written on the flyleaf. On the first lined, ledger page, at the top, was written in Ben Stringfellow's hand, "B: Ben Stringfellow, M: Miranda Street." Then,

July 17, Evening (Nantucket Hospital)

B: Miranda, yesterday I gave you Thomas Cope's account and the story of your rescue as told by Captain Chase. I wonder if you have any ideas on either or both?

M: I found Mr. Cope a sincere and perceptive man. My responses to his ideas were certainly, in part, brought out by my need to be thought responsible and of solid, family lineage. Yet, at the time he was here, the miracles of the wreck and the birth were quite far behind us and the wonderful Yoho had not managed to work its magic for a considerable length of time, at least, as Skipper Chase would say, on anyone who stayed sober. Those accounts Mr. Cope wrote down are about as I heard them, and I heard them quite often as you can imagine. Not too much happened out at Tuckernuck, then or now, so people talked a great deal about a very few events.

B: Yet within a short time you were once again deeply involved with Muskeget?

M: I certainly was, and after Horace saved me from the schooner, I had no doubts about the peculiar and powerful influences of the island. None whatever. I can still give no explanation as to why such an influence exists there, but I think I finally understand its purposes.

B: Can you give me the reasons why you are certain that what you call an influence exists on the island?

M: Because on three different occasions it was able to bring about a basic alteration, or perhaps better, an expansion, of my mental abilities. When Horace carried me into the humane house at the height of the blizzard, after we reached shore in the dory, I found that I was gradually able to see, or really to enter, into Horace's inner self, to actually read his mind. It was a tender and wrenching and very extraordinary thing.

B: And did Horace also seem to have gained a similar ability?

M: He had, and I was able to sense that expansion happening inside him as well. That is, I was able to see my whole self, both my inner and outer self, focused through Horace's own consciousness, in his mind. I cannot possibly describe how precisely we perceived each other during those long moments, for that meeting passed with a slowness and a detail that I had never experienced or even imagined. Much has been written about the special awareness of lovers, but this sensitivity far transcended anything of that sort.

B: And did you and Horace talk about this later? Did he agree that you were both in the grip of an extraordinary influence?

M: When I was a little girl, oh, I guess seven or eight, I was up in town visiting my oldest brother, Nathan. He was already a fine carpenter and he was then rebuilding the stairway of a huge, old house up on Main Street, right near the three Coffin brick homes. They were rich, New York, summer people who owned the place and in the children's playroom was a big, wonderful dollhouse. It had porches, gables, everything. I suppose it was built for some fancy New York toy store. I couldn't take my eyes off that house. The whole time I was there, I just stared at it, walked around it, and touched it. Nathan saw that, and next Christmas a dollhouse was my present. Nathan and Father had gotten together and made the parts, then assembled the thing on Christmas Eve. It was every bit as nice as the one from New York. That was the most wonderful Christmas I ever had, and for weeks afterward, I didn't really play with the dollhouse at all. I just sat in front of it, looking at it and touching it. Just *having* it was enough, and though my family joshed me about my being afraid to get it dirty, it was done gently since they could see how deeply and profoundly that present had satisfied me.

That night on the island with Horace was sort of the same thing. We didn't discuss it or refer to it afterward, but we each had it tucked away inside of us where we could consider it and touch it whenever we wanted.

But there was another part. We knew each other in ways that I don't think anyone else can ever imagine. You have to draw back from that, living day-to-day. Most people have things inside them they don't wish to share. Horace and I had, for a long, remarkable moment, shared *everything* between us. In a way, it was not so much the wonderful triumph of the rescue that made what came afterward seem small, but that sense of totally knowing each other's selves that made us both, perhaps, too careful not to throw those doors open again. So, like anything that is wonderful and very intense, it had its two sides.

B: Do you believe that the island influence did this as a gift or reward to you and Horace, or as part of its own attempts to understand or control us, I mean human beings?

M: Neither. It wished to create, record, and then store away an intensely experienced event.

B: What exactly do you mean by "record" and "store"?

M: The sound of an orchestra can be recorded on a phonograph record. That record can be stored and the music re-created at any time. It is evident to me that the island influence has that ability with regard to our experiences and memories.

B: This would be in addition to its ability to help you to see inside one another's experiences, I gather?

M: Correct. That ability enhanced and enriched the rescue, for Horace and for me, but having done that, the influence was then able to have me repeat the complete experience exactly at later times.

B: You mean repeat it in your mind, like a recalled memory?

M: Not exactly like a memory. Much more accurate and detailed than that. A memory of even the most important sort of event is very incomplete, at least with me. I think most people tend to bring back certain textures and aspects, but not the whole thing in exact duplication. This is difficult to write out clearly.

B: And did the influence do that the rescue night you were there with Horace, to you or to Horace?

M: No, that happened much later, that last day we were on Nantucket, before Horace went to France.

B: Miranda, I think we've overstayed our time. I hope we can speak this way to each other again tomorrow. I find this all very interesting and challenging. Psychic auras based on love are uncommon.

M: As, you might imagine, do I. Good night Rose and Ben. This has been enjoyable.

July 18, Afternoon

B: Before you describe what happened in 1917 when you and Horace returned to Nantucket, do you have any more ideas about the rescue?

M: I have thought about it now and then, and it seems to me that some parts of it, the whole emergency I mean, might have been contrived.

B: Contrived in what ways?

M: Well, first of all, they only sent the first half of the message about Mother from the town telegraph office. I knew that Mother had been ill for some days, so when I read in the wire that she'd been taken to the hospital,

I was quite distraught. The rest of the telegram said she was resting comfortably and that I should not worry, but of course, worry is exactly what I did after reading that half-a-message. Then, where they wrecked that schoo-er simply made no sense. Those men must have realized that even if they got rid of me, the authorities would soon discover that there were no tea crates or logwood floating around in Nantucket Sound, so their theft would have been revealed. In fact they were so utterly demoralized, in such a total state of panic, that when we struck on Tuckernuck Bank, and I went below to put on a cork life jacket, they just locked me in the mate's cabin and went off, shouting and reeling, in the jolly boat. The storm simply hadn't gotten that fierce at that point, and I have never understood how they became so unable to handle and tack the vessel. They seemed in a state of complete bewilderment by the time we struck the shoal, with the wheel untended, the schooner lying alee and broadside to the gale.

B: Were they drunk?

M: Some of them were, but not all, I think. They seemed to be seized by a state of confusion. Men like that can usually handle a vessel, even when they are almost staggering from liquor, but this was quite different.

B: Then, you're suggesting that they were under the island influence, they and the telegraph operator in Nantucket town too?

M: I don't know. It almost seems too complicated to imagine such a variety of controls over so many people. Yet if that influence had been able to show those hard men their mutual fears and suspicions, in the same way it showed Horace and me our mutual affection later, the results might have been very much what I saw. By that, I mean a total inability to work together with continual raging disagreements amongst them all.

B: Then you conclude that the influence wished, and thus organized things, to get you and Horace to Muskeget?

M: It seems beyond reason or belief, does it not? Yet that *was* the final result of it all.

B: Might Horace's seeing your light have also been assisted by an outside force? And what about Chase letting a man go alone into that storm?

M: You have paid attention to all this, Ben! Horace did have wonderful eyesight but I have wondered sometimes if his impulsive setting out that night might have been contrived in some indirect way. As to Skipper, he said a thousand times after that, to anyone who would listen, that he had never done, and would never do again, such a stupid thing.

B: Then at some point, on the beach at Coskata perhaps, both Captain Chase and Horace were being manipulated, at the same time. Rather like a play or story with the aura, the author.

M: Yes, and there were other plays to follow. But remember, the way I acted to Horace that previous summer might have put him in a mood to do almost anything to distinguish himself. Perhaps the influence helped him to see the light, but perhaps that was all that it had to do.

B: Can you tell me now about what you described as the "recording" of the rescue aftermath and its "re-creation" later?

M: In the summer of 1917, Horace and I returned to Nantucket as it says in the Yankee storybook. We had never been able to have children, as Skipper mentions, and I think his other thoughts are perceptive, if a little bit personal. Horace and I had led a very interesting and challenging life together, and we had enjoyed many good times, but I now think we were truly overmastered, in a number of different ways, by that night of the rescue. Yet I loved Horace very much and I love him now. His death in France was devastating to me, Ben. Especially when it occurred so soon after our last day on the island. That day was so sweet, so renewing and so fruitful, that I really saw us starting out on a new, better relationship after the war.

B: Tell us about your visit, Miranda. Your face is alight.

M: Yes, it certainly takes a memory like that one to flush my cheeks at this stage in my life. Horace had been ordered to New York, but then he got a five-day leave because his troopship sailing was delayed, and we decided on the spur of the moment to visit Nantucket. We came over from New Bedford on the *Sankaty* and Captain Merriman was an old friend, so we spent most of the trip in his stateroom or in the wheelhouse, chatting with him and other, overdressed, portly and important people. Horace had wired ahead and we found that the Sea Cliff Inn had given us their best room, up under the roof where you can see in three directions, out over the whole island. I asked John Coffin to try and get that room for you. I hope you have enjoyed it.

R: (Rose Stringfellow) I would just like to write down here that the view from that lovely room is the nicest part of this very nice visit, and I want to thank you, Miranda, for doing that.

M: Rose, now you know what Horace and I saw. It was a perfect visit. Everybody spoke to us and looked after us. The manager of the Sea Cliff Inn made her rig available, with a boy to drive, and she, with Skipper Chase and John Coffin, Sr., arranged things wherever we went. When we got into 'Sconset on the train, there was practically a parade up the bank with three men on cornets and two young drummers. They marched us to my old place, much bigger now and called the Beach Walk House, where we all had a wonderful lunch. There were some speeches, and then Horace's response. Horace had put on a little weight in the twenty-or-so years since the rescue, but with his uniform and his stern moustache, he was quite romantic looking, and he made a warm little speech reminding everyone that there were eight men in a lifesaving crew and that the other seven had saved over a dozen men that same night he saved me. Then he took my hand and said something to the effect that to give a man a medal for saving me was rather like handing a strawberry ice cream soda to a man who was already sitting "plumb in the middle of paradise." It was a very sweet and pleasant moment. Everybody stood up and cheered. I wept a few tears and kissed Horace's cheek.

The next day, Mr. Coffin took us out to Coskata by way of the Head of the Harbor in his catboat. Skipper had sent a message to the lifesaving station, so they were certainly more than ready for us. They put on a very smart Lyle gun drill and then fired some of the experimental line-carrying rockets for us to watch. I thought we would have to go back to the Wauwinet House to eat lunch, but the keeper had arranged a wonderful clam chowder and lobster spread at the station, with wine and everything. Afterward, Horace climbed into the tower and told them how he saw my light, and then he walked to the beach and showed them where the dory had been kept and how he had dashed off on that wonderful blizzard night. He didn't say anything about that other time when we had been together at the station end-of-July party, but after the lunch and the lecture, we walked alone behind the sand hill where Horace had tried to kiss me that other time. We kissed warmly and it was a good moment for us both. We had a fine supper at the Wauwinet House and a long, languid sail home to town, ending in the bright moonlight. It was another magical day for us, but the next day was far more magical.

B: That was your last day on Nantucket?

M: Yes, when we got back from Muskeget in the late afternoon the next day, Horace found telegraphed orders at the Sea Cliff Inn desk for him to be in New York the next morning.

B: The nurse feels we should let you rest, Miranda. I hope that tomorrow we can finish your account of that pleasant-sounding visit.

M: Rose and Ben, I hope your visit is going as nicely as ours did back then.

July 19, Evening

M: The next morning after that day-sail to Coskata, Mr. Coffin took us to Muskeget with a picnic lunch. Horace and I rowed ashore from the big catboat and tramped around the island. It was still shifting eastward slowly, year by year, yet it seemed little different, nothing but beach grass, sand, and poison ivy. The day was warm and bright. We ate our picnic sitting on some tumbled foundation stones and got the idea for a swim. We had brought no towels or bathing suits, so we decided to undress in the ramshackle humane house, then go and paddle in the little bight of a harbor on the south shore, opposite from the side where the catboat was moored. What happened in that shack exactly duplicated what had happened the night of the blizzard. Exactly! It was like running a play on the second night after the opening.

B: Did you see Horace as younger? Did he change for you?

M: I saw him as his younger self, and as he was in 1917, both at the same time. Everything went very slowly.

B: What other visual effects seemed different? Was the shack in both forms too, or wavering between its two parts, at the blizzard and in 1917?

M: I've never thought much about that. I guess it was sort of a combination of the two. Like a dream with three or four pieces from different places combined.

B: But Horace was seen in both forms?

M: Yes, and at the same time. Horace and I completely duplicated that night of the blizzard, simply went through it again in total and exact detail. We said the same things, felt the same things, saw each other's joy in exactly the same way, did, sensed and thought everything exactly as on the blizzard night. And, in addition, we still knew ourselves as we were then, in 1917. So, in one sense, we watched our younger selves all the while totally experiencing this from our older vantage point. Because of this added perception, the moment was even deeper than the first time, and I could actually sense that in Horace and he in me. We were overcome by it, unable to even speak for what seemed a great length of time afterward. The influence had again somehow expanded our perceptions and made time pass very slowly. Eventually we found our way down into the warm, shallow water of the southern bight of harbor and we felt the slowness and the deep, almost stark, joy pass gently from us. Again, we did not discuss what happened as we lay in the water, holding each other, but we were, the two of us, far more attentive and loving for the rest of our time together before Horace sailed for France. We would have come back there, Ben, if Horace had lived and come home. I can't imagine what our life would have been like, but his loss then was the most bitter and dismaying of chances.

B: Then this re-creation of the earlier event included both physical duplication of what was done and a duplication of what you felt?

M: Yes, and it was total, complete. I saw Horace as he was at the time of the blizzard and I saw him as he was at that moment, a handsome, middle-aged, army major. We moved and spoke in exactly the same way because we were living through it again. And of course we wanted it, yearned for it, so we were the most pliable of subjects for something that can work such a miracle.

B: Did anything else that was unusual happen while you were there? I mean, on the island.

M: No, not really. After our swim we dressed in the little house, but that part of it seemed to go along at a normal pace. The wind had picked up a bit so the sail home was brisk and breezy. We found the telegram at the Sea Cliff Inn and the hotel rig got us down to the dock in plenty of time for the evening trip of the *Sankaty* to Woods Hole. This time we found that Captain Merriman had provided us with the best stateroom, courtesy of the line, and when we got in there we found a vase of flowers and a bottle of champagne in a cooler from the captain. We left Nantucket at dusk, waving from the top deck to our friends, and then went to our roomy stateroom and passed the most pleasant evening. Of course the *Sankaty* was passing relatively near Muskeget since in those days they went on a quite direct route, south of Cross Rip, if the weather was fair. But I don't believe we were influenced then. The day, the whole visit really, had renewed us. If I had dreamed that Horace was to soon die abroad, I don't believe I could have lived through the day and a half that remained to us. Horace reported for duty to his ship the next morning, but there was more delay, so we had one more day together in New York. By then the Muskeget experience was more distant, but still like a warm, immensely dear possession.

B: Miranda, we can see that this is difficult for you. If these memories are too painful, please let us go on to something else.

M: My tears aren't for those few, perfect days at the end, Ben, but for that moment next winter when the telegram came from the War Department. I had no inkling of it, no sense that Horace was even in danger. It broke me. I was lost. There were days, weeks, afterward that I cannot now remember at all. Fortunately, there were friends to help me through it.

B: Why do you feel the influence touched you and Horace again in 1917, that day you went back to the island?

M: Oh, probably several reasons. To reinforce and also remind us of the rescue night, to prepare us, or perhaps, me, for what it almost did last fall, and maybe to just try its ability out on us.

B: And what did the influence almost do in the fall?

M: Pierce and stop my heart. It could do that, I think. With enough detail and the stretching of time that goes with it, the influence could amplify the sweetness, the tenderness, until it became stronger and deeper than anyone could ever stand. I don't mean you would not *want* to stand it, and would not *try* to stand it, but I don't believe, finally, that it would be possible. It would have been an ending to redeem my life.

What I went through last year was incomplete, yet wonderful. I think I'm ready, Ben. I know there are many people who have had far more continuously happy lives than I have, but few, I think, who have seen that sort of intensity. It is beyond description. It is more valuable than anyone could imagine.

B: Miranda, I think we must say good night. We hope you sleep well and forgive us the tears we brought.

M: I weep often by myself. It is pleasant to do it with good friends, now and then. Good night.

Eve sighed and blinked, then put the book, carefully open, down next to her on the bed. She drained the ice water from her drink and got up to fix another, for her stomach was a hollow knot of uncertainty and anticipation. She stopped, in the thin light of the bedroom, before the long mirror hanging on her closet door. The darkness concealed the small but undeniable sags and wrinkles and made her seem very beautiful and very young. She cupped her breasts as Jack had done in the cockpit of the yacht and turned while watching her shadowy shape and movements. What had that young man said at her party when Noel asked what we might get from crossing space? A *good* aphrodisiac? But we didn't even have to make the trip, she thought, watching herself pivot and touch herself. That thing brought us one, not just good, but the very best.

She let her hands drop and stood, now almost at attention, looking at her face and her body in the dark mirror. But what had the old physicist said, a *safe* aphrodisiac? Eve shook her head. That was a contradiction in terms, she thought. If it was truly good, then it could not also be safe.

She walked into her kitchen, mixed her drink and, almost reluctantly, padded back to her bed and the ledger. Though Eve's astronomical research centered mainly on photography and computer analysis, she knew something of electronic and electromagnetic theory, at least in practical applications. Could the Muskeget visitor, she wondered, read and store such a vastly complex and detailed episode, from two different points of view, while at the same time amplifying both their personal sensitivities and feeding the moment-to-moment output of each of the participants to the other? What a miracle of signal processing and signal separation that was! Eve had a solid grip on Information Theory and she wondered about the gigantic bit-transfer rate that was involved. And how the hell would the alien store all that stuff so that it could be retrieved, not just in perfect sequence, but absolutely in sync with Horace and Miranda together? But then she shrugged and picked up the ledger again. Even we can get something like a full symphony orchestra completely down in binary form with its color, harmonics, dynamics, the whole thing. The real miracle was not the data processing and storage, but the thing's sensitivity, its ability to read out such a complicated experience with so much detail and completeness, entirely from the weak and tiny signals emitted by human brain activity. Eve focused her eyes again on the journal.

July 20, Evening

B: Miranda, can we talk now about your final experience with the island last summer?

M: After I went to Boston for my throat operation and knew I had only a few weeks or months to live, I decided to go to Muskeget and die there. I had no clear vision of what might happen, or whether I would again be with Horace, but I had hope that some sort of meeting might happen, even if only at the moment of death. John Coffin, the son of the man who took us there in 1917, was most kind and helpful, and he arranged for Marcus Dunham, the caretaker who worked for the Muskeget gunning club, to refurbish the humane house for me. John sailed me there toward the middle of June with all my gear, and I knew before we landed that I had done the right thing. The pain in my throat faded away and I felt stronger, and, yes, happier. John soon had me settled and even he could see that I was feeling better. "Memories, when they're pretty ones, sure beat aspirin," he said and then went back to town.

B: Did the influence contact you during the summer in any obvious way?

M: No, not directly, not till the storm, but my sense of physical well-being and that constant happiness were signs enough. I began to wonder if the island itself might be my lover, in some deep, nearly unsensed way. And there were other things. Muskeget is a very buggy place, with greenhead horseflies and other biters around most of the summer. Mr. Dunham had tacked up some screening on my shack windows, but he shook his head and said he was afraid I wouldn't be able to keep the "pesky critters" out. I was never bitten that summer. There was never a bug in my little house.

Then, Mr. Dunham said he had never seen such a summer for lobster and bass. Men came in catboats and fished off the south shore, casting out, you know, and they got so many fish that they always cleaned one for me. My appetite came back and I guess nobody ever ate more or better seafood than I did those three months. Marcus used to bring me great crocks of fresh-shucked scallops with the lobsters and clams and one day, toward the end, I think it was the first week of September, he said an odd thing to me. He had a large bowl of tiny scallop eyes and they were the sweetest and tenderest I had ever tasted. We were both of us eating them raw, picking them out of the crock. I both patted and rubbed my stomach, my sign of thanks and delight that I used often when Mr. Dunham brought me good things, and he said, "Them scallops are comin' up, Miranda, to take a look around. Why, I just dipped them up with a dang crabbing net, if you can believe it. Can't imagine why they'd do that so early. Why it ain't really fall yet."

I should write, Ben, that in the late fall, in November or December, scallops, which can move by snapping their shells open and shut, often rise to the surface of the water, making little splashes as though it were raining. The old-timers, like Marcus, claimed that they came up to consider the weather. If it looked like it was turning cold, they said, the scallops knew it was time to move to deeper water where the ice could not trap them. I wrote down something to the effect that they were probably coming up because there were so many lobsters and bass on the bottom that it was too crowded for them. Mr. Dunham shook his head. "No, they come up to look at you, Miranda. They come up to look at the queen of Muskeget."

Mr. Dunham was almost eighty, friendly and talkative, but still a shy, solitary man and this was a remarkable and unlikely thing for him to say. One of the loveliest of the Indian stories is about a Capowak princess who was so beautiful that the scallops would rise to the surface of the water when she walked by on the shore. In so doing, they turned their watery, inedible bellies into the white, firm "eye" that you eat, which is really a muscle, of course. You see, the beauty of the princess was so perfect that it conferred on her tribe, and on all the Wampanoag nations, a great blessing, the sweet, white eye of the scallop. One day, the princess was coming back to the Vineyard in a long canoe with many braves, led by her lover who was the mightiest warrior in the Capowak nation. A great storm carried them off and, ever since, when the days get dark and the water chill, the scallops rise in the water to peer about for the princess, for they know that if they should ever see her walking along the shore again, the winter will not come and they can live in the warm shallows forever. I wrote this legend out at length for Marcus, while we continued to eat his scallops, and he read it over for some time in thoughtful silence.

Then he said, "I never heard that one, Miranda, but what I said was true. They come up when you walked by. I was out splicing a line on a mooring shackle and I seen it happen. You were heading around to the point, looking for shells, and as you went by, them little pips began on the water's surface. I rowed over quick, only had the crab net in the dory, and fished the little fellers out as fast as I could scoop. As soon as you moseyed around the point, they stopped rising but by then I had buckets full. I never saw the like of it.''

B: This all sounds very much like the business with the fish just before your birth?

M: Rather less spectacular, but the same sort of thing. Was it showing some sort of love for me with these gifts? In a sense, I think it was. I had gone to the island to seek my death and instead I had gained a sort of extraordinary life. Yet, even if the scallops had seen a local, and rather ancient, princess, November would still come and I wondered, not with any fear or dismay but simply with anticipation, if I would see it at all. And then, about two weeks after the scallops, came the hurricane.

B: Did you have any warning or sense that the storm was coming?

M: No, but I certainly knew something was going to happen. It was a warm, dark, blustery morning. Mr. Dunham was over working at the clubhouse, and I began to feel an increasing sort of acute sensitivity. The day was getting very dark. Gradually it came to me that though I had lost my pain and nausea when I came to the island, my moment was finally arriving. I lay down on my bunk and went immediately into a reverie, remembering Horace and all the things that had happened to us. And I was happy, simply filled with happiness. Oh, Ben, I hope I can remember that sense when the moment truly and finally comes. The wind was picking up, but I had no sense of fear or apprehension about it. The wind was part of the whole thing. I knew that.

B: Miranda, our time is up again, but we will see you tomorrow. I find this more and more fascinating.

July 21, Afternoon

M: As I wrote above, the wind was really starting to pick up around noon, and as it did, my reverie became deeper and more profound. And I realized that whatever was there, that spirit of the island, was going to enter my soul, become a partner with me, and that the storm made this possible. You see, it could not come over to me unless it was terribly threatened, unless the island itself was threatened, and so it had brought me there to await the moment that it knew, or perhaps hoped, would come.

B: The idea then, was that it would escape the catastrophe by merging with you, with your personality?

M: You don't understand yet, Ben. Whatever lived on or in the island didn't want to escape. It wanted to die. It didn't just possess me, take me over, so that I would walk to a boat and leave. It took me back to those two other times, with Horace. The illusion was total, absolutely complete, and I lived in both those times, the blizzard night and the day in 1917, simultaneously. Things went even more slowly than the other times. I knew then that I could not withstand those scenes for a third time. The reality was beyond anything I have ever experienced. But then, as the moments lengthened and the detail became ever more complete, I began to see with delight that my final instant with Horace would not actually end, that it would always continue to happen. Yet I knew also that I couldn't possibly withstand such a never-ending moment and that in this way, we would, together, perish in a moment of transcendent joy.

B: Extraordinary! But what happened? Why did the influence's plan fail?

M: It miscalculated the storm track, I think. If the sort of waves that struck the south Rhode Island coast last year had come over Muskeget, the island would have been destroyed, swept into Nantucket Sound.

B: Then its ability to reproduce your experiences with Horace in such complete detail was used to keep you passive while the storm mounted? To insure that you did not try to escape once it had entered your consciousness?

M: Yes, I think that was the whole point, but not so much to keep me, Miranda, from running. I was, and I am, dying, Ben. I would have stayed without the visions. I think that it needed that final, blinding vision to mask its own needs and reflexes. Had we gone on with that deepening experience, I think nothing on heaven or earth could have brought me back. Brought us back, I should say.

B: Yet you did come back?

M: Things did not continue as I anticipated. At some point the experience began to fragment. I literally felt the influence leaving me, pulling back away, and as it did so, my experiences with Horace began to come apart, to fade into pieces and brief bits of remembrance. And as that happened, I became aware of the horrible howl of the wind, the wild slatting of the house shingles and tar paper as they beat against the house and then tore off. The water rose as though I was in a bathtub and was soon swirling around my bunk and through the crumbling shack. I was terribly disappointed, yet so warm and filled with delight at the partial experience that I waited without fear, knowing the shack would last only a few minutes as the water came up. I was prepared then, and I focused my thoughts on Horace, trying as hard as I could to see his face when the moment I was swept into the sound arrived.

Instead, it was Mr. Dunham and some of the men from Tuckernuck who arrived and carried me to the higher ridge at the west end of the island where a powerboat was anchored. By then the water was up to their waists, and it was a wild struggle to get over to Tuckernuck. The scud was blinding and the endless hurricane roar simply covered every other sound. I almost collapsed before we made shore, but the wives put me to bed with much whiskey and warm bricks at my feet. I dozed, wept, and then fell asleep when the wind dropped.

B: Did you go back to Muskeget again?

M: My health had suffered from the storm effects and I was in and out of the hospital all winter. In May I felt strong enough to ask Mr. Coffin to take me to Muskeget on a calm day. I felt nothing at all, the whole time I was there. Mr. Coffin carried me ashore and helped me to walk up to the ruined floor of my little house, but I had absolutely no sense of either physical improvement or any mental changes. My aches and concerns were continuous and unabated. I was no longer the queen of Muskeget.

B: Might the storm have done its deadly work on the influence, even though the island remained?

M: I don't think that happened. I think my part in it, my chance, had simply gone by. I was no longer needed or useful. I feel it would be a mistake to assign too many human values, such as friendship, association, or gratitude to what is there. As my dear mother so astutely said to Mr. Cope, the Yoho is itself and has its own purposes.

B: Before we leave today, Miranda, I want to propose a question that you may think about until we talk this way again. Mr. Cope, the night he gave me the journal with your parents' stories, suggested two things. The first was that this planet, our earth, had been visited by a gigantic ship almost two hundred years ago. He claimed to have proof, but I did not see it. The second was that what we now call an influence on Muskeget Island is, in fact, a living being left by that vessel. You, of all the people who have been affected by what is there, have the most scientific education, and surely the closest associations. I wonder what you think about such a theory?

M: That idea has never occurred to me, Ben. It will take some thinking about. Have a pleasant evening, both of you.

Eve took several deep breaths, shut her eyes, and let her head fall back to the cool headboard. She was in this really deep, she knew, much deeper than Miranda. There was a terrible, horrifying difference between that storm and the one to come. When Eve's storm came, things had to work, because there would be no third chance. It would not take the clever men now unloading electronic racks on the Muskeget beaches very long to decipher at least some of the thing's tricks.

Eve grit her teeth and shook her head in disgust. Nobody was going to play Iphigenia in this little interstellar tragedy. If the sort of electromagnetic influences that thing was capable of exerting could be analyzed and duplicated by signal-generating equipment, then what might become possible? Not just the damn fish and the scallops and who knows what else wiped out in a year or two, but what about the passions and disagreements that could be stirred up by a megawatt of broadcast power? Posthypnotic-type suggestions showing up months or years later in a congress or parliament. A schooner, a whole navy, a country set to fighting itself. Glandular activity altered, emotions set awry, mental confusions broadcast everywhere, all by tiny, unfelt signals filling the world with mad commands. Nobody would ever get to Barnard's Star if that happened! Forget the biology and the space-crossing stuff. The thing's physics was mischievous enough! And the most terrifying, outrageous thing of all would be that nobody could ever be sure they weren't being acted upon by some greed-ridden, malevolent system or ideology. Talk about gurus flowing out of a television set!

Eve thought a long time about another drink, but finally turned from that. Where is the storm? she wondered. I think I can do this, but, oh God, don't make me wait too long. She shivered in the warm, stuffy room, but then, remembering Prissy, her shivering stopped and she soberly turned the ledger page to the last interview.

July 22, Evening

M: When I first started thinking about your idea last night, Ben, it seemed too fanciful to even consider. But understand that through our meetings, and at the one years ago with Mr. Cope, I've been trying to look at what happened to me, to us, from your point of view. I mean, from the idea of the occult, psychic influences left from past events, possession by spirits, and all those sorts of things. But if you once look on the influence as something living, with unimagined abilities, yet abilities still lying within what science understands, what happened to me takes on an entirely different aspect.

B: In what way? Which parts of the stories, specifically?

M: Well, the fact that the most intense experiences happened at a single, rather small location, and that the farther you got from that center, the lower the level of effect there was, is scientifically reasonable. Take Horace spotting my signal light on the schooner. What a tiny bit of suggestion it would take to convince lonely, lovesick Horace that he saw something, even if it was faint and far away. Coskata lies about twelve miles from Muskeget. And surely the momentary distraction of a telegraph operator is not too difficult even if the town lies nine miles from the island. But making the men on the schooner almost berserk with rage and suspicion, so willing to act against their own best interests, would take more power, and the schooner was within two or three miles of Muskeget when she stranded. Finally, Horace and I spent our wonderful times at the center, directly above where the creature probably lies, under the island. What could it be but some unimaginably evolved creature with huge intelligence, able to use radio waves in ways we cannot conceive of?

B: Can you think of any other evidence in your experiences to support Mr. Cope's theory?

M: I lay awake thinking about such connections. I wondered if such a visitor, left by its people alone and unprotected for so many years, might have very strong self-preservation instincts. Everything that it did shows that its race has a vastly greater understanding of mental science than we do. Surely they would be able to impose on their explorer whatever behavior they wanted, and remaining alive and functional would have to be primary commands.

B: I see where you're going. You're saying that the influence had to protect and save itself, even if this meant shifting its own personality into some other host, through some sort of radio wave transfer of mental capacity?

M: But if it brought with it certain other things, such as the totally detailed experiences of Horace and me together, it could overcome any preservation commands set into its own personality. And it could. I will attest to that. Nothing, no inner force, could have drawn me back from that endless moment I was to have with Horace. If Mr. Cope is right, and his ideas certainly fit the facts better than any occult theories I know about, then my sense that it wanted to die is probably correct. Its people must have gone away without it. Maybe it was injured or lost. But what a terrible gift they left it, an utter inability to end its own life! And it waits there now, Ben, for what? Another hundred-year storm to blow away its home and end its sadness? What a dreadful finish for such a bold venture! I wish the hurricane had tracked as that creature anticipated.

B: I think Rose and I must go to Muskeget, even if we sense no more than Mr. Cope. All these years I have sought for that perfect apparition, the one that comes when you call it. This is probably not one of those, but we must go and see.

M: I'm afraid the greenheads will be all too real and unghostly. Still, there lies the source, the center of what you came to study. I think you should go. Who knows what may happen, and you may be the first to visit the island suspecting its secret.

B: And it would be able to sense that knowing, do you think?

M: That seems a small enough miracle to set against the others. Yes, if it could obtain the detail from Horace and me that it did, it could certainly sense thoughts readily. Pick a good day and a good captain. Mr. Coffin may have a charter, it's his busy season, but he will find you a trustworthy boat.

B: We will be leaving in two days, Miranda. The war is coming in Europe. We will try to stop in tomorrow night or the next morning before the boat leaves.

M: Ben, I must finally ask you a question. I thought about it last night and today. What will you do with this information? I feel strongly that whatever is there should be left undisturbed. I sensed that we humans have already injured it with our cruel and rough ways. I wonder what you think about this?

B: I entirely agree with you. It is your story and not mine to tell. I have followed it from Scotland to Nantucket and put what Mr. Cope speculated and you experienced together. The answers seem beyond the occult. No one would believe it anyway, but they will have no chance. That visitor means us no harm, and we would only turn it to evil ends.

M: Yes, I feel better seeing you write that down. Perhaps it will discover some other way to bring about that sad boon it seeks. I am deeply grateful that you brought this to me, Ben and Rose, this strange idea of Mr. Cope's. It gives a marvelous and melancholy color to my life that I cannot yet really comprehend. Have a lovely time on your visit to Muskeget. I will envy you that and think of you.

July 24, On Board the Steamer, Naushon (to Woods Hole)

We returned too late from Muskeget (a *wonderful* trip and though no visitor actually appeared, we did notice a decided psychic aura about the place, a remarkable sense of cheer and jollity) to see Miranda yesterday evening, and found this morning that she had suffered a bad night and was not strong enough to write more than a few words. We could only give her our heartfelt farewells and accept her hugs and some tears, which we tried to josh away by telling of our so-happy day on Muskeget. This soon had her smiling and so we parted with warm smiles and waves.

I will correspond with Miranda about this matter, but I will take it no further than that. To share such an extraordinary secret with such an indominable woman is entirely sufficient for me. I only wish that Mr. Cope might have shared in this triumph of logic and imagination. His connecting of the space vessel over Scotland and the incidents at Muskeget is the sure act of genius in our investigation of this matter. As to the Star Visitor (Mr. Cope's phrase) on Muskeget, it seems to me so immensely powerful yet so immensely weak at the same time, that I can find no ethical or moral way to deal with it other than leaving it alone.

Benjamin Stringfellow, Esq.

Eve put the closed book softly down on her nightstand, but her thoughts were hard and bitter. Misanthrope Drummond, wise old Cope, and ethical Ben Stringfellow were inspired amateurs, blessed with good luck and open minds. No snotty journal staff refereed their stuff. No tenure committee of time-serving deans and half-smart professors sifted and handled it. And it never occurred to Ben, when the Muskeget puzzle finally sorted itself out, that he had found a secret beyond all price. Well, he and Miranda didn't have Ph.D.s, they had character instead. Forty years later, things were very much reversed. The technology to make waveform analysis of the thing's activity was probably in place, or would be in a short time. The fact that the visitor meant us no harm, as Ben put it, would signify exactly nothing to the bright, cool men from Cal Tech and from her institution, and from all the other nasty, smart places where almost any mischief can be cooked up, if you just pay them enough.

Eve turned out the bed lamp, but she remained sitting up in the dark for a long time. She would not take the ledger to Ed. Not until the storm. In the end, this was her decision alone, and she knew she could not withstand Ed indefinitely, and probably Ian too, if Ed phoned him. Her heart constricted. Eve sat in the warm darkness, her skin cold, and she remembered steering the yacht, that wonderful, blustery, wild day, and making love with shy Ian, and the excitement of the auction. Do I really have the guts for this? she wondered.

She flipped on the light and reached for the ledger, to read it through again, and as her fingers touched the cover, she realized there was no real choice and no turning back. Cope, the Macys, Miranda and Horace, the Stringfellows, those were her people, that was her family. Queens had rewards and they had duties. It was as simple as that.

·12·

A Return
to
Muskeget

A few days later, on the morning of the third of September, Eve heard a first report on tropical storm Daisy, gaining strength off Miami and having the potential of striking the American East Coast. By nine that night, Miami Hurricane Center had posted a hurricane watch as far north as Cape Cod, and Eve knew, with a sinking heart, that the time had come to go and face Ed Berry.

Her small apartment was still hot and humid, the whole month had been terrible, but she stared around it with both affection and sadness. The old, leather volumes lining her bookshelves drew her back from her stern purpose, and she lifted out the Bion and opened it to a plate of elaborately scrolled and embellished astronomical quadrants. How had they come from that beauty, she asked herself, to the vast, unhuman, ballistic weapons systems, a near-infinity of technical horrors?

She closed the book and walked to the door of her apartment. Behaving properly, through your whole life, had never been simple and it wasn't easy now, she thought. Yet to blink might unleash an evil beyond all calculation, bring about a world in which behaving properly could become simply impossible.

She hesitated on the street below for a moment, tempted to take a cab to Ed's and so invite them to seize her now, but that was a cowardly way out and instead she walked briskly down busy streets to the Harvard Square subway station, surrounded and protected by unseeing, scurrying people.

Eve stood on the subway platform, staring about at all the other, different persons, and she was both frightened and human enough to think suddenly that maybe they just weren't worth it. Most of the time, she thought bitterly, they, hell, she too, had little enough self-control and would probably live with few regrets in a world in which emotional and mental freedom was removed or manipulated. She grimly stared at the approaching train. That, she realized, was hardly the point. If they had to *earn* their deliverance from mental meddling by the cruel and ambitious men who ran the world, then they were controlled anyway. The simple right-to-be-left-alone was orders of magnitude more important than any four, or forty, other freedoms. She stepped quickly into the subway car and, ten minutes later, was giving two quick rings on Ed's doorbell.

Ed immediately let her in and she could see at once that he was distressed, almost angry. He muttered a greeting, then led her quickly and silently to his small book-lined sanctum at the rear of the store. As she settled herself in an overstuffed and bursting old arm-chair, Ed brusquely handed over a single, folded sheet of paper. "From Ian," he said in a low voice. "Came in today."

Eve opened the paper and read

Dear Ed,

I finally got an answer to my letters to Mrs. Stringfellow. It turns out that she (a) found the Miranda Street account behind a bookshelf, (b) is now visiting relatives in California, and (c) gave said book to Eve in Boston on her way west almost a week ago. Ed, what in hell is happening? Why didn't you call me? Pay attention, for God's sake, Ed!

Best, Ian.

She looked up and saw Ed peering at her from frowning, sober eyes. "Eve," he said quietly. "This is no time to play the lone hand. We may have a hurricane up here within twenty-four hours."

Eve looked steadily back at him. She reached into her large handbag, pulled out Ben Stringfellow's interview account, and handed it over. "Read it. Then we'll talk," she said.

Ed reached for another sheet of paper on his desk and handed it to Eve. "Okay, you read that while I go through this."

The single sheet Eve now held was entitled, "Escape Plan for Leaving Boston in the Face of a Hurricane Threat." Underneath she read:

I own the next house to this one, and have a way of getting into it from the cellar. In its small garage is a panel truck I leased this summer, to take us out of Boston. My first thought was to drive north and west for Canada, but I realized that, even if we got out of Boston, they would have hundreds of miles of road on which to chase us, or lie in wait. Instead, my plan is as follows:

We leave in the truck and head north over the thruways to Cape Ann. (I have a disguise. You will be hidden.) I have leased an outboard powerboat and put it in a marina slip on the north coast of Cape Ann. When we reach the marina, we will leave the truck and head north, out to sea, in the boat. I have done all of this three times this summer, at different times of day.

The storm will probably catch up with us at some point, but if it does, we will simply run the boat ashore. I have picked out places along the Massachusetts and New Hampshire shores where we can safely abandon the thing to the storm and the underwriters. By then, we will be able to represent ourselves to the local citizenry as shipwrecked yacht persons and, given the dislocations of the storm, will be able to hide out as refugees in somebody's house, or in the local high school gym, or whatever. The point is, by remaining in the storm's path, we make its confusion our ally. If we can once get out of the marina in the boat, I doubt that they could ever take us in time to get you to Muskeget before the storm passed over.

I have a pistol and have practiced with it. Obviously, I am no match for several, professional police-

men, but my age and benign (feeble?) appearance
might give me an edge, at least in some situations.

The document was signed, "Ed C. Berry, Secret
Agent."

Eve quietly wiped her eyes as she read this. She
finished and reached over to put a hand over one of Ed's
and when he looked up, gave him an open and teary
smile. He smiled warmly back, then continued his careful study of the ledger.

Ten minutes later he finished reading, closed the
book, and looked up at her, and she saw that he was also
close to tears. "Nobody is indispensable, Eve," he said in
a small, choked voice.

She shook her head. "You don't know that, Ed, any
more than I do. Suppose it transfers itself, because I'm
not there at the final moment, to one or more of the
people at Muskeget now, the ones the Coast Guard is
protecting? The point is, Ed, we don't know what is
possible and what may happen. What we *do* know is that
the fat is in the fire. The visitor can't be hidden any
longer!"

Ed pointed a steady finger at her. "Everything you're
thinking and saying right now may be totally conditioned
by that thing. How can you even consider making a
freewill decision on this?"

Eve pointed down at the ledger in front of him.
"You're a document expert. Is that a fake or a forgery?
Has all this been cooked up out of nothing, all two
hundred years of it?"

Ed sighed and shook his head. "No, I'm sure the thing
is there, and I guess Miranda had as good an idea of what

it wanted as anyone. But what if they seize you, after the . . . the personality transfer or whatever it is, and get you away from the ending the alien wants? They won't just let you sit in that shack to die while that storm sweeps over Muskeget, Eve!"

Eve blinked and wiped her eyes again, but she looked steadily at Ed. "Has it made any false moves yet, that we know about? Other than misjudging the thirty-eight storm? Don't you think it's considered that possibility? And remember, as far as we know, only three people in the world understand what the visitor truly desires: you, Mrs. Stringfellow, and me. Ed, you're smart and you've lived a long time. If our government gained the kind of power over humans and animals that this visitor has exhibited, it would be horrible, terrifying, beyond imagination! And what about the Russians, and the nasty East Germans, and the P.L.O. and Israel, and South Africa and most of the Third World? And, oh, God, Ed, almost anyone? It would totally corrupt our lives and our leaders. I'm going to do it, Ed. Please understand why! Please!"

Ed blinked and bit his wrinkled lower lip. "Ian isn't here. What will I say to him? How can I face him? I *have* to speak for Ian, Eve!"

"Then speak," said Eve, staring down at her shoes.

Ed peered at her and big tears began to run steadily down his cheeks, yet his voice was oddly young and steady. "Come live with me and be my Love, and we will all the pleasures prove, That hills and valleys, dale and field, And all the craggy mountains yield.

"There will we sit upon the rocks, And see the shepherds feed their flocks, By shallow rivers, to whose falls Melodius birds sing madrigals. There will I make thee beds of roses And a thousand fragrant posies, A cap of flowers, and a kirtle Embroider'd all with leaves of . . ."

But Eve had stood up, weeping openly, and now stamped her foot. "No, damn you! Stop it! You damn book people can always find a Marlowe or a Shakespeare or a Herrick to do your stuff for you!"

Ed stopped speaking at once and also stood up to face her. Eve stepped around the desk to him and took him in a warm and strong hug. "Ed, *please* let me go, Ed," she said, pressing her cheek against his. "You have to tell Ian and Julia and the others what this was all about. Please, please, Ed. I'm wounded and it never really healed, hurt by Prissy's stupid, senseless death, by brave Johnny Finn's fall. Ed, that thing can give me Prissy back! It *has* to do that, to make the whole thing work. Read what Miranda said! It won't be an end for me, Ed, just something sweet and tender that goes on and on."

Ed put his arms around her and the tears poured down his cheeks. "Then I can't come with you, to Muskeget?" he said softly.

Eve kissed his wet cheek. "Knowing you're here and safe, ready with your brave and beautiful plan to save me, that will help me, give me strength, Ed. I don't want to hurt anybody, including me. Let me go, my dear, dear friend!"

Ed dropped his arms and stepped back. Finally he nodded. "I will be here," he said, his face distorted with grief. "If it doesn't work, or it's the wrong storm, or whatever happens, I'll wait." His face twisted in pain. "I knew I didn't have the courage for this sort of thing. If I were a younger man . . ."

Eve seized his hand and pressed the palm to her cheek.

"If you had been younger, younger when I was younger, perhaps it might have been different, brave Sancho Panza. But when the windmill is finally still, the giant slain by its own sadness, the name of Ed C. Berry, Antiquarian Bookseller, and a few others, will be graven on the true and eternal list of the Saints of God. I know that is true!"

"Assuming that such a list exists, outside of a Vatican computer file," said Ed, his face pinched and grey with anguish.

"You and I have lists like that inside our skulls," said Eve. "You know what has to be done as well as I do."

She walked through the small shop to the front door, followed by Ed, then turned and gave him a light but long kiss on the lips, hugging him tightly. Finally, she whispered in his ear, "The shepherd swains shall dance and sing For thy delights each May-morning: If these delights thy mind may move, Then live with me and be my love," and as he stood, now totally unable to speak, said, "Good-bye, dearest Ed," and stepped out the door.

Beacon Hill was dank and dark and Joy Street deserted when Eve stepped out of Ed's building. A large, low-pressure air mass hung sullenly along the New England coast and the air conditioners along the street whirred and dripped. Eve had decided to walk over the top of the Hill to Park Street, to see if she could tempt them. But as she walked quickly along in the oppressive heat, her face now a shine of sweat, she wondered what she would do if nothing happened, if she just got on the subway and went home, and no one was there either. She had thought about this before. Only that visitor knew if this was the right storm. If she went herself to the island, she thought, what would the men there do with her? She *had* to trust the visitor, she felt. And it *had* to get her there, or tell her when to come.

But now as she walked, she heard first the sound of footsteps coming along behind her, then the quiet engine noise of a car. It was a roving cab and Eve had a sudden sense of everything coming together.

On impulse, she stepped to the curb and hailed the prowling cab, just as the man walking behind her came up. The taxi stopped and Eve opened the back door to see a man sitting quietly on the far side of the rear seat. "Sorry," said Eve, "I thought this cab was . . ." but his hand came at her faster than she could avoid it and seized her right wrist. At the same moment, the man on the sidewalk caught her other arm and shoulder, doubled her over, and pushed her into the cab. "Dr. Pennington," he said in a low voice, "we're federal agents. Please don't make a fuss."

The door shut and the cab moved off swiftly. Eve found herself sprawled on the rear seat between two, large, business-suited men who seemed to be holding out identical wallets with identical gestures, each with a badge for her to inspect. Eve got herself sitting up, tucked her blouse back into her slacks, and rubbed her wrist where the man had seized it. She paid no attention whatever to the wallets or badges. "If either of you hurt me again," she said through her teeth, "I'll knee you in the balls. This is a kidnapping. I intend to put you both in jail."

The men put their wallets back into their inside pockets with identical gestures, and the one on her left dropped large, sweating palms down on even larger thighs. "We believe that you know perfectly well why we took you into custody, Dr. Pennington," he said in a flat, midwestern voice. "You can play charades if you choose, but don't expect us to join in."

"And where are we going?" said Eve, trying to sustain her anger and indignation, yet increasingly filled with excitement as she saw how closely events were duplicating what she had anticipated.

The large man stared at her in expressionless menace. "To a seaplane base over near Logan," he said in his flat voice. "From there we'll fly to Cape Cod."

They went rapidly through the tunnel and were soon pulling up to a dark and seemingly deserted dock complex where several seaplanes were located between two piers. A small, concrete-block building at the water's edge had a bit of light showing around some close-fitting shades. The two men, with the phony cabby right behind, walked Eve to the door of the building, each of them holding one of her upper arms in a light grip. When the door was swung open, the first person Eve saw standing by a desk was Jack Goldman.

Her eyes narrowed in renewed anger and she turned to look at the rest of the group. There were three other men, obviously not police officers but apparently bespectacled science-types or bureaucrats, and, next to Jack, stood Marta Hoerner in a trim pants suit, her eyes cold and focused, staring at Eve.

"Sorry to have to do this thing in such a manner, Dr. Pennington," said Marta Hoerner, "but I'm afraid you've been playing a little, solitary game with something rather important to world science."

Eve paid no attention to her. "Jack, why are you here?" she said in a frigid voice.

Dr. Hoerner answered for him. "Dr. Goldman has been most cooperative in this matter, once we explained the situation to him. We needed somebody to let us know where you were during that cruise in Maine. If the need had arisen, we would have had you back here, quite quickly."

"So, you've betrayed me to these insects, Jack," said Eve in a hard, bitter voice. "What was your price? Four more grad students? Extra time at Palomar? Two sabbaticals back-to-back?"

Jack's heavy lips twisted and his expression was sullen. "You're fooling around with something a whole lot bigger than either of us, Eve," he said, staring down at the floor. "You're supposed to be a scientist. What in hell did you think you were going to do? Hide the thing from us?"

His voice trailed off and Marta Hoerner spoke crisply. "Dr. Goldman knows that if we can achieve this contact and learn from that alien thing at Muskeget, all of astronomy, all science, may well be transformed."

"What utter bullshit!" said Eve, still glaring angrily at Jack.

Jack found this gaze difficult to withstand and he spoke again. "You might have been nicer to me, you know. You might have been more friendly. People get what they give."

"You mean that if I had put out on the cruise, you might have told me you were their fink?" said Eve hotly. "You're a liar and a weak bastard!" but Marta Hoerner held up her hand.

"I think we've had enough discussion on this subject. We're leaving for Martha's Vineyard at once, Dr. Pennington," she said in a loud, commanding voice. "I don't want to handcuff you in the plane, but if you are objecting to this, I see no choice."

"I never told you I objected to going to Muskeget, did I?" said Eve. "Damn right I want to go, so let's do it!" but she saw that Marta Hoerner had been made both thoughtful and concerned by this needless bravado, and added quickly in a low voice, "I don't want to be handcuffed in a plane. I won't interfere with the trip. You have my word, for whatever it's worth."

Marta Hoerner nodded curtly, then turned to the others. "Very well. Dr. Pennington and I, plus you two . . ." she gestured to the silent, hulking policemen, "will go in one plane, Dr. Goldman and the rest of you in the other."

For a moment, Eve frowned in dismay. She had gradually realized what would probably happen, indeed what must happen, on Muskeget, and had tried to ready herself, but Jack Goldman was, in spite of his treachery, another matter. "Jack is going too?" she asked in a small, almost-frightened voice.

Marta Hoerner turned to stare suspiciously at Eve. "He's deeply involved in this, Dr. Pennington. We think everybody should be there, all the people who have had, shall we say, relations with the island."

Eve nodded, steeling herself, and they all trooped out on the dark piers to the two float planes at the end, which now had been pulled alongside the docks so the passengers could climb aboard. Marta Hoerner and Eve were settled in the middle of a six-passenger, single-engined Airtraveler with the two big police officers located one up front with the pilot and one behind Eve in the rear seat. The plane taxied away from the dock, the engine revved, and they took off, roaring down a bright, moonlit path of calm water and up into fog wisps that hung just above the land-sea junction.

As soon as they reached cruising altitude and the engine noise had dropped away, Eve turned to Dr. Hoerner. "Did you people kill Noel Fenwick?" she said in a calm, frozen voice.

The older woman looked at her from dark, hooded eyes. "Hardly. It was the other way around, I'm afraid. Dr. Fenwick apparently turned against us. Two of the men lost off that yacht were my closest colleagues. Fenwick tried to convince me to come on that junket too, but I was suspicious after his drugged performance at your place in Hampstead."

"Then there is no alien in the Western Isles of Scotland?" said Eve, trying to maintain an air of modest, if hostile, interest.

Marta Hoerner shrugged. "We believe there probably was one there, but it clearly expired from storm effects or natural causes fifty or more years ago. Noel Fenwick, being the only one who was able to directly communicate with the Muskeget alien, as far as we know, had us at a disadvantage. By that I mean he could tell us things that we had no way of verifying independently ourselves. No bodies from that yacht were ever found. My belief is that Fenwick killed our people and the hired captain, threw them over the side, and went over during the storm himself."

"Why would he do that?" said Eve.

"For the same reasons that you have apparently decided to go your own, private, little way in this matter. A hundred years ago they called people like you Luddites. Fortunately, most of us believe that intellectual progress and scientific truth are the rational, the only, paths in the present situation."

"How did Noel communicate with the Muskeget

alien?" asked Eve, managing to hold her temper strictly in check.

Marta Hoerner's stern, old face twisted in disgust and contempt. "Last summer, Fenwick and a young, male friend went ashore on the island. Fenwick had chartered a yacht to cruise around Cape Cod waters. They engaged in repetitive, sexual activity there, augmented by the alien's electromagnetic intervention, and at some point, Fenwick . . . he was a secret heroin addict in addition to his other defects . . . found he could write whole messages on the beach sand to himself, apparently by simply letting himself go into a drug-induced, or sexually induced, stupor."

"What the psychics used to call automatic writing," said Eve in a low voice.

Dr. Hoerner nodded. "The alien suborned Fenwick, bought him body and soul by feeding him a succession of sexual kicks. In return, Fenwick did it some favors, such as setting up the book auction situation. We were already watching the island and this summer we made common cause with our British associates. They finally realized that if they were to gain anything from this, it would have to be as our partners since, geographically, we control the area and any access to it. I had hoped to have Fenwick, drugged if necessary, as a possible communications link with the alien, but his madness and self-hatred have made that impossible."

The plane flew on through the hot, dark night and Eve was silent for a minute. She took a deep breath and turned again to Dr. Hoerner. "Can you communicate with it in any way?" she asked.

Marta Hoerner shook her head. "The complexity of the thing's mental-projection abilities is simply staggering, yet it either cannot, or will not, attempt any direct sort of mental conversation, beyond what it did with Fenwick. This month we have finally installed a receiving and detection system on Muskeget that lets us determine when it is mentally active. That is, when it is doing something, but the problem is to assign a given purpose or intent to these immensely complicated signals. It modulates across the entire electromagnetic spectrum in all three ways simultaneously; phase, frequency, and amplitude, but we are unable as yet to separate out specific components as they activate human mental processes. I believe that it is able to stimulate brain activity, in higher life-forms at least, so that we actually broadcast, or read out, parts of our thoughts or memories to it. There's a definite suggestion of some sort of activation and scanning technique. Of course the electromagnetic signals generated from our heads are weak indeed, but reception sensitivity is obviously the alien's most remarkable ability."

"So that's how it reads minds," said Eve thoughtfully, "by forcing us to broadcast specific things back to it. And we never know when that is happening."

"Think what that would mean to the criminal justice system," said Marta Hoerner, "providing we can modernize the self-incrimination amendment. Or maybe that wouldn't be necessary. Proving intent, detecting intent, is the whole problem! There are dozens of revolutions hidden under that Muskeget sandbar!"

Eve bit her lip to stop an angry retort. "How do I fit into this?" she said finally.

Dr. Hoerner's eyes narrowed and her mouth became a hard line. "Oh, I think you know that perfectly well, Dr. Pennington. You and the hurricane are coming to

Muskeget together. Noel Fenwick knew that, since the thing told him that it needed whoever bought that book at the auction and that the book would explain why. Your friends, Mr. McPherson and Mr. Berry, surely understand it, as did Miranda Street, whose history we have followed with the same interest that you have shown. We can see only one explanation. When its home is threatened, it is programmed to electromagnetically transfer its essential self, that is, its mental instructions and abilities, away from danger. The attempt to do this with Miranda Street failed, obviously because the storm failed to destroy Muskeget and the transfer was unnecessary. But its marvelous senses and computational abilities have told it that another storm is chronologically close, and it has carefully prepared its line of retreat . . . you."

Eve's heart gave some wild, extra beats. How *much* they knew! she thought in silent panic. Yet, what had the bitch said, a line of retreat? They knew most of it, but not the essential, final part; that the alien didn't want to retreat, that it wanted to die.

She waited to speak until her voice was calm. "But why would you even want me to participate? It must be obvious that I despise what you're doing, and will never cooperate in unleashing this awful stuff on the world?"

Dr. Hoerner stared out at the black sky. "If it could accomplish this escape with anyone, it would hardly go through such complicated preparations with each of you. I believe that it finds the kind of mental affinity it needs to make a transfer in very few humans. Furthermore, it seems to need a very close and intimate nearness to prepare both itself, and the human mind, for what will come. Miranda Street had what was clearly an intense sexual experience with her husband-to-be on Muskeget. You and Jack Goldman engaged in intense, sexual activity on Muskeget last summer. In fact, you discussed this exact visit with Dr. Goldman during your Maine cruise this summer, and at considerable length."

Eve's eyes frosted over. "Dear me, I'm afraid that Jack has kissed and told. What a naughty boy he is," she said in her coldest and thinnest voice. "But, how do you know it isn't Jack that the alien wants to join forces with, since he seems to be the one who claims our screwing was so terrific?"

Dr. Hoerner turned to look at Eve with a narrow smile. "We *don't* actually know, Dr. Pennington. That's why Dr. Goldman is in the other plane."

Eve rubbed her hands and stared at her lap. "So you plan to whisk us away after the big moment occurs, but before the island is submerged, is that the idea?"

"Of course. It seems unlikely that the transfer will occur too late. That would make the whole, elaborate preparation involving first Miranda Street, then you, completely meaningless. And we have positive and reliable ways of escaping from the island, even close to its final moments." Marta Hoerner's eyes glittered in excitement. "I believe that Fenwick was correct in his assessments of the alien. It is a constructed thing, with abilities perhaps even more remarkable than those of its constructors. They would have to plan for a transfer to a new, local, and mobile host involving at least some of its many powers. But after this has happened, we will have a combined alien and human, something or somebody with whom we can talk. In other words, we can monitor brain activity at the same time that the host will be, perhaps, reading our minds. Once that kind of correlation, signal-to-effect, becomes possible, what follows will be, quite simply, revolutionary, perhaps even leading to a world that finally runs in a safe and rational manner."

Eve made no answer, though her heart grew cold, and they flew on in silence.

The moon was low when they came in to land, but Eve recognized the place as Cape Pogue Bay on Chappaquiddick Island, just east of Martha's Vineyard and west of Muskeget a few miles. Marta Hoerner turned to Eve as they skimmed over the water to touch with a mild thump. "From here we'll go to Muskeget in two water-jet boats. We can put them right up on the beach there. And they can make almost forty knots if we need that, so we should be able to get clear of the storm, unless the alien simply miscalculates and waits too long." Dr. Hoerner's eyes were bright and her face intent.

The two planes taxied up to a lighted pier, where several men waited to tie them up. Eve saw that this compound of docks and small, white, prefab buildings was backed by a high, barbed-wire fence, and that several signs had been set up in the pond itself warning boaters not to come near the piers or the secured shore. The two large policemen made no attempt to stay near her, and Eve saw that she was completely on the enemy's turf from now on. They entered a small building where a coffee machine, plates, and other eating equipment rested on tables.

"I think we all should have some food," said Marta Hoerner imperiously, indicating the icebox and other parts of the makeshift kitchen. She then quickly introduced Eve to the three men who had flown with Jack in the other plane. They turned out to be two academics from the Coast and one from England, all with Ph.D.s, and Eve, though two of them tentatively held out their hands, nodded stiffly at each one, her hands stiffly down at her sides. They were obviously nervous and uncomfortable, and Eve dearly wanted to give them the same "you will go to jail" threat she had used on the policemen, but she saw no point in making things any more complicated than they seemed to be getting already. Were they corrupted by fear, about their jobs or their reputations, bought by promises of academic sugarplums, or were they besotted, like Marta Hoerner, with the idea of running the world in a scientific manner? One would soon get you to the others, Eve thought, and her gaze was so steady and contemptuous that the three men, and Jack too, escaped to a table where they became very busy making sandwiches and heating frozen French fries in a microwave oven.

After the late meal, Eve was conducted to a small bedroom where she was locked in. I'll never sleep, she thought, yet when her head touched the pillow, she was seized by a pleasant lethargy, a feeling of complete relaxation. If you're doing that, she thought to the alien, thanks.

At dawn they came and roused her, and gave her a slicker and a life jacket. Once again she went in the lead boat with Marta Hoerner and the two policemen. The jet boat was driven by a twelve-inch-diameter column of water that squirted directly back from the stern just above the water surface. The jet was steerable and the boat, though over thirty feet in length, could run in water only deep enough to supply its pump intakes. They soared out of Cape Pogue Bay and then around the lighthouse at the northern end of Chappaquiddick. The course was direct to Muskeget and they passed rapidly through rips and over shoals only one or two feet deep. Marta Hoerner drove the big speedboat with a commanding air and soon they were abreast of Muskeget. She turned them suddenly, slowed up, and ran the boat up onto a smooth, sandy beach.

A gangway was dropped, which allowed them to walk down onto the sand, and as Eve turned toward the small complex of low concrete buildings that surrounded and joined with an older wooden hut, she saw that the two policemen, though still dressed in business suits, were obviously knowledgeable about preparing the boat for a quick departure. They set several anchors out on each side of the jet boat to hold it perpendicular to the beach line, so it could back right out rapidly when the moment came.

Marta Hoerner led the way into a much-repaired wooden hut, and inside, Eve saw that high tech had finally arrived at tiny Muskeget. There were racks of signal-processing and display equipment, the hum and chuff-chuff of a generator running nearby, and fluorescent lights in abundance, so that the whole room was bathed in a cool, white blast. Only one young man was there, sitting at a large and complex console of multiple scopes and multichannel tape decks.

"What about the storm?" asked Dr. Hoerner in a tight voice.

He shook his head. "They're still predicting that it will come by to the east, putting us on the calmer side, Dr. Hoerner."

"Look!" she said in a harsh, angry voice. "We're

assuming it's going to drift west. The point is, how long until it gets here?"

The young man peered at some numbers and then at a satellite weather map. "Eight hours at present velocity," he said, "but it's definitely accelerating."

"Could it be four hours?" said Marta Hoerner intently.

He nodded. "Yeah, I think so. If you take the present acceleration and the present velocity, four hours or so comes out."

By now the people off the other boat, plus the two big policemen, had arrived, and Marta Hoerner suddenly lifted her head and shouted, "Bring him in!"

Eve looked up startled. Who? Bring who in? In a moment she saw who, for a door opened from an adjoining room and she caught a sudden glimpse of a familiar figure. "Oh, *Ian!*" she said in complete shock. She almost added, "You too?" but then she saw him fully, his nose smashed down and broken, his shirt dark with bloodstains, his clothes torn and his face battered. He was handcuffed to another large, silent man in dungarees and a wool shirt.

"You bastards!" shouted Eve at the top of her voice, turning to run to Ian. "What in hell are you doing!" but the two policemen held her tightly, if carefully, and she lunged to get out of their grip.

"You shut up!" said Dr. Hoerner in a loud and harsh voice. She turned to Eve and now her face was completely cold and hostile. "I tried out one of our little theories on you in the plane, Dr. Pennington, but you seemed quite noncommittal, almost uninterested. The fact is, we think you know quite accurately what it is that the alien wants. Mr. McPherson probably does too, but he has been stubborn with us. Don't underestimate us, Dr. Pennington, the stakes in this are higher than you can possibly imagine!"

"I don't know what you're talking about, you old bitch!" said Eve through clenched teeth. "You've all gone absolutely crazy! Is this the way you're going to talk with something from another star . . ."

Marta Hoerner stepped up to Eve and suddenly caught one of her cheeks in a painful grip, pushing her face close to Eve's. "Shut up, I said! We're running out of time and I'm running out of patience. If what the alien needed to keep going was simply, uniquely you, then why would you remain in Boston? Why would you say you wanted to come to Muskeget? Why didn't you just go someplace else in the world and hide until the hurricane season was over and the alien eliminated? Why? Because that isn't quite what it wants or intends. Now, you're going to tell us exactly what it does want from you!"

She nodded at one of the men holding Eve, and he dropped her arm and stepped over to silent Ian, then suddenly ripped open his right shirt sleeve to the shoulder. The policeman lifted a small metal device, which looked like some sort of complicated handcuff, off a table. He suddenly closed it over Ian's forearm and activated a switch. In an instant, Ian gave a penetrating scream of pain and fell to his knees, his face awash with sweat, his eyes blind with agony.

Eve gave a great shout of anger and a great wrench and broke free of the large policeman holding her arm. She fell on her knees next to whimpering Ian, cradling his battered head in her arms. "Oh, darling Ian, I'm sorry! Oh, forgive me, dear Ian . . ."

"Get her away from him," said Dr. Hoerner in a

steady, ice-cold voice. "It shouldn't take long to find out what she knows. He has another arm and two legs."

But at that moment, an interlocking series of events were set in motion, implacable and deadly. First, the man at the data processing console gave a sudden grunt of surprise, then said in a loud voice, "Dr. Hoerner, we're suddenly getting all kinds of activity from it. I've never seen such strong signals. Hey, they're increasing . . . !"

Marta Hoerner turned to stare at the young engineer, but what she saw was that he had already half-risen in his chair, and his arms were stretched straight out from his sides, trembling and shaking. He tried to speak but could only manage a terrible confusion of, "*Help . . . uh, uh, aggghh, hel-l-l, uh, ahhgh . . . ,*" as he struggled, half-erect, his face distorted in terror. His arms came unsteadily forward, moving uncertainly and jerkily, until his hands hooked around the two, U-shaped handles of one of the rack modules in front of him, not in any sort of grip but more like two flabby hooks. The moment the hands were in position, the man's body stiffened and he gave a violent lunge directly backward. The two hands and fingers were now locked rigid and they jerked the module, which was the main power supply for the entire console of instruments, out of its rack, trailing snapping cables and blue sparks. The man's body jackknifed open as he went over backward, and the heavy power supply unit smashed down on his face and head as he hit the floor. The sparking short circuits shut down the generator and the bright fluorescents dimmed, blinked and went out, to be replaced by four emergency battery lanterns up in the room corners. The little space was now much dimmer and more shadowy.

"Oh, no, you don't!" said Dr. Hoerner in a sharp,

savage hiss. "Stop this or I'll kill her! Stop! I swear I'll kill her!" and she lunged toward Eve with a pistol she had taken from her handbag. The gun swung toward Eve's head as Marta Hoerner's face distorted in fear and rage, but the motion was never completed. Instead, Dr. Hoerner began to gag and mewl and froth in a quite dreadful way, fighting her own gun arm as it began to slowly turn toward her own face.

A similar thing was happening to the man handcuffed to Ian, who had also pulled a gun from an upside-down armpit holster with his free hand. No one else seemed able to move, as both Marta Hoerner and the policeman gasped and gagged and fought their own betraying muscles. The guns turned slowly and irrevocably toward the two distorted, terror-filled faces and both mouths wrenched open in a gagging rictus to accept the muzzles. Their fingers, which had been locked immobile until then, closed convulsively on the weapons' grips and triggers.

Eve buried her face in Ian's shoulder with a sharp suck of breath as the back of Dr. Hoerner's head blew off with a spatter of blood and bone. A moment later the second explosion came from the man standing next to them and his bigger weapon, not quite so well aligned when it fired, took out most of the left side of his head plus his left eye.

The man fell like a sack beside them, but Dr. Hoerner's corpse did not fall. Instead, it turned, one foot sliding awkwardly in front of the other, and began a tentative shuffle toward the outside door. Its hands fell to its sides. Its gun dropped on the floor, and it moved unsteadily forward. The body of the young engineer, who had pulled out the power supply, rolled over and got up on its knees. After several clumsy attempts, though its face was now little more than a mass of blood and bone from the smash of the heavy, metal module, it began a shuffling, agonizing crawl toward the door as well. And the others were moving, tentatively but unmistakably, one foot in front of the other, all heading for the door at various slow rates of progress.

Eve felt Ian's arms close tightly around her and his lips caress her cheek and ear. "It took away all my hurts," he whispered. "Look! Oh, my God! See how quickly it learns to walk them! See! See!"

It was true. Even the mobile horror that had been Dr. Hoerner was moving more rapidly, its shuffling steps longer and more assured, but Eve turned from that and peered at Ian's left arm, which was still handcuffed to the fallen policeman. "We've got to get that handcuff off you," she said urgently. Turning her head away from the man, she knelt and patted his pockets. "Damn! Where are his keys?" she muttered, forcing herself to push her hands deep into his dungaree and shirt pockets. "Where in hell are they?" she muttered. She jumped up and darted over to where Dr. Hoerner had dropped her small gun, seized it and dashed back to kneel in front of Ian, trying not to look at the man lying next to him.

"Oh, lordy," she said, half to herself. "Johnny, did we ever do cuffs like these? Oh, help me, baby!" She lifted Ian's arm and the cuff and smartly hit the latch three times from different angles with the gun butt. It instantly flew open. "Thanks, Johnny," she whispered, then gave a small scream of fright, for the dead man, now free of Ian, was trying to turn from its back to its stomach. It finally succeeded and began a slow, awkward crawl after the others.

Eve and Ian got unsteadily to their feet and stood staring at the shuffling, crawling throng. "We're in a damn zombie movie!" breathed Eve, but then she saw that Jack too was moving with halting steps along with the others, but where they all stared straight ahead, he looked back at her, his face a mask of imploring terror. "Oh, Jack!" she breathed, but she did not move toward him, and suddenly Jack's head was twisted forward again, inexorably and jerkily, and when he reached the door, he followed the others out into the beach grass.

Eve and Ian, their arms tight around each other, followed slowly behind the shuffling group. Some had fallen in the sand and were now crawling since the alien still seemed to lack the control to get people up on their feet, but the procession was moving more and more rapidly, down through the beach grass and poison ivy and down across the sandy beach, heading for the northwestern tip of beach around which a rapid tidal current swirled. The walkers reached the water's edge first, with Marta Hoerner's corpse in the lead, and it did not pause but moved on, one foot sliding in front of the other, and the water rose to knees, then to waists. The Hoerner body suddenly fell forward and was swept out of sight immediately, but Jack Goldman, the two large policemen, and one of the California scientists continued unsteadily on, until they could no longer make headway against the current. As he finally fell over, Jack managed to look back once more, but it was too dark for Eve to see his expression. As soon as his mouth went underwater he convulsively inhaled a full inspiration of seawater and drowned at once, as did the other three men.

The crawlers moved more slowly, but once in the shallow water they were swept off, one after another. In a few moments, Eve and Ian stood alone on the dark, blustery northern shore of tiny Muskeget Island, tightly hugging each other, paralyzed by shock, shivering in fright, yet taking comfort in each other's nearness.

Without a word they turned and walked back into the dim, disheveled room, and as she reached the door, Eve's eyes lit on the torture device they had used on Ian's arm. In a sudden, blinding rage she ran and seized the small, heavy thing, then ran back to the door and threw it as far as she could out into the water where the walkers and crawlers had disappeared. "Take your filthy toy with you, you rotten stinking bastards!" she shouted, wishing for a second that they were back so she could watch them drown themselves again.

Ian seized her shoulders. "We've got to get away from here! Can you run one of those boats, Eve?"

She hugged him to her, kissing his lips and cheeks. "Ian," she said, "we have a little time yet. Oh, my darling Ian, listen to me now, my beloved. You *must* listen!" They found a small bunk room adjoining the electronics work space and sat down on a cot, still hugging each other tightly, and Eve, with much kissing and murmuring, told Ian what Miranda Macy and Ben Stringfellow had concluded. All through it, Ian's head shook, back and forth, and he murmured, "No, no . . ." in a soft voice, but Eve, feeling stronger and more certain with each moment, persisted.

"Then I'll stay here too," said Ian positively when she finished.

"Ian, you still don't understand," said Eve, tears welling in her eyes. "You've become as much a part of this as I have, but staying isn't your role. I *have* to stay. It would never let me leave now because it must have someone here when it sees danger, and I'm the only one it can control at the end. If you stayed, it might, partly, come over into you too, and with those boats there, you'd run. It couldn't stop that with you, the way it can with me. And it might have to treat you like the others, and I simply couldn't stand that. The whole business might come apart. You've got to save yourself! The alien will help you drive the boat. It can *do* that! Ed is waiting, Ian. He'll get you back to England safe. You and Ed will comfort each other, tell others what happened, live and remember me. Ian, you must truly promise me you will escape and live. Truly, truly! That will make things happen the way it wants, the way I want. Promise, Ian. Without your promise, we're lost!"

Ian kissed her passionately but she persisted. "Promise me, Ian!"

He dropped his arms and shut his eyes tightly, squeezing out his tears. "All right, I promise," he whispered, then blinked and gasped.

"Beloved, what happened?" said Eve.

Ian peered at her, then around the room. "They broke my glasses while they were beating me up on the plane. But now, I can . . . can *see* as though I had them on!"

Eve hugged him. "It knows how much you mean to me, and it's helping you." She drew back and looked at him. "Can you bear to make love with me, now, for a moment, knowing you'll never see me again? It will help us with that too, I think. It won't be like Miranda and Horace, but it will be sweet, perhaps very sweet."

Ian nodded, rubbing his eyes. "I've got to stop crying first," he said in a choked voice, as she unbuttoned his shirt and then reached to open his belt.

As they lay together undressed on the cot, touching each other, Eve smoothed his bruised forehead and smiled at him. "Those nasties didn't help your handsome face, poor Ian, but the rest of you is still firm and strong," she said breathlessly. "Oh, come into me, my darling. See . . . *see* how slowly it's going! See . . . see . . . ahhh, you're bursting with love for me, my Ian!"

And though he knew that later the longing and the regret would be almost unbearable, Ian at that instant saw only beautiful Eve Pennington, saw into her open joy and her brave soul and her gentle boldness. He gave himself up to their pleasure completely and, though only a few actual minutes passed as they strove urgently and lovingly together, a lover's eternity passed for Ian and he knew that the alien had given him a final, perfect gift to take away and cherish.

After their long, intense moment passed and time began to run at its more normal pace, they lay together whispering and kissing, not wanting to end it. But the southeast wind was rising, blasting around the corners of the building with a fitful, sullen strength, and so Eve finally sat up and reached across Ian for her heap of clothes so rapidly discarded on the floor. They helped each other to dress and, finally, holding each other tightly, they walked back into the electronics space where Eve suddenly released him and ran to seize her purse from a table. She pulled out her wallet. "Here," she said. "This has almost a hundred dollars and the keys and directions to get you into Ed's secret side door. That's plenty of money to get you to Boston. Just tie the boat to some pier in Nantucket Harbor and get away from it, but try to be careful that no one sees you land who might identify you later. It should be easy. By now this storm will have most of them running in tiny circles of panic."

She handed the wallet to him, but then drew it back and reached into a pocket to remove the dangling shooting medal she had found on Muskeget. "I'll keep this here," she said. "Ed was right. Things have to be symmetrical, especially at the end."

She pushed the wallet into one of his pockets and gave him a slicker to put on.

"How will I find Nantucket Harbor?" said Ian, listening to the wind scream with a landsman's apprehension.

Eve just grinned. "Your course is one-twenty degrees magnetic, but it will get you there. Just stay alert and let things happen," she said in a positive voice. "Come on. This wind is starting to cook," and her face was filled with a firm anticipation.

Outside the blustery wind was warm and occasional gusts were strong enough to make walking difficult. The day was even darker, with thick, torn clouds blowing by close overhead. Eve led Ian to the first jet boat, then turned and kissed him in a final, loving farewell, but when he hesitated, she gently pushed him up the gangplank.

"I know you'll be sad, my beloved," she said, "but the sadness will fade and the hurts will heal. And what an adventure we've lived together, Ian! Holmes and Watson never imagined anything half so wonderful! Give my best love to dear, romantic Ed, and to Julia, and tell her old, corrupt Noel was a real hero after all. Good-bye, my Ian."

He climbed into the boat and pulled up the gangplank. "Start your engine," called Eve. Ian found that he knew, or his fingers knew, how this was done and soon the big diesel rumbled into powerful life. Eve ran around the boat, pulling out anchors and throwing them up over the gunwales, and when the boat was free, gave it a big push on the bow while shouting, "Reverse, Ian, reverse!"

He pulled back on a lever and a series of small, forward-aiming jets at the stern began to shoot water against the sand. "More throttle!" cried Eve and the boat suddenly scooted backward, while Ian turned the wheel to back it around, peering in bewilderment at his compass.

A grey-black rainsquall swept toward them, and Eve walked quickly over the sand back to the open door of the building, never taking her eyes from Ian and the boat. He got it turned southeast in a big slow circle, then began to go away from her faster and faster, and as he roared off into the squall, Eve had both hands up over her head, waving them rapidly in great sweeps until long after he was gone from sight.

She turned, went inside, and walked back to the cot on which she and Ian had made love only a few minutes before. "All right," she said in a firm voice, as she lay down on her back and let the shooting medal fall on the pillow next to her cheek, "I'm ready."

·13·

Two
Chronosequences

Hurricane Daisy was hooking to the west, heading for Buzzards Bay and the eastern Massachusetts shoreline. It was not an especially large storm and its rotary velocity was not exceptional, not much more than sixty miles an hour, but its forward velocity was also equal to this speed, so that winds on the eastern semicircle, where the velocities added, were blowing well over a hundred. But, in addition, the high forward speed piled up the ocean ahead of the storm and great waves began to run as forward consorts of the storm's eye, aiming their violent energies at the south coasts of Martha's Vineyard and Nantucket.

Muskeget Island was older than the Visitor by a hundred years or so, having been mainly piled together from an earlier, nearby sandspit called Sturgeon Island during some forgotten, stormy cataclysm. The chronosequence of its ecology, though interesting, was not especially varied, for the place was small and few species could prosper on such a thin, spare, and wave-swept strand, especially one that continuously moved. Yet this modest place had domiciled the most wonderful zoological specimen to ever live on the earth. At last the Visitor prepared to end its long and melancholy existence.

As the danger probability hardened rapidly, the Visitor began to enter Eve's conscious mind, to work with her forebrain. She fell into a quiet reverie as its scanning modulation became more intense. The one place where its Makers had allowed it almost total freedom of choice was in the matter of what data would be transferred in an emergency. Eve could not, nor indeed could any naturally evolved creature anywhere, contain and access the huge information store held by the Visitor. Its Makers had realized that only a Visitor, immersed in its particular, local situation, could judge what must come across to a local host and what must be left behind, although the basic, self-preservation and escape commands would always, and automatically, transfer. What the Makers had failed to realize, not that it mattered, since their huge vessel was lost and its constructed crew dead, was that these essential, first-priority commands could be overridden, in the particular cases of Eve and Miranda and perhaps a few others, by even stronger emotional interferences. On this modest programming, or structural, flaw, the Visitor had based its hundred-and-fifty-year search to terminate itself. It was programmed, at a totally determined level, to provide itself a host when danger threatened, and it had done so twice. But it chose the hosts. It was a small sliver of freedom, but an essential one if the Visitor was to succeed.

As the danger probability approached unity, the Visitor's automatic transfers of basic skills and survival imperatives to Eve's mind began, but simultaneously with these came, in a marvelous and intricate itemization only possible with designed, artificial, biological memories . . . other, detailed visions.

Eve looked from Miranda's eyes at the storm. She felt Miranda's fear, her impatient anger at herself, everything! She and Miranda were one, but with a huge difference. Eve knew what would happen, where it was all going; Miranda did not. So Eve savored the girl's fear, her shivering in the blast of the blizzard snow, her plucky hoisting of the lantern.

Eve peered with Horace into the white smother, the dory bucketing ahead, swooping and swaying over the steepening waves. Horace's gut was a tight knot of fear and he was wondering, quite forlornly, what mad vision impelled him out on such a dreadful night. He stared and stared ahead into the blinding, white sheets of snow. The dory was oversailed, barely steerable, and running wildly, much too fast for the ten-yard circle of visibility given by his masthead light.

Eve and Horace stared out, eyes pinched and streaming, to . . . what! Something black and big dead ahead! Horace shoved his tiller hard over but he was up on the wreck so quickly that he couldn't turn the dory up to windward fast enough and struck the side of the stranded schooner a heavy, glancing blow. Thump!

Thump! Eve heard that noise with Miranda too, and felt her heart squeeze in quick terror, for she thought the vessel was already starting to break apart. She dashed to the starboard side and peered over.

Horace, wincing at the sharp smash of the collision, staggered to his feet and reached to seize the side of the schooner, his dory pitching, banging, and rolling against it. He quickly reached up to tie his painter to a deadeye. Eve waited in both of them for that first, tender, astonishing moment.

Horace looked up. Miranda looked down.

"Horace!"

"Miranda!"

Eve's own heart expanded mightily with the sudden, uncontrollable joy that exploded inside Horace. How happy he was! How amazed! His courage was suddenly that of the fiercest lion. But in Miranda, her relief, gratitude, her own sudden happiness were mixed with something more intimate and deep; a lovely emptiness that would have to be filled, a lovely tenderness that would have to be shared.

For a long, perfect moment they peered, up and down, at each other in the frozen, blinding snow, and Eve felt the Visitor begin its gentle, powerful work on both of them. Miranda quickly hoisted her thick, long skirts and climbed capably over the schooner's rail with a brief, dim flash of petticoats and long, white-stockinged legs that set a thunderous pulse going inside Horace as he reached to catch her.

"Here I come," she called in her high, strong voice. "Ready or not!" and she jumped down to where he held his arms up. Horace caught her, felt her strong, soft body slide through his arms, felt her warmth against him, felt her own arms clutch his shoulders and one hand brush his cheek in what, to Horace, was a touch of fire, so that he caught his breath in a semiparalysis of delight.

Miranda, feeling that wide, strong chest against her softer one, seemed to stumble in the banging, bumping dory and clutched him all the tighter, looking up into his face and saying with almost a sigh, "Oh, thank you, Horace."

They stood in the thumping, rolling dory together, sharing that first embrace, until Miranda blinked, then grinned up at him. "Can we get to shore, Horace?" she said. "Muskeget must be about to leeward?"

Horace, intent on her close and dear face, also blinked and finally managed a fairly stern, if perfunctory, "Is there anyone else aboard, Miranda?"

She shook her head and spoke angrily. "They locked me in a cabin and ran away in the only boat. They're wreckers, Horace!" But since nothing seemed to be happening grinned at him again. "We'd better start," she said softly. "It's getting worse."

Horace absently shook his head, then collected himself, nodded, and let her go. "Stay on that middle thwart and hang on with both hands. Keep your head down. Here we go!" He untied and then pushed off the dory from the schooner, weathered around with a tremendous bang of sail and booms, then set off rapidly downwind, the blizzard screaming at their backs. The collision with the schooner had split several of the planks at the dory's bow, and Miranda was soon down on her cold, wet knees in a foot of chilly water, bailing steadily.

Horace watched his compass and fought with his tiller, now cursing himself for not shortening sail while he was at the schooner. With each of them rode Eve, seeing with growing pleasure how the two, beautiful flowers of lust and desire and love were opening their petals. The Visitor was creating a masterpiece of tenderness, of surrender, step by step, and the bluster and roar of the storm, the cold, wet run of the dory, the freezing water splashing all about them only served its purposes with perfect efficiency.

Horace saw that the waves were shortening, becoming steeper, and he stared out, his eyes aching from the concentration. The world was completely white. He was steering in a white smother. Then, the darker loom of shore appeared in a flash ahead of him, and they came in at tremendous speed, riding the crest of a big breaker.

"Hang on, Miranda!" he shouted, then gave a triumphant, exultant, small-boy *"Wheeee!"* as the dory scooted up the Muskeget beach like a toboggan on the slick, new snow, stopping with a sudden jolt only when its bow struck the rise of a low ridge of grass at the edge of the bank. Miranda, paying complete attention to her bailer, was taken by surprise and thrown down on the floor of the dory into the water and was now completely soaked.

Horace jumped out of the dory in an instant, spent ten seconds dropping and lashing the sail and tossing an anchor out into the grass, then reached and scooped Miranda into his arms and began a run to the humane house that lay about fifty yards to their right.

By the time they arrived, the run had turned into a rapid walk, but panting Horace did not put her down until they reached the door, and by then his warm fingers had a sense of her trim yet pliable waist and the smooth length of her round thighs.

They pushed in the door, gasping from cold and excitement, and peered about the little room. "I'll get a fire going. I've got some lucifers," said Horace, "and you find some blankets or something. Your dad still keeps this place in shape." Like all surfmen, who never know where they might come ashore, Horace always carried a waterproof match case. Soon a fire of shavings and twigs was roaring in the big, iron stove and Horace was loading in larger pieces of driftwood.

Miranda, shivering now almost uncontrollably, lit a kerosene lantern and opened a wooden chest in the corner with trembling hands. "Oh, good! Here's some cotton blankets," she muttered through chattering teeth. She lifted several out and ran back to Horace at the stove. "I've got to get my things off, Horace. I'm soaked and freezing," she said. "Here, you hold the blanket up so's I can stand next to the stove. . . . No peeking now," she added coquettishly.

But now Eve found herself within two additional personalities, Major Horace Street and his stylish, handsome, middle-aged wife, Miranda, alone on a hot, balmy summer holiday, their picnic ended, undressing for a swim. And in an instant, Eve knew them completely, as completely as she knew their younger selves and, though there was pain and sadness and disappointment in this older pair, Eve paid no attention to that.

Major Street and Surfman Street were both holding a blanket high so that both Mirandas could drop their clothes, one garment after another, on the floor, and what one man knew would happen, the other dearly hoped would happen, and both were filled with a near-unbearable anticipation.

The Mirandas shed their clothes as fast as they could be removed, but as the final underthings were dropped, they undressed a bit more slowly. Old Miranda looked down at her younger body with her younger self, and down at her own, older body as well. She saw them both to be shapely, soft and desirable, and they merged in a kind of dream of shapes, one slipping roundly into the other. The two Mirandas briefly yet warmly touched themselves and stared at the blanket with expressions of, almost, impatience.

Then, each reached with two hands and took the dangling blanket from the two Horaces. Young Miranda wrapped herself in it and reached to hold up a second one for Horace, but old Miranda simply took the same blanket, standing naked in the warm summer air behind it. Each said in a soft, breathless voice, "Now it's your turn to get your wet stuff off, Horace."

For the young Horace Street, this undressing became a matter of great embarrassment, for it was obvious when he wriggled out of his long, wet underwear that he was immensely excited, and so he turned to put his back to the blanket. He felt dismay lest Miranda should peek, catch a glimpse, and possibly faint. Major Street did this too, but he savored and delighted in his own, earlier embarrassment. The two Mirandas said to each of them, in voices so soft and filled with such desire that the men's hearts melted, "Turn around, please, Horace. You are wonderfully handsome. I want to see all of you."

Most of the Visitor's activity was directed by its underlying programming. It was bound to activate, and with increasing strength, the escape commands it had transferred to Eve. The timing was now clearly urgent and the mental alarm bells were ringing loud underneath the humane house episodes. Eve had proved wonderfully able to accept and process the Miranda and Horace details, even though the Visitor had carefully prepared her for this through the documents, but now she was starting to twitch in and out of the experiences.

The wind had become a heavy, menacing roar and this sound of menace tended to assist the programmed escape imperatives. Eve wondered about the roar.

The Visitor had anticipated this and it was as ready as it could be, considering the unlooked-for death of Priscilla Pennington and many other difficulties. This was the Visitor's final card, its final and strongest interference, for it was Eve's own experience. The Visitor began its most detailed information transfer yet into Eve Pennington's fragmenting mind.

Eve now joined with two more personalities, two young, gawky, pretty girls in shorts and T-shirts, walking to have a picnic lunch in the tiny, decrepit, wooden house. Eve gave a sigh of total recognition. Prissy's sweet, heart-shaped face was so dear to her that for a moment she was overwhelmed by the nearness of it, the total completeness of the vision. Except that it was not a vision. It was happening, all these things were happening and happening together, and she was at the core of them all, inside of everyone.

They each gripped a handle of the big, swinging picnic basket. "We will be the queens of Muskeget," said Prissy, with a huge smile at her sister, and Eve looked in delight into her own, younger and smaller face, her big white teeth and the freckles on a tilted, peeling nose.

"And the little house will be our castle," said young Evie at once, "and the birds our subjects and courtiers. See, they go to announce our return." The girls entered the dim, little house with their picnic hamper and carefully set out the feast, using an old blanket to cover the shattered, splintery floor, and as they did so, older Eve saw how gently and yet urgently the Visitor joined them, how the sense of happiness and love grew large and round between them. As they ate, they peered into each other's faces, laughing and giggling at first, but then with more and more loving and tender expressions. The sandwiches had never tasted better, nor the lemonade sweeter.

Finally, Prissy looked into Evie's soft eyes with her own soft glance and rubbed her sticky hands together. "I'm done for a minute, Evie. Those were yummy!" she said in her young, sweet voice.

"Let's save our last sandwiches and go for a swim now," said Evie. "C'mon, let's get undressed and go skinny-dipping. The water's like a bathtub!" and in a moment they had peeled their clothes off into two small piles on the blanket and they stood, close together, staring at each other's slim, nicely budding form with a love that older Eve welcomed, even though she knew it would finally consume her.

As Muskeget's chronosequence neared its end, Eve Pennington's essential, inner chronosequence diverged from that of her surroundings. The rate processes that she was experiencing were so detailed and stretched that her inner time began to run more and more slowly. The hurricane was lunging north and west, its eye now aimed at a landfall on the west side of Buzzards Bay, but as the terminal phase of its place of exile neared, the threatened Visitor was able to use more and more extensive data-transfer rates. Eve's own personality began to completely fragment as she received the Visitor's stored data with ever-greater detail. Her sense of being an observer, an all-knowing and withdrawn participant, remained, but all control on the direction of her thoughts or the use of her mind slipped away, and she became totally and simultaneously submerged in all six of the personalities that the Visitor had so lovingly stored, awaiting this moment. And all six of these recalled individuals were moving, at slower and slower rates, toward their individual, and collective, piercingly sweet surrenders.

Horace turned and saw, with embarrassed delight, that Miranda was not wrapped in a blanket, nor did she hold one in front of her, but that she stood, empty-handed, with her arms out toward him. Her beautiful body was completely open and he took, and was given, an eon, vast stretches of time, to contemplate her shape, the round perfection of her breasts, the gentle curve of her belly. And as he stared, Miranda saw her lovely self along with him, and she delighted in all the special curves and shapes that he found and studied, the shadows and edges and soft junctions he continuously constructed out of her beauty, and the fierce desire it all drove like a roaring engine inside him.

Yet Horace was a shy and modest young man, and his face burned as he peered at his beloved, for he knew he stood close in front of her, huge and rampant with desire. But that flush gradually faded for now he could see himself from inside Miranda, and he saw and felt how that thing that so shamed him, only passionately excited her. How *much* she desired to share that strong and ready part of him! Tears flowed in Major Street's eyes as he also saw these things, as they were and as they had been, but they were not tears of regret at a loss, but tears of joy that they could at last renew the wonderful desire they had shared so long before.

And both Mirandas reached and gently took their lovers where the core of their desire stood, and moved closer to sweetly join themselves with their men. "You have saved me, darling Horace," they said. "Now you must completely fill me with your love. I desire you passionately. I love you dearly, my hero, oh, *hero* of my heart!"

Prissy sank gracefully down on the blanket and held up her hand to her sister. "Let's talk a minute before we swim," she said quietly, and as Eve dropped down beside her, she gently touched Eve's breasts. "You're going to be lovely up there, Evie," she said in a loving, passionate voice. Eve deeply saw how much Prissy loved her, how much she wanted to touch her, and she delightedly touched her in return.

"Oh, you too," she said. "Yours are so high and nicely far apart. How beautiful you are, Prissy! I love you dearly!"

They did not speak for a while, but kissed tenderly, then more closely, and as they hugged, they lay down so they could touch more fully along their thin, smooth bodies. "How happy we are!" sighed Prissy. "I can see your happiness, Evie, inside you. Oh, and you can see mine!"

"I've never felt like this, have you, Prissy?" said Evie. "So *happy*. So beautifully, wonderfully happy!" and the two sisters looked into each other's faces from solemn yet tender expressions that seemed to young Eve something she could not bare to watch for even a second, yet something she would never wish to leave.

The tremendously long waves leading the hurricane, driven by the unusually high forward velocity of the storm, were coming over the edge of the continental shelf, and as they felt the bottom, they began to rise and shorten. Up they mounted, larger and steeper, as they drove wildly toward the shores of the south Cape Cod islands. The Visitor's probability estimates had reached one-hundred percent. There was no longer doubt. Muskeget's chronosequence was absolutely ending. The Visitor increased its bit-transfer rate to Eve to its maximum, rapidly moving all the essential skills and identity keys into its new host. The original Visitor would, of course, be destroyed when the waves struck, but it was reconstituting its basic self inside Eve's mind. The second jet boat hung in the blasting, screaming wind, still hanging on its anchors, now completely afloat in the rising water, but the original, or Muskeget, Visitor continued to prevent what had become the Eve Pennington Visitor from taking any self-protective actions by continuing the transfer and reconstruction, ever more detailed, of the six personalities.

Eve's personal chronosequence was approaching a zero-rate process, and the detail and time stretching she was undergoing were beyond anything a human being had ever before experienced. Eve was becoming, within her own inner context, immortal.

As the Mirandas felt the Horaces enter them, a millennium of delightful sensations passed through them all. They saw the wonderful, sought-for junction mirrored in each other's minds and bodies. The detail was slow, the complete firm and gentle thrust taking longer than an entire age of the world. It seemed possible then that they would succeed where all other lovers had failed, to utterly possess one another, forever.

But now, at the center of the experiences, Evie and Prissy set forth on their final, tender journey. Geological time spans opened as they caressed and kissed. Whole cosmos spun into life, evolved, and finally flew off into nothingness. And though it never seemed that it would finally happen, Prissy and Evie felt twin bubbles, expansions of joy, growing and blooming, and Prissy said breathlessly to her sister, "Something lovely is going to happen to us! I see it in you too, Evie!"

The approaching joy opened and bloomed in them all, stretching and extending, finally becoming so large, so ready to burst them asunder, that Horace could only say, taking nearly forever to say it, "Ahhhh, Miranda, we're finally, truly one, aren't we?"

And Evie, feeling her pleasure growing larger than her body, larger than Muskeget or the whole world, gasped, "This little kingdom will be just ours. We two. Say that it will, Prissy!"

The first great wave lifted and curled as it came over the coastal shallows, mounted ever higher in the screaming, roaring wind, rising in stormy rage against the blocking islands. But for Eve Pennington it never actually struck, for her spiritual chronosequence had almost completely stopped. The bubbles of joy inside them all were finally bursting, endlessly bursting, bursting forever. When the Mirandas and Prissy answered their lovers at that final moment of climax with the single word, "Always!" they defined the meaning of that word in a way never before or again achieved. It was always for Eve and it lasted forever, but in the chronosequence of the world, in the briefest instant, the wave struck Muskeget Island a savage, irremediable blow, scouring it down to cobbles and sand, sweeping vegetation, houses, and boats away in a fifty-foot-high white horror of total destruction. Yet what it finally swept off was only a dead, useless husk, for in that final moment, Eve Pennington's warm and gallant heart burst apart.

The Muskeget Visitor, or parts of it, lived a few moments longer, for it was the third of the huge, hurricane-driven waves that had achieved the most fear-some and deadly energy integration, and it crested gigantically south of the island a hundred yards or so, coming down and across it to smash and disperse the glacier-deposited stones and cobbles completely away to the north.

So shattering was that explosive landfall that seismographs throughout the country recorded in tiny ink squiggles the most devastating and powerful wind wave ever to strike the New England coast, at least during the four-hundred-year chronosequence of Muskeget Island.

Where the island and its sand shoals had stood now lay an open roadstead, a new passage into the sounds from the ocean, ten feet or more deep. Yet when its sought-for ending came in that huge smash, the Visitor did not expand its own, inner chronosequence, but leaving behind its failures and its loneliness, faced and welcomed the huge wave with a final, intense satisfaction. It had learned from men and women, over the centuries of its visit, the terrible nature of cruelty, pain and despair, but these it set aside at last, so that in its complex and intricate mental structures, it held foremost during that final millisecond only to what Eve and Miranda had finally taught it; only sweet joy and sweeter surrender.

·14·

EPILOGUE

Julia Stetson had waited all day for Ian, so when the buzzer finally went in her Hampstead flat at ten in the evening, she dashed to push the lock button, then opened her door and rushed out onto the landing to look down the stairwell. As Ian trudged around and upward, now peering up at her, she gave a loud, "What in hell happened to you?" for Ian's nose was heavily bandaged and the rest of his face was still puffy and blue in spots.

He finally reached her floor, gave her a long hug and a light kiss, and grinned around some cheek bruises. "Just a little American law and order," he said cheerfully. "Listen, can I have a big drink? They kept trying to dose me with cheap scotch at M-6 or M-9 or wherever the hell I was, but I wanted to stay sober then. Now I don't."

"Me neither!" said Julia, darting out to her icebox. "I was ready to call the Foreign Office again. They kept you ten hours down there! I'm already quite a ways out in front."

Ian slumped into an armchair and looked around the flat with a melancholy glance as he pictured Eve and

304 • HILBERT SCHENCK

himself there on those two treasured and intimate
nights. He reached for the stiff gin and tonic, then the fat
hash reefer gratefully. "Coffee too, please. We've got to
talk, Julia. I want you to know it all in case those
wonderful Yanks come and find me again, all of a
sudden."

"So, our people are back to those nasty tricks?" said
Julia. "Somebody must have cloned Nixon."

"Well, they bit off more than they could handle, for
once," said Ian, leaning to take a sandwich off a heaped
plate that Julia put by his elbow.

She stood looking down at him. Finally she spoke in a
small and empty voice. "It's really true? Eve is really
gone?"

Ian nodded and blinked back some tears. "I was there,
the last to see her. I knew the exact moment it happened,
Julia."

Julia dropped into a low, soft chair across from Ian
and took a long pull on her joint, then a longer pull on
her drink. "Okay, give me the whole thing," she said.
"Eve always thought I was tough as hell. Let's see how
much of this I can handle."

Julia knew most of the earlier parts, about the books
and the first contact with Mrs. Stringfellow, so Ian went
on with what he had learned in Boston from Ed Berry
and what Eve had quickly told him on Muskeget about
Noel Fenwick's last cruise.

Julia sighed and frowned. "Poor, old Noel. So he was a
hero after all?" she said.

"Quite a large one, actually," said Ian. "One of those
men he, uh, removed was a Nobel-level big shot in
neurological data processing. Of the bunch of them, that
fellow might have made some dangerous discoveries on

Muskeget before the end of the summer. As it was, only nasty Marta Hoerner was left out of the original project group and the alien finished her off in a trice. Well, we'll get to that."

Ian went on to describe Eve's Boston visit with Mrs. Stringfellow, then what the Miranda Street account told. Julia shook her head in wonder. "The damn thing just wanted to end it all, huh? But how in hell did it figure out that storm was coming?"

Ian shrugged. "That's one of the nine million things about it that we'll never have an answer to. It obviously drew on information sources that we can't even imagine."

As he got closer to the ending of his story, the night deepened and the north-London streets got still and Ian began to pace around the silent flat. "They pulled me right off the street here, four days ago. Kidnapped me right into an electrical-contracting van and whisked me out to an American air base. I was blindfolded, of course, but it was obvious from the accents of the people talking around me. On the way to America, in a cargo plane with bucket seats, they did this business," and he pointed to his damaged face.

Julia grunted in anger and disgust. "Did they ask you questions while they punched you? What in hell were they trying to do?"

Ian shook his head thoughtfully. "Not really. The questioning seemed halfhearted. They must have realized that Eve probably knew better than anyone else what it, the alien, wanted with her. Anyway, at this point, I didn't even have the answer myself since I hadn't yet seen Miranda's account. No, I think they just wanted to make me look awful for Eve, so she would realize they weren't fooling around. They waited to use a hell of an effective electrical torture device on me in front of Eve. They obviously wanted to get at Eve through me."

Julia's eyes glowed in anger. "I thought that Hoerner bitch was wrong one way or another. You ought to get the damn American consul into magistrate's court, Ian!"

Ian shook his head. "I agreed not to do that, with the Whitehall and Foreign Office people. Julia, we won! We beat the bastards, so who needs the finger pointing? Anyway, the three men who did it are all dead, as are their immediate superiors. Now try and get anyone else in the entire U.S. federal establishment to admit they knew a thing about it."

Julia made them some more coffee and Ian went on with the story of the last hours on Muskeget. As he described the final moments of Marta Hoerner and the rest of them, Julia's mouth opened in astonishment and her eyes narrowed in shock. "My God!" she breathed finally. "Jack Goldman was there and the thing walked him into the water too? Why . . . why, I didn't even know he was dead!"

"Because of the shark problems," said Ian, "the casualty lists for the storm are still uncertain and, I suppose, will remain so. They probably picked Jack up at his office and took him directly to Muskeget, so no one else knew about it, except the others who died."

"Shark problems?" muttered Julia.

Ian sighed and his face showed his distress. "The storm struck early and much harder than expected. There was considerable loss of life, several dozen people. Immediately after the hurricane eye had passed, a great many large sharks entered the sounds and bays from the deep ocean to, uh, uh, to feed on the bodies." Ian took a deep breath. "Of course the alien must have produced that effect, brought them close and made them hungry before it died, to make sure there were no slipups."

Ian shook his head. "Eve thought she might have saved Jack, intervened with the thing strongly as it was marching Jack out, but she said she didn't see how I could get away with him alive to tell the whole thing the moment we got to Nantucket."

"That wimp!" said Julia disgustedly. "And he totally betrayed her! He was never worth ten minutes of Eve's time." She sighed and grinned at Ian. "Listen to me. I should tell *anyone* who to date!"

Ian went on to finish Eve's story and when he said, simply, "We made love before I left," he dropped his head and wept. "It was wonderful, slow, like Miranda described," he said in a choked voice, "but Eve was looking for something beyond that. Something completely transcendent."

Julia got up and went over to hold Ian in a gentle hug. She kissed his swollen cheek lightly. "Why don't you stay here for a while, Ian? I'm no Eve Pennington, but you can be in there with me, or out here on the daybed, and either way will be just fine from my side. I know you'll be safer here. I can shop and cook while you write this all down before you stop believing in it yourself."

Ian nodded. "Maybe I will. You're a good person, Julia, an honest person. That's someplace to start, anyhow." He poured another drink and sat down again.

"Eve was right about it showing me how to run the boat. I had no problems, but as I got closer to Nantucket harbor, I could see all the lights and activity. I suddenly thought that if I left the boat on a dock, the baddies would realize that at least one person escaped from

Muskeget, and maybe come looking. The moment I thought that, I knew what to do. I turned in and kept the breakwaters that line the ship channel to my left and zipped the boat right up to a big, deserted sandy beach near the town. As soon as it touched, I shut off the engine and jumped off the front, got wet up to my waist, then turned and pushed it off the beach. The wind was from the south, directly out from me, and the rain was so heavy you couldn't see much. So the boat just blew north right off the beach and disappeared in a minute.

"I was pretty scruffy looking, but when I arrived in the town, nobody was paying much attention. They were really running around, doing all sorts of things. Suddenly, somebody noticed my face, grabbed my arm, and shouted, 'Hey, Red Cross is over here, fella. Lemme help ya,' and I did let him help me and gave them a big story about losing my way in the storm, hitting rocks and wading ashore in surf. They set my nose, got me bandaged up, and found me a room in a boarding house, but I couldn't sleep. There was too much sense of preparation, so I walked around watching it all at the docks. It was almost noon, but so dark the cars all had their lamps on and people were using flashlights to get their boats ready. The rain squalls came and went.

"I've never seen wind blow like that. Chimneys and trees began to come down and fences and skiffs went up through the air, even though the harbor faces north and the wind was from the south. The harbor water was rising very rapidly, boats were beginning to drag, and it seemed to me impossible that it could get worse, yet it did."

Ian looked down at the floor. "I should say that when I promised Eve I would save myself, the alien instantly

fixed my eyesight . . . the coppers broke my eyeglasses
. . . and as I walked around the town of Nantucket I saw
everything quite clearly, so I knew the thing was still in
contact with me. Finally, it got dangerous to be outside,
and I went to my rooming house in the center of town
and stood with the landlady in her parlor windows
watching the trees fall, when the ground suddenly shook
like an earthquake, and my vision was instantly changed
back to what it's always been. Those were the waves that
struck the south shore of the island that made the
ground shake, but I knew better than anyone what had
happened. Julia, you can't imagine the roar of that wind,
even in the house. But that thing spoke to me over the
roar and announced its end, and the end of Eve
Pennington."

Julia went and sat on the arm of Ian's chair and put an
arm around his shoulders. "You two did live a great
adventure, Ian," she said warmly. "Eve said that at the
end, and it's true. So weep and weep again, my friend,
but don't despair."

Ian breathed deeply and blinked several times. "I got
to Boston with a whole lot of other storm refugees,
packed on buses, and used the stuff in Eve's purse to let
myself into Ed's secret side door. I found Ed still up
watching two TVs and, of course, astounded to see me.
We wept a good deal when I told him about Eve's ending,
drank a great amount of vodka, and ate a tremendous
number of bagels with strawberry jam, which Ed seemed
to feel was Eve's favorite dish." Ian now half-grinned at
her.

"By the next day, Ed was cheerful again and he did his
secret agent stuff to get me home. I had no passport, so
he went off to the Boston British Consulate in his

business suit and Phi Beta Kappa key. Spent all day there and when he came back, he told me we were driving to Canada that night in this van he'd organized to spirit Eve away. Julia, he had a pistol, for God's sake! Old Ed! In Massachusetts where they promptly lock you away for that! He had a disguise, a washerwoman getup, and the van had a firm name, Mops and Slops, with a great bucket of water sloshing across a floor painted on both sides.

"We went out that night, with me in a small, locked cabinet and Ed in his wig, dress and lipstick, but once we got onto the back roads, I got out and sat behind Ed. He had a route figured out that was roundabout but would let us see if we were being followed. At a Canadian border station, this rather dashing Colonel Forsythe of the Mounted Police joined us. He had a high-collared coat and his own gun, so of course he and Ed got on famously. In fact, before we got to Montreal, Forsythe had enlisted Ed's assistance in catching international book thieves who've been picking good things out of libraries and peddling them off in other countries. Ed changed in the back of the van and we all walked into the Montreal airport where the colonel had two first-class tickets for London waiting. He was coming over to be Canada's man at the briefing I had agreed to give in London if they got me back safe. That was the worm Ed dangled at the consulate."

Ian sighed and smiled. "It was quite a tearful parting with Ed at the airport, but he'll soon be over to talk about Eve and go further into the Thomas Cope thing and, I suppose, eat more bagels."

Julia stroked his hair. "Did you tell them all of this today, the little bastards downtown?"

Ian nodded. "Everything except about Eve's sister. Only you, Ed, and I know that and it isn't written down anyplace. I implied that she either had a tender scene with a boy there during her Nantucket summer or had gone there with Johnny Finn. Actually, that side of the story didn't interest them all that much. They asked many more questions about what I felt the alien could do, about the shellfish and porpoises, what the potential was for directing or influencing people, both consciously and unconsciously, all that sort of thing. And, of course, they were riveted by its final moments, when the alien, as one of them put it, finally turned against mankind."

Julia snorted. "What crap! How did they like the idea that it was mankind putting that torture thing on your arm that got the alien up and twisting its own arms?"

Ian grinned. "They were fascinated, completely. I think up until then, the idea of it wanting to die, and needing Eve to block its survival reflexes, was a little too complicated or poetic for some of them. But they could all see the cause and effect of Eve breaking loose from a thug to comfort her brutalized lover, and the alien playing sudden Marshal Dillon with the baddies. They had vast contempt for their American counterparts and endlessly bemoaned the losses to the world brought about by a few mad Yanks in Reaganland, or something like that. Well, you know the sort of veddy-British fluff we poof around now and then."

Julia shook her head. "They really are crazy, most of them." She hugged Ian strongly and kissed his cheek. "This was a close call, hero. You know that? Damn close!"

Ian smiled up at her. "You're not the first to say that. After ten hours of talk and questions, they just let me walk away. Everybody shook my hand, thanked me, and said, bye-bye. So I walked out into an underground garage and this one old man, who had been there all day peering at me from the end of the table, but never saying a word, motioned to me from a big Daimler with a grey-liveried chauffer driving, obviously a real big shot but I didn't recognize him.

" 'Where are you headed, Mr. McPherson?' he called and when I said north, he opened the door to invite me in and I gave your address to the driver. We swept up the ramp onto the street and as soon as we were in traffic, the old man turned to me. He had such pouchy eyes, so many wrinkles, that I couldn't even see his pupils.

" 'The world has had a narrow escape, Mr. McPherson,' he said. 'Please accept my deepest thanks for your responsible and sensible behavior in this moment of extraordinary danger.'

" 'Your colleagues wouldn't put it quite that way,' I answered him, but he quickly leaned closer and almost hissed in my face.

" 'They are not my colleagues, sir! They are the idiot children spawned by a ruthless and irresponsible scientific establishment! Bad enough that one or another of them comes up with the destabilizing wonders and horrors they do, but to try and pick interstellar brains . . . ugh!' His mouth wasn't two inches from mine and his face seemed a thousand years old. 'Mr. McPherson,' he said, 'you and I both know what is true; the world owes your lover, Dr. Pennington, a debt impossible to discharge. Whatever your loss, what has been saved is incalculably greater!'

"I thanked him for that and when we got to your building he told me that, as long as he was functioning, whatever that means, he would see that I was not bothered."

Ian shrugged. "Well, it has a hopeful sound, I guess. He did make me feel better. Sometimes it seems like the smart and powerful people have all gone crazy."

Julia stood up and peered out the window. "Wow, look at that. The dawn is peeping. We've been up a whole day and night. You must be broken in half, Ian."

He came to stand beside her, looking down the hill to London in the first glimmer of dawn, and she put an arm around his waist. "Ian, if you want to shut your eyes and imagine Eve there on Muskeget with that storm roaring around you, I mean, in there with me, I wouldn't mind that. Not a bit."

Ian put his arm around Julia and leaned to kiss her cheek, and as he did so, they both heard a sudden clatter of hooves and looked out to see two long columns of brown, unsaddled horses pounding up the center of the road, while several outriding young soldiers galloped along the flanks of the two columns to keep the lines straight. It was the mounts of the Royal Horse Guards being taken up for exercise on Hampstead Heath in the early morning. Leading the columns was a tall, fair young man in boots and khaki cavalry clothes. He rode hard, leaning well over the left-hand leader, beating its flanks with his peaked hat to urge it to a faster pace, and shouting across at the other leader to stir it to ever more effort.

They whirled by below the window with a great, romantic hoof rattle, and as he passed under them, Ian stared down at the boy's excited, intent face as he flogged and galloped his long columns up the hill. Ian saw that he was not simply moving some royal show horses to exercise in a London public park, but galloping his battery through ruined Mons, or some six-pound Napoleons through the Valley with Stuart in action ahead and shouting for cannon.

"Look at that boy's face, Julia!" cried Ian excitedly. "What a wonder the human imagination truly is! Everything is possible inside our heads."

Julia grinned at him suddenly. "Come on, survivor," she said, seizing his hand and leading him toward the bedroom. "Maybe you'll need a little imagination cooked up out of your own head and I'm afraid there's no alien left to help, but old Julia can provide the rest of it, the nonimaginary parts. Reality can be nice too, Ian!"

He looked down at her wide lips, her tired yet handsome face, and he leaned to kiss her. "We've got to remember, it was love that redeemed the world, Julia," he said and his eyes were bright. "Death, yes, but love most of all. Suddenly that seems to me a very, very hopeful idea!"

They walked, arms lovingly about each other, into Julia's dim bedroom and Ian pulled the door shut behind them.